PLAYERS

TERRANCE DICKS

Published by BBC Worldwide Ltd,
Woodlands, 80 Wood Lane
London W12 0TT

First published 1999
Copyright © Terrance Dicks 1999
The moral right of the author has been asserted

Original series broadcast on the BBC
Format © BBC 1963
Doctor Who and TARDIS are trademarks of the BBC

ISBN 0 563 55573 4
Imaging by Black Sheep, copyright © BBC 1999

Printed and bound in Great Britain by Mackays of Chatham

Cover printed by Belmont Press Ltd, Northampton

For Steve Cole:
an editorial raft in the stormy sea of deadline.

Credo

Winning is everything – and nothing
Losing is nothing – and everything
All that matters is the Game.

Chapter One
Mudlarks

Outside the palace wall, the sewer-hatch slowly began to rise. Two figures crawled out into the murky, drizzling gloaming of Rigel Seven.

The first was substantial, the second somewhat smaller. Since both were covered in thick black slime, it was difficult to make out much more.

The smaller figure spoke. The voice was feminine, the language English, the accent American, and the tone cool with an undertone of suppressed fury. 'When I was a kid, Doctor, there was this comic called *Swamp Thing*...'

The larger figure's voice was robustly masculine, with a note of repressed irascibility. 'Interested as I am in your native culture, Peri – if culture is the word – may I remind you that we are still hunted fugitives. If we don't find the TARDIS before the Palace Guard find us...'

'This *Swamp Thing* was kind of *made* of mud,' Peri went on calmly. 'I know just how it felt. Come to think of it, old Swampy would fit in very well on this planet. Blend in with the natives with no trouble at all.'

'Rigel Seven is a planet with plenty of rich fertile soil and a heavy rainfall,' said the Doctor defensively. 'Naturally there's a lot of mud about. The Rigellans *like* mud. You might almost say they worship it. They regard it as the primal ooze from which flows all life.' He looked up at the huge mud wall looming above them, and gazed around the swampy desolate landscape.

'This way, I think. Come on.'

'The Rigellans may like mud, but they certainly don't like us,' muttered Peri as she followed him along the muddy trail. 'What was all that "Cast them into the deepest dungeon!" bit, back at the palace? You said we'd be honoured guests here.'

'I'm afraid I failed to allow for the changing political situation.'

'Come again?'

'Years ago, I helped old King Adelebert put down a palace revolution, led by his son. How was I to know the poor old boy had died and the son was on the throne? He always was a nasty, vindictive lad.'

'He certainly had some imaginative plans for you,' said Peri. 'That stuff about the red-hot spikes, the boiling oil and the poisonous spiders was very inventive.'

'He had plans for you as well,' the Doctor reminded her, and nodded as she shuddered. 'Not quite so bloodthirsty, but just as gruesome in their way. It's lucky for both of us that the main sewer runs right under the deepest dungeon. A little digging with my Gallifreyan Army knife and – *Voilà!*'

'How did you know about the sewer – and that escape hatch?' asked Peri. 'More luck?'

'I designed the sewerage system for them,' said the Doctor modestly. 'At the time I was a national hero.'

'Hail Doctor,' muttered Peri mutinously. 'Bringer of peace, justice and flush sanitation!'

'The Rigellans live mainly on fruit and beans, Peri. Believe me, they *need* flush sanitation.' The Doctor peered through the gloom. 'There she is, just by that clump of swamp-oaks. Come on!'

From somewhere behind them they heard a hoarse voice bellowing. 'Halt in the name of the King!'

They turned and saw a group of very large lumpy figures squelching determinedly towards them through the mud. The Palace Guard wore heavy mud-spattered armour, and carried an assortment of ugly-looking weapons amongst which spike-studded iron balls and jagged saw-edged blades featured prominently.

'Run!' cried the Doctor, succinct for once.

Unencumbered by arms and armour, and spurred on by the thought of red hot spikes and a place in the new king's harem respectively, the Doctor and Peri made better time than their pursuers. Soon the Doctor was struggling with the door of the TARDIS.

The Palace Guard lumbered closer.

'Hurry, Doctor!' urged Peri. 'They're nearly here!'

The Doctor heaved open the door, shoved Peri inside it and dashed through after her.

As the door closed behind them, the Palace Guard caught up.

'We have you now!' bellowed the Guard captain. 'Useless to hide within this flimsy hut! Smash it, men.'

Surrounding the blue box, the Palace Guard hammered it with their assorted weapons – to no effect at all.

With a sucking, squelching sound the TARDIS disappeared.

Some subjective time later, Perpugilliam Brown, Peri for short, late of Pasadena, California, and currently the Doctor's travelling companion, was feeling much, much better.

She had stripped off her mud-soaked clothing and soaked for ages in an enormous hot bath, scented with oils, unguents and potions from all over the galaxy. She had washed and brushed and arranged her hair, and applied a little make up. She put on a Grecian-style gown in heavy white silk, with a jewelled brooch at the shoulder.

Looking at herself in her big bedroom mirror, she decided she looked terrific and went to find the Doctor. She had something to say to him.

The Doctor was in the TARDIS control room, freshly scrubbed and groomed, his face clean and shining. His mop of curly fair hair was restored to its usual springily uncontrollable state, and he wore one of his horrible multi-coloured three-quarter-length coats. He seemed to have an endless supply, each one just as ghastly as the last.

He was tying an eye-scorching cravat, red with big blue spots. It clashed perfectly with his yellow trousers, purple spats and green shoes.

Peri wondered, not for the first time, why this Doctor insisted on wearing an outfit like a slap in the face. Maybe that was why – an opening statement of defiance. Like it or hate it, this is me and here I am!

The Doctor gave Peri an approving nod. 'That's better. I must say, you do clean up nicely. Feeling better, I hope? You were getting somewhat pettish out there.'

'I'm much better, thank you, but I'm still feeling – well, disgruntled, actually.'

'I'm sorry to hear that,' said the Doctor with unusual politeness. 'What will it take to gruntle you again?'

'I'll tell you,' said Peri. 'Since we first met leaving Androzani Minor…'

'We met long before that, Peri.'

'That was a different you…'

Very different, thought Peri. As she surveyed the flamboyant figure before her, his gentle predecessor seemed to fade away in her memory.

Determinedly she went on with her speech.

'Since we left those lousy caves, we've visited a planet ruled by paranoid gastropods, a London invaded by Cybermen, and a Punishment Dome dedicated to torture and death – heaven knows what else…'

'All right, all right,' said the Doctor irritably, waving away any further examples. 'I admit we've landed in a few hot spots, but that's the way the cosmos crumbles.'

'Well, I've had it with hot spots, Doctor. I need a change.'

'What are you after, Peri?' said the Doctor exasperatedly. 'Exactly what is it you want?'

'I want elegance!' said Peri explosively. 'Culture, civilisation, champagne and charm! The ballet, the opera, society balls. Somewhere they won't shoot at us or throw us in dungeons, or threaten us with a variety of fates worse than death. Somewhere – *nice*, Doctor!'

The Doctor sighed. Somewhere nice. The request of his female companions through the ages. Heaven knew he'd tried to provide it, but so often fate seemed to conspire against him.

For a moment he considered offering Peri a trip to Metebelis Three. Then he thought perhaps not. Somehow those Metebelis Three trips never quite worked out.

He looked thoughtfully at Peri. She'd been having quite a hard time lately and wading through those sewers hadn't helped her mood.

Generously, the Doctor decided to indulge her.

'Elegance you shall have, Peri,' he promised. 'I know just the time and place.'

He moved to the controls.

Chapter Two
Attack

Captain Aylmer Haldane came out of the Command Tent and looked around the railway station yard, now filled with orderly rows of army tents.

Dusk was falling rapidly, and the South African twilight was brief. Very soon it would be dark.

Instinctively, Haldane studied the ring of hills surrounding Estcourt. The enemy was on the other side of those hills – somewhere.

The British, two battalions of them, had pitched camp at Estcourt Station, nestling in a little cup in the hills. Captain Haldane wasn't happy with their situation. The little hollow was a refuge that could easily become a trap.

As he strolled through the rows of tents, Haldane saw someone hurrying towards him. It was his friend the war correspondent, a medium-sized, almost stocky figure in breeches, boots and tunic, a forage cap stuck on the back of his head.

'I say, Aylmer,' called the war correspondent. (His lisp turned the words into 'I shay'.) 'Any news? A few crumbs of information for a poor devil of a correspondent?'

He was hopping up and down with sheer impatience.

Captain Aylmer Haldane, tall, elegant, as languid and utterly conventional as a British officer should be, grinned affectionately down at the energetic figure.

He and the war correspondent, totally different in temperament, had been friends for quite some time. They had fought on the Indian Frontier together when they were both young subalterns. Haldane had always regretted his friend's decision to resign his commission and go in for politics. He'd tried to talk him out of it. Not that he'd listened, of course… Typical! The fellow was able, energetic, and completely harebrained. Once he got a new idea in his head he was off.

Some time later, Haldane had heard of his friend being adopted as parliamentary candidate for some town up north – and of his defeat in the election. Now he'd turned up here in South Africa, bouncy and bumptious as ever, covering the newly-begun Boer War as the accredited war correspondent for the *Daily Mail*.

How he'd managed it, heaven alone knew. Charm and cheek probably, as usual. And connections, of course. When your late father had been a Cabinet minister and your mother was still a famous political hostess, there were always strings to be pulled.

Anyway, here he was, larger than life as always.

'Well?' said the war correspondent impatiently. 'Dammit, Aylmer, there must be some news.'

'Nothing very much,' said Haldane. 'Our revered commanders can't decide whether to advance, retreat or stay where we are.'

'We must advance,' said the correspondent decisively. 'We cannot stay here, the position is untenable. And there is no occasion to retreat. General Joubert is ensconced on the Tugela River, he is unlikely to risk an attack. We must seize the moment and attack him first!'

'I know, I know,' said Haldane. 'I heard you telling the Colonel all about it over dinner last night.'

Typically the war correspondent had arrived with his own tent, his own cook and a liberal supply of food and drink. Most nights he entertained a selection of senior officers to dinner. Quite frequently he ended up telling them how to win the war.

The war correspondent frowned. 'We have consistently

8

underestimated the Boers and we are paying the penalty. We have suffered many defeats and now Ladysmith is besieged. But this is no time for despair. We must be resolute.'

'All right, all right,' said Haldane. 'Stop addressing me like it's a public meeting. You gave up politics, remember?'

The war correspondent grinned sheepishly. 'It would be truer to say politics gave up me.'

'The Colonel's decided we need more information,' said Haldane. 'I've been ordered to take the armoured train out on a reconnaissance patrol, first thing tomorrow. Want to come along?'

The war correspondent hesitated, and Haldane knew what he'd be thinking. He had been on such trips before. Almost invariably, nothing happened. You chugged out of the station on an armoured train crowded with troops. You moved cautiously along the line, until you were as close as was considered safe to the border of enemy territory. Then you stopped, reversed the engine and chugged even more slowly back. If you were lucky, some enterprising Boer enlivened things by taking a few pot-shots at you from behind a rock, but that was about the only entertainment you could expect.

'Well?' said Haldane. 'We set off tomorrow morning. Five a.m. sharp. Are you coming?'

The war correspondent shuddered. 'I'm more fond of late nights than early mornings, but, well, I suppose I might as well.'

Haldane smiled. 'Good man. Until tomorrow, then.'

Once again, Peri stood looking at herself in front of her big bedroom mirror. This time she was wearing a costume chosen for her by the Doctor.

She wasn't crazy about it. A long skirt, a severely tailored jacket, a high-necked blouse, a parasol and a broad-brimmed hat, all in dark subdued colours. It was sober and elegant, but it really wasn't much fun.

She went off to the control room to find the Doctor, only to receive a considerable shock. He too had changed into an equally formal outfit. Now he was resplendent in dark trousers and a frock coat, open to reveal a waistcoat complete with gold watch-chain. A white shirt with wing collar and a flowing black bow tie completed the ensemble. On the TARDIS console rested a glossy black top hat.

Peri knew she was staring at him, but couldn't stop. The transformation was extraordinary. Out of his habitual garish clown outfit and, dressed like this, the Doctor looked powerful, dignified, important. He looked like *somebody*. Which, of course, reflected Peri, he was. Several somebodies, in fact.

The Doctor stuck on the top hat at a jaunty angle and grinned at her.

'Well?'

'That's quite a change, Doctor,' said Peri cautiously. 'You look almost – respectable.'

'Quite right – and so do you.' He flicked some switches on the console apparently at random. 'We're going to visit a very respectable age.'

'I feel like I'm dressed for my grandmother's funeral,' grumbled Peri.

'Nonsense, my dear girl. You're wearing the walking-out dress of a fashionable late-Victorian lady.'

'Victorian?'

The Doctor nodded. 'London, 1899. The last years of *fin-de-siècle* elegance. Garden parties, Henley Regatta, society balls and country-house weekends. Elegance galore, Peri, you'll love it. We'll take a house in Town and do the Season. I might even get you presented.'

'Oh yeah?' said Peri suspiciously. 'Presented to who?'

'To the Queen of course. Mind you, I can't guarantee it – not with you being *American*. But it's possible.' The Doctor bent over the TARDIS console, and made a few last-minute adjustments. 'Not long now.'

Peri watched with her usual mild apprehension as the time rotor slowed its rise and fall and then came to a gradual stop. The Doctor studied dials and meters for a moment, and then straightened up looking smug.

'Perfect! Even if I do say so myself. 1899 on the dot!'

He touched a control, the doors opened and bright sunlight flooded into the TARDIS.

'Ah yes,' said the Doctor happily. 'That glorious summer of 1899! Come along, Peri.'

He strode towards the door, checked himself, took Peri's arm and escorted her gallantly from the TARDIS.

As they stepped out into the blazing sunlight there was the sudden crack of a rifle.

A bullet blasted the Doctor's top hat from his head.

The war correspondent was leaning against the hot metal side of an armoured train-car, smoking a cigar and wishing he'd stayed in bed.

Everything was happening exactly as he'd predicted. The train was chugging across the bare and rocky South African veldt. The sun was climbing high in the sky. It was already too hot for comfort, and soon the heat would be unbearable.

Trains such as this one, sheeted with ramshackle armour, had been improvised by the British Army when they realised how rapidly the Boer commandos could move across the veldt. They appeared from nowhere, launched brief, devastating raids and then vanished like ghosts.

This particular train consisted of an ancient steam engine and a number of open-topped armoured trucks, each filled with hot and sweaty riflemen. Firing slits had been pierced through the heavy metal sheets protecting each carriage. One of the trucks held a field-gun, manned by a detachment of naval gunners, on loan from the Senior Service. To protect the engine – steam engines were in short supply in South Africa – it was placed towards the middle of the train, so that some trucks were pulled and others pushed.

The war correspondent was riding with Captain Haldane in the front truck. They reached Frere station with no sign of the enemy, and, according to orders, moved on to the next station, Chievely. It was only a few miles down the line, on the other side of a range of low hills.

As the armoured train came to a shuddering, clanking halt, a soldier ran from the station office clutching a telegraph form. Saluting, he handed it up to Haldane.

The war correspondent watched as Haldane studied the form.

'Message from HQ,' said Haldane. 'There's a report of Boer troops sighted here some time last night.'

The war correspondent looked around. Everything was peaceful. The little station, which consisted of no more than a signal box and a hut, lay baking quietly in the African sun.

'No sign of them now.'

'We wouldn't necessarily see them if they were here,' said Haldane grimly. 'We're ordered to go back to Frere and await further orders – "taking care to preserve our safe retreat".'

The war correspondent yawned. 'Advance – retreat! We go forward – we go back again. Honestly, Aylmer, this is the most *boring* war! The North-West Frontier was much more fun!'

Captain Haldane gave him a withering look and sent a message to the engine driver.

The driver, a stolid middle-aged railwayman called Wagner, received the message in much the same spirit as the war correspondent. He looked glumly at his stoker.

'All the way here – all the way back! What's the point? War!'

He reversed the engine and the armoured train began chugging back towards Frere.

What had been the front truck now became the rear one. From it Haldane and his friend surveyed the bare and rocky landscape.

'I'll be happier once we're past those hills,' said Haldane. 'If I were setting an ambush...'

There was a bright flash and the *crump* of a heavy shell detonating. Haldane shaded his eyes and peered forward.

'Men and artillery, up on that hill!'

More shells rained steadily down on the armoured train, and the front truck was torn wide open by a huge explosion. From the other trucks, the riflemen and the naval gunners began returning fire.

'Sounds as if they've got two or three guns up there,' said the war correspondent coolly. 'If the engine driver keeps his head we may be able to run past them. Luckily it's a down gradient.'

Already the train was picking up speed. Still under heavy shell-attack, with the riflemen and naval gunners returning fire, it sped towards the safety of Frere – straight into a pile of heavy boulders blocking the track.

There was a screeching, clangorous crash and the armoured train rattled bone-jarringly to a violent halt.

Captain Haldane and the war correspondent picked themselves up, jumped down from their truck and ran forward to assess the situation.

It wasn't good. The three trucks now in front of the engine had been derailed. Worst of all, the already badly-damaged foremost truck, the one that had actually struck the boulder, lay slewed across the track, barring the train's escape.

'We must get the track cleared,' said Haldane. 'We're outnumbered, and out-gunned, we can't hold them off here for long.'

'You can leave the track clearing to me,' said the war correspondent.

'Dammit, man, you're supposed to be a civilian.'

'So I'll do a bit of civil engineering. Come on, Aylmer, someone has to do it. You go and command the counter-attack. Give us what covering fire you can.'

Not waiting for Haldane's reply, the war correspondent ran towards the group of able-bodied soldiers who had crawled out from the wrecked trucks and who were now milling about confusedly beside the track.

'All right, men,' he called, in a surprisingly loud voice. 'Now listen, we have to get those trucks off the track. So all together now, and heave for all you're worth.'

The men were still half-dazed from the crash, but the energy and authority in that voice were irresistible. They stumbled over to the trucks and began to heave.

The Doctor reacted instinctively to the rifle-shot, hurling himself on Peri and throwing them both to the ground.

They found themselves rolling over and over down a steep slope, finishing up wedged behind a massive boulder where they lay gasping for a moment, taking stock of their situation.

They were halfway down a small, roughly conical hill, one of a number scattered around a group of larger ones. Behind, and quite a way above them, was the TARDIS, wedged in a narrow crevice close to the top of the slope they had fallen down.

Below them was a steep-sided railway cutting with a wrecked armoured train on the track. Three derailed trucks were blocking the track and a party of soldiers was trying to shift them – by the look of things – under heavy enemy fire.

On top of a hill on the other side of the railway track was the source of the fire, a battery of three heavy field-guns supported by riflemen, some mounted and some on foot.

From the shelter of the train, more riflemen were shooting back at the gunners on the hill, doing their best to cover the men working on the track. The air was filled with the crack of rifles and the thudding of artillery.

The Doctor surveyed the scene with calm interest. 'Yes, of course,' he said suddenly. 'I see!' He sounded almost pleased.

Peri rubbed her face and spat out dry, choking dust. 'Doctor...' she gasped.

The Doctor turned to her, his face alive with interest. 'Don't worry, Peri, I've worked out what must have happened. A slight spatial error, that's all. We've reached Earth in 1899, all right. Unfortunately we've landed in South Africa, not London – just at the beginning of the Boer War!' He studied the scene below them. 'There's quite a little battle going on down there.'

'Well, it's not our battle, is it?' said Peri crossly. 'For heaven's sake, let's get back inside the TARDIS.'

They ducked as a shell thudded into the hillside above them.

'That could be a little difficult,' said the Doctor ruefully. 'That hillside's a bit exposed at the moment. The Boers will think we're British, and the British will think we're Boers and they'll both do their best to shoot us dead. Better to wait here till the fighting's over and *then* make our way back to the TARDIS.'

Peri looked down at the battle with horrified fascination. It was like having a seat at the Royal Tournament, only the ammunition was live and the blood, the wounds, the *dying* were all real.

She saw one of the men heaving at the trucks stagger back and drop. A soldier ran forward to drag him to safety, and another took his place.

'What do you think will happen, Doctor?' she whispered.

'If they can get that track cleared, the British will be able to get away on this occasion – some of them at least. Otherwise the Boers will overwhelm them and they'll all be captured or killed.'

'Do you think they can clear the track?'

A cheer floated up from below as one of the trucks tipped over, away from the line.

'They will if that red-headed chap's got anything to say about it,' said the Doctor. 'He's organising the whole thing.'

He pointed to a figure running up and down the track, rallying the men and urging on their efforts.

'The funny thing is, he looks familiar,' the Doctor went on. 'I've met him before somewhere – before or after. Only he was different then – and so was I of course…'

Peri was struggling to make some kind of sense of this when her eye was caught by a movement further down the slope.

'Doctor, look!'

A man was moving across the side of the hill below them. He wore a tweed suit with plus fours, and a deerstalker. A long leather case was slung over his shoulder.

Moving with calm deliberation, he found a boulder, much like their own but smaller, and settled down behind it.

He opened the case and took out a long gleaming rifle equipped with telescopic sights. Then he took a handful of long bullets from his pocket and loaded the rifle. Calm, deliberate and precise, he leaned forward against the boulder, resting his elbows on the top and brought the rifle up to the aiming position.

'Who is he, Doctor?' whispered Peri, urgently. 'One of the Boers?'

'I doubt it. That's a Mannlicher rifle, worth a small fortune. No commando ever carried a gun like that. Besides, he doesn't look like a soldier.'

The unknown marksman peered through the telescopic sight, making some minute adjustment. He wet a finger and held it up, testing the wind, then settled back to the aiming position.

'He looks like a hunter,' said Peri. 'A big game hunter.'

Another cheer went up from the soldiers below as the second truck slowly tilted and fell away from the line.

The marksman shifted his aim, singling out the directing figure standing a little apart from the rest.

'Not a hunter, Peri,' said the Doctor suddenly. 'An assassin! He's trying to kill our red-headed friend down there.' He stared at her, his face impassioned. 'Of course! It's just like before!'

Scrambling to the top of the boulder, the Doctor yelled, 'Hey, you, stop that!'

The astonished marksman swung round, raising his rifle – just as the Doctor launched himself into space.

Chapter Three
Capture

The assassin fired, and Peri ducked as the bullet ricochetted off the boulder.

Before the unknown marksman could fire again, he was struck by the Doctor's substantial bulk. The speed of the assault sent the pair hurtling down the hillside.

Peri watched in horror as the two men rolled over and over in a cloud of dust and stones. They came to a halt against another boulder and immediately began a ferocious struggle. It ended abruptly as one man disentangled himself. It was the assassin. The Doctor lay at his feet, a trickle of blood on his forehead.

The assassin was still clutching his rifle and, to Peri's horror, he raised the butt high in the air, about to smash it down on the Doctor's skull. Peri jumped out from the cover of the rock. 'No!' she screamed.

The assassin froze, rifle raised high, staring at her in utter astonishment, giving Peri her first clear look at him.

He was thin and dark, Spanish or South American, perhaps, with a pencil-line moustache.

Suddenly he smiled, and made a saluting gesture. Scrambling back up the slope, he collected his rifle-case and his deer-stalker, and disappeared around the side of the hill.

Peri ran down the hillside to the Doctor. To her vast relief he was already recovering consciousness by the time she arrived. She helped him to sit up, wiping the blood from his forehead with a lace handkerchief. There was a shallow cut and some bruising but the injury didn't seem very serious.

'It's a good job you're so thick-headed,' said Peri shakily.

'What on earth did you think you were doing? Are you all right?'

The Doctor put a hand to his forehead and winced. 'Pretty much, I think. I got a crack on the head from this rock, didn't take much in after that. Where's our marksman?'

'Long gone,' said Peri. 'And so should we be. Let's risk trying to get back to the TARDIS, Doctor, anything's better than staying here.'

The Doctor shook his head, wincing again.

'I can't just leave, Peri. I've got to warn our friend down there that there's an assassin on his track. Wait here, I shan't be long.'

Struggling to his feet, he began running down the slope towards the railway track.

'Doctor, come back!' shrieked Peri.

The Doctor ignored her.

He's mad, thought Peri. Or maybe he's concussed. Whatever, he's in no state to be left alone.

She ran down the hill after him.

'Heave!' yelled the war correspondent. 'Heave! One last try, men!'

They heaved, but it was no use. The last truck, the one still slewed across the track, resisted all their efforts.

'Rest for a moment and we'll try again.'

A voice called, 'I say, sir. You there!'

The war correspondent turned. To his utter astonishment he saw two complete strangers hurrying towards him.

In the lead was a man in a frock coat, a smear of blood across his forehead. He had bright blue eyes and an unruly tangle of curly fair hair. Behind him came a young woman, dusty and dishevelled, but still extremely attractive.

Astounded as he was, he still managed to exclaim, 'Who the devil are you?'

'Never mind that,' said the stranger, his voice strong and carrying over the rifle fire that filled the air. 'I came to warn you – someone's trying to shoot you.'

An involuntary smile came to the war correspondent's lips.

'It can scarcely have escaped your notice, sir, that there are a number of Boer gentlemen assembled on that hill over there. I assure you, they are *all* trying to shoot me! Happily, they have not as yet succeeded.'

As she ran up to him, Peri looked hard at the man the Doctor was so determined to save.

Not particularly tall, he was strongly built, with reddish hair and a wispy moustache. While the soldiers about them looked pale and weary in the middle of the battle, this man looked vividly alive.

'You seem very cheerful about the situation!' said Peri.

The man smiled. 'Few things are so exhilarating as being shot at without result!'

'This is no time to be facetious,' said the Doctor sharply. 'I was speaking of a rather more individual attempt to kill you.' He gave a brief account of events on the hillside.

The man shrugged. 'The Boers must have sent a solitary sniper to work his way to a vantage point and pick off the officers. It's a common enough tactic.'

'It wasn't *like* that,' said the young woman.

'My dear young lady, why should anyone go to the trouble of assassinating me in the middle of a war? There's a good chance the Boers will do the job anyway. I'm simply not important enough.'

'Not yet, perhaps,' said the Doctor enigmatically.

'Do I know you, sir?'

'Not yet,' said the Doctor again.

The two men measured each other for a moment, and it suddenly struck Peri how alike they were. Not so much physically, though there was some resemblance even there. It was more a matter of temperament and zest. Both had a sort of cheerful truculence about them.

Dauntless, thought Peri. They were both dauntless.

A tall officer came running up to them, addressing the red-haired man. 'We can't hold them off much longer. One of their shells has knocked out the naval gun. How's it going?'

'Not too well, Aylmer,' said the man. 'This last truck continues to defy all our efforts.'

Peri noticed his slight lisp, which turned the last word into 'effortsh'.

The officer, Aylmer, it seemed, suddenly noticed her and the Doctor.

'Who the devil are these two?'

'Never mind that now,' said the Doctor suddenly. 'You need to get that truck shifted right away, you know! Stay here much longer and it'll be too late to get away.'

'That is indeed our intention, sir,' said the man sharply. 'But, as I said, it refuses to budge.'

'Use the engine,' said the Doctor.

'What?'

'Use the engine to barge it out of the way.'

'Dammit!' said the man. 'That might just work.'

'Of course it might!' said the Doctor. 'Now let's get a move on!'

'One slight hitch,' said Aylmer. 'The engine driver's out of action – shell fragment got him in the head. And the stoker's cleared off – made a run for it.'

'I'll drive,' said the Doctor.

Aylmer stared at him. 'You can drive one of these things?'

'I can drive anything,' said the Doctor simply.

He jumped up into the cab of the engine, knelt by the unconscious driver and examined him briefly.

'Just a graze, he'll come round pretty soon. Now we must get that boiler fired up, I'll need all the power she can give us!'

The man nodded. 'I'll see to that.' He put his revolver down beside the coal box, grabbed a shovel and set to work.

The Doctor studied the old-fashioned controls. 'We'll need to uncouple the engine.'

'The Boers have done that for us,' said Aylmer. 'A stray shell blew the couplings clean off.'

'Right,' said the Doctor. 'Now, I'll have to back her up a bit, get a run at it.'

He was completely caught up in the situation by now, and Peri knew it would be pointless to argue with him. She could only stand back and watch.

Aylmer took her arm and led her back from the track. Sheltered by one of the over-toppled trucks, they watched as the engine backed up laboriously, shunting backward the unattached trucks still on the track behind it.

It stopped for a moment, giving out great clouds of steam.

Peri could see the man they'd come to warn shovelling frantically, and the Doctor heaving on the heavy controls. The engine began to move forward, gradually gathering pace. Faster and faster it sped along the track. Peri watched the two men brace themselves as the engine crashed into the obstructing truck at full speed. One end of the ruined carriage rose high in the air and hung there, poised for a moment while the engine and its tender passed triumphantly beneath. Then it crashed back down again.

'Stop her!' shouted the war correspondent. 'We're leaving the others behind.'

'I'm trying,' yelled the Doctor indignantly. 'This isn't a London taxi you know, it doesn't stop on a sixpence!'

The engine was some distance beyond the barrier by the time the Doctor managed to bring it to a juddering halt with a screeching of metal.

The Doctor and his companion jumped out of the cab and looked back down the track, surveying the result of their efforts. Behind them now, the wrecked truck still lay slewed across the track, blocking it even more thoroughly than before.

'What you might call a partial success,' said the Doctor ruefully.

'It doesn't really make much odds,' said his companion. 'With the coupling smashed we can't take the rest of the train anyway.'

They ran back down the track, past the obstructing truck and found the officer and Peri.

'Well, you saw what happened,' said the Doctor, grimly.

Aylmer said, 'Never mind, old chap, you tried.' He looked down the track at the truck-like tender attached to the engine, the bullets still raining down about them.

'That tender will hold most of our wounded. If we can get them and the engine safely back to Frere we'll have salvaged something. Wait by the engine and I'll start sending the wounded along.' Enthusiastically he shook the Doctor's hand. 'Many thanks, sir. I don't know who you are, but you've been damned useful!'

Aylmer turned and ran back up the track while his soldiers offered renewed covering fire.

The Doctor, Peri and the man they had come to warn ran down the track to the engine. When they reached it, the red-haired man turned to the Doctor.

'Will you drive the engine back to Frere for us, sir? I can assure you of a hero's welcome.'

The Doctor looked worriedly at Peri. 'That's rather difficult, I'm afraid. I have other commitments.'

A voice from the cab said thickly, 'I'll drive.'

They turned and saw the engine driver struggling to his feet.

24

'Are you sure you're all right?' asked the Doctor.

'Got a hell of a thick head, but she's my engine. I'll get her back to Frere for you.'

'Good man,' said the red-haired man enthusiastically. 'I'll see you get a medal for this!'

Wounded men began arriving in twos and threes and the Doctor and Peri gently helped them aboard the engine tender. All the time shells and bullets screamed above their heads and clanged into the engine.

When the tender was full, the man called up to the driver. 'Better get moving, we don't want to lose the lot to the Boers.' He turned to the Doctor. 'Are you sure you don't want a ride? You'll be safe at Frere – you and the young lady.'

The Doctor shook his head. 'I've made – alternative arrangements. Why don't you go yourself? You've earned a place if anyone has.'

The red-haired man smiled and shook his head. 'Can't leave Aylmer in the lurch. Old friend, you know! Off you go, driver!'

Peri watched the engine chug away with agonising slowness. Her ears were ringing, her muscles straining from helping lift the wounded. As another shell impacted noisily into the ground, the red-haired man turned to the Doctor.

'I say, I don't even know your name.'

'Smith,' said the Doctor. 'Doctor John Smith. This is my ward, Miss Perpugilliam Brown.'

The man bowed. Peri suddenly had a thought – in all the chaos, she hadn't even remembered to ask his name.

'We don't know your name either,' said Peri. She glanced at the Doctor. 'At least, I don't. My friend the Doctor seems to think he knows you already.'

'Churchill,' said the war correspondent. 'Winston Churchill, very much at your service.' He looked at the Doctor. 'I don't think we've met before, sir, have we?'

'We will, Winston,' said the Doctor. 'We will!'

Churchill gave him a puzzled grin, and a nod of farewell. 'Doctor, Miss Brown.' Then he turned and ran back up the track.

The Doctor said softly, 'In fact, we already have!'

Peri was watching the disappearing figure with some awe. 'Was that really – *him*, Doctor? "We shall fight on the beaches," and "Blood, sweat and tears"?'

'That's right,' said the Doctor. 'Old Winnie in person. Young Winnie at the moment, of course. He's got a long way to go before England's finest hour. And someone seems determined to stop him being there...' He hesitated for a moment and then sighed.

'Well, I suppose we shouldn't interfere too much here.'

'Yeah, right,' said Peri dryly.

'Come along, Peri,' said the Doctor, ignoring her, 'Let's see if we can get back to the TARDIS before the Boers claim it for themselves.'

Winston Spencer Churchill, ex-army officer, failed parliamentary candidate and currently war correspondent for the *Mail*, ran along the railway track, still filled with the exhilaration of achievement. They'd got the engine away at any rate, and the wounded. Maybe they could still fight off the Boer attack.

Odd chap, that Doctor fellow. A good sort though, even if he was a bit bossy. And damned useful. Girl was pretty too. American. Nothing wrong with American girls, of course. Though come to think of it, *they* could be a bit bossy as well.

He smiled, thinking of his formidable mother.

Suddenly he saw two men walking down the track towards him. They weren't Haldane's men either... Boers!

As they raised their rifles, Winston Churchill turned and dashed back along the track towards the engine. The Boers must have swooped down in full strength and Haldane been forced to surrender.

Churchill pounded along the track, sweating in the baking heat. If he could only catch up with the engine and ride into Frere...

He heard the crack of the Boers' rifles and the sucking of the air as their bullets whizzed past, one either side. He was in a deep cutting with no cover to be had.

Swerving suddenly to the left, he scrambled up the bank and crawled under the barbed wire fence, ripping his clothes on the wire. He was on the edge of a bare stretch of open veldt. But a few hundred yards ahead, a narrow river ran through a deep gorge. There was plenty of cover along its banks. He decided to make a dash for it.

As he straightened up, he saw a horseman galloping furiously towards him. Instantly Churchill revised his plan. If he could stop this Boer and take his horse...

He'd been shot at so much today, it would make a nice change to shoot back.

Churchill stood crouched, waiting as the Boer galloped towards him. Slowing down, the Boer reined in his horse, calling out something Churchill didn't catch.

He was a very young-looking soldier. Pity to have to kill him but, then, war was war.

'Just a little closer, my friend,' thought Churchill grimly. 'Closer... Now!'

As the Boer reined his horse to a halt, Churchill grabbed for the revolver at his belt.

With a shattering sense of anti-climax, his hand closed on an empty holster.

He had left his pistol in the engine.

The horseman raised his rifle, fixing him in his sights. Ruefully, Winston Churchill raised his hands.

The Doctor and Peri hurried away from the track, conscious that the rattle of firing was dying away.

'Sounds as if it's all over,' said the Doctor. 'We're only just in time.'

They worked their way around the side of the little hill, climbing towards the ledge where they'd left the TARDIS.

They almost reached it.

As the ledge, and the TARDIS, came into sight, a little group of Boer horsemen rode onto the top of the hill.

They looked at the TARDIS, then at the Doctor and Peri. Almost casually they levelled their rifles.

The Doctor sighed, and raised his hands.

Interlude

'*I appeal to the Adjudicator!*' *The man's voice was angry.* '*There was interference. Blatant interference as I made my move.*'

The woman's voice said calmly, '*Not from me. It was hazard.*'

'*I demand to repeat my move!*'

'*No!*' *The woman's voice cracked like a whip.* '*You made your move and failed. The next move is mine.*'

'*I appeal, Adjudicator. A replay.*'

'*Appeal denied.*' *The third voice was that of a much older man.* '*You will continue to make your moves in strict alternation. And remember – the Pieces must never see the Player's hand.*'

'*To kill a man on a battlefield – what could be simpler?*' *grumbled the man.* '*How can I kill him, safe in prison?*'

'*How can I free him?*' *said the woman.*

'*A test of ingenuity for you both,*' *said the old voice.* '*Repeat the Credo.*'

> '*Winning is everything – and nothing*
> *Losing is nothing – and everything*
> *All that matters is the Game.*'

Chapter Four
Prisoners

'This is a disgrace, sir,' thundered the Doctor. 'I am a civilian, a non-combatant. My ward, Miss Brown, is a citizen of America, a country neutral in this conflict. I demand that you return my property, and release me at once.'

'I am a civilian, an innocent and harmless non-combatant,' growled Winston Churchill. 'I was unarmed when captured. I am an accredited war correspondent. My newspaper, the *Daily Mail*, wields a great deal of influence. It will harm your cause in the eyes of the world if you detain me here.'

Peri sat quietly in her chair. The Doctor and Churchill, both on their feet, both gesticulating furiously, were doing more than enough talking. Not that it was doing them any good. Behind his desk the prison Commandant looked singularly unimpressed.

It was rather like being back at school, thought Peri. Hauled up in front of the Principal for some terrible crime. Particularly since the room they were in had once been a headmaster's office.

They were in the States Model School at Pretoria, the Boer capital. The school, a large and impressive building, had been converted into a prison for the duration of the war. Prisoners took their exercise in what had once been the school playground, and sentries patrolled outside the iron railings.

After their respective captures, the Doctor, Peri and Churchill had been reunited for a brief forced march.

'Rounded up and herded like cattle,' grumbled Churchill. 'Doctor, this is the greatest indignity of my life!'

Peri had been allowed to ride in an ox-cart with the TARDIS.

It had been tantalising to be so close to a means of escape. Tantalising but useless, since the Doctor had the key and he'd been some distance away under heavy guard, marching beside Churchill with the main group of prisoners.

They had been marched to the nearest station, loaded on a train, and shipped here. The only consolation was that the TARDIS was stored somewhere in the same building.

Most of their fellow-captives were British officers, who accepted their imprisonment philosophically. The Doctor and Churchill, however, had created a tremendous fuss from the moment of their arrival. They had demanded an interview with the prison Commandant, and had finally been granted one – probably just to shut them up, thought Peri.

The Commandant waited until the Doctor and Churchill had finished their protests. He was a wiry little man with a stiff leg, sun-baked skin, bristly grey hair, and steel-rimmed glasses. He didn't look, thought Peri, like a man who could be fooled, bluffed or frightened.

He wasn't.

'Lies,' he said. 'Deliberate, shameless, calculated lies!'

The Doctor and Churchill glared indignantly at him. Both opened their mouths to protest, but the Commandant waved them to silence.

'That will do, gentlemen. You have had your say. Be good enough to sit down and be quiet.'

With identically aggrieved expressions, the Doctor and Churchill sat. The Commandant surveyed them coldly, like a teacher dealing with two particularly delinquent pupils. He turned first to Churchill.

'You, Mr Churchill, took an extremely active part in the defence of the train. It was largely as a result of your efforts that the engine itself escaped our capture. We are short of engines!'

'I naturally did my best to escape from so perilous a situation, and save my life,' growled Churchill. 'My conduct was the same as any of the civilian railwaymen – and they have been released!'

The Commandant sneered. 'More lies! You rallied the troops, you organised the unblocking of the line. You carried a revolver, and were seen to use it. If you were unarmed when captured, it was only because you had contrived to lose your weapon.'

Churchill lapsed into a sulky silence. His lower lip stuck out in a pout. He looked, thought Peri, like an oversized angry baby.

'Your countrymen have chosen to make a hero of you,' the Commandant went on. 'The English papers are full of your exploits at the train.'

Churchill cheered up immediately, preening himself a little. 'Indeed? That is most gratifying.'

'My Government considers you a very dangerous prisoner,' said the Commandant coldly. 'You will certainly not be released. Indeed, you will be fortunate if you are not shot.'

Churchill's face fell.

The Commandant turned his attention to the Doctor.

'As for you, Doctor John Smith, your conduct is puzzling indeed. You appear from nowhere, and you wander on to a battlefield like some idle tourist, endangering the life of this young lady. For some reason, you chose to aid the prisoner Churchill in his efforts.'

'As a doctor, I was engaged in a humanitarian mission, helping the wounded,' protested the Doctor. 'And may I point out that I was most certainly not armed. I never carry weapons, I don't approve of them.'

'You drove the engine, sir,' thundered the Commandant. 'You engaged in an act of war!' He calmed himself. 'Then there is the matter of this mysterious blue box. You refuse to open it, and it defies the efforts of our engineers. Does it contain weapons?'

The Doctor said nothing.

'The box bears the word "Police",' said the Commandant. 'Are you a member of the English police force?'

'Certainly not!'

'The box is clearly a piece of police equipment. Either you are an English policeman and an enemy of the Boer State, or you are a thief, and an enemy of society. In either case, prison is the best place for you. We shall hold you here, Doctor, until you and the box give up your secrets!'

The Commandant turned to Peri and spoke more gently. 'Your case, Miss Brown, is rather different. You are female, and have a claim on our chivalry. Whatever the English say, we Boers are not barbarians. Moreover, you are American, a citizen of a neutral country and one with which my Government wishes to maintain good relations. Therefore, I am prepared to release you, and to arrange passage back to your native country.'

Peri had a sudden nightmare vision of being shipped back to the America of – when were they? 1899! Fighting back her panic, Peri managed to shake her head calmly. 'Thank you, but no.'

The Commandant was amazed. 'You do not wish to be released?'

'I couldn't think of leaving without my guardian, the Doctor,' said Peri firmly. 'Unless you let him go you'll have to keep me here as well.'

The Commandant rose, his patience evidently entirely spent. 'There is no provision here for female prisoners. I am sure after a few days here you may be willing to change your mind. Until then, we clearly have no more to say to each other. I bid you good day. Sentry!'

The armed guard outside the door came in and took the three of them away. He escorted them to the playground, which was filled with strolling groups of prisoners.

When he was out of earshot, Peri looked at her two companions.

'Well, that didn't do you much good!'

'I never thought it would,' said Churchill cheerfully. 'However, the effort had to be made.'

'Quite right,' confirmed the Doctor. 'Always worth trying a bluff. Sometimes they even work!'

'The Commandant was quite right, wasn't he?' said Peri.

'What about?'

'You were both lying your heads off in there. "Harmless non-combatant! Humanitarian mission!"'

'Well, of course we were,' said the Doctor. 'No point in half measures.'

'Love and War, you know, my dear young lady,' said Churchill.

Something else they had in common, thought Peri. When it suited them, they both showed a complete lack of scruple.

'Only one thing for it,' went on Churchill. 'We must escape! Are you with me, Doctor?'

'Well, in spirit certainly,' said the Doctor.

Churchill looked disappointed. 'In spirit only? I had hoped that we might engage in this hazardous enterprise together.'

'It might be best if we split up for the actual escape,' said the Doctor hurriedly. 'Less chance of getting caught, you know!' He turned to Peri. 'You'll probably have a bit more liberty than we will. Do you think you could possibly –'

'Find out where they're keeping the TARDIS?' Peri nodded and looked ruefully down at her sombre and dusty clothing. 'I'll make eyes at one of the guards.'

Churchill was looking puzzled. To distract him, Peri said, 'That was a pretty long train ride, Mr Churchill. How far are we from anywhere that would be safe for you?'

Churchill considered. 'The nearest neutral territory is Portuguese Mozambique.'

'And how far away is that?'

'About three hundred miles!'

'Quite a stroll,' said the Doctor drily.

'You have some alternative scheme, Doctor?'

'It's not fully worked out yet,' said the Doctor hastily. 'Now, I suggest we all lie low for a day or so. We've made ourselves rather conspicuous, and we need to lull the Commandant's suspicions. We must pretend we're resigned to being prisoners. And we must meet only casually. It won't do to look as if we're plotting together.'

Winston Churchill heaved a sigh. 'I shall endeavour to follow your advice, Doctor. But it will not be easy. Do you realise, I shall soon be twenty-five? Twenty-five! And what have I achieved in life? A few years of military service, a failed attempt at politics, a brief career as a war correspondent. I refuse to rot in this prison for the remainder of the war.'

'No, no, of course not,' said the Doctor soothingly. 'Just a little patience, is all that is required. We must bide our time. Now, as I say, we'd better separate.'

Churchill nodded, and strode away.

'He's going to be quite a handful,' said Peri.

The Doctor nodded. 'At least I can try to keep an eye on him while we're in here.'

'In case he does something rash?'

'In case someone tries to kill him,' said the Doctor. 'There's been one attempt already, remember. There may well be another.'

Chapter Five
Plans Afoot

Following the Doctor's advice, the three inmates saw little of each other over the next few days.

Conditions, although far from luxurious, were not intolerable. Prisoners had a reasonable amount of liberty inside the school and in its grounds. Accommodation and food were simple but adequate. The main enemy was boredom.

The prisoners were allowed to subscribe to the Transvaal State Library. Winston Churchill had signed up, telling the Doctor that he hoped to improve an education which had not progressed very far at Harrow and Sandhurst.

'My scholastic performance was not distinguished, Doctor,' he said wryly. 'It was a time of discomfort, restriction and purposeless monotony.'

'Not unlike prison?' suggested the Doctor.

Churchill smiled. 'Yes indeed, Doctor. For one who has endured the horrors of an English public school, a Boer prison can hold few terrors!'

All the same, it was clear that Winston Churchill did not intend to endure prison for any longer than he could help. The Doctor noticed that he spent a great deal of time with his friend, Haldane, the officer with whom they'd been captured, and a certain Sergeant-Major Brockie. They were often to be seen with their heads together and it was perfectly clear to the Doctor that they were plotting escape. He just hoped it wasn't equally obvious to the prison authorities.

One warm South African evening, as they strolled around the playground, the Doctor confronted Winston Churchill with his suspicions and Churchill owned up quite cheerfully.

'Aylmer Haldane and Brockie plan to escape over the wall,' he said. 'I am endeavouring to persuade them to allow me to join them.'

'And what will you do, once you're over?'

'We shall walk to Portuguese Mozambique.'

'All three hundred miles?'

'There is no alternative.'

'Sounds a harebrained scheme to me,' said the Doctor frankly.

'Perhaps so, but it is the only one available to us,' said Churchill. 'Besides, Brockie comes from Johannesburg and speaks fluent Dutch. That will be of great assistance to us.'

'When do you make the attempt?'

'It is not yet settled. At the moment they are reluctant to include me in the scheme.'

'Why's that?'

'The objections come from Brockie.'

'What's he got against you?'

'Nothing at all.' Churchill did his best to look modest. 'He feels, however, that the escape of so distinguished a captive as myself will be the sooner noticed – and the resultant hue-and-cry all the more vigorous.'

'He may have a point.'

Churchill shrugged. 'Perhaps so. But I am determined to join them all the same. I am confident that my friend Aylmer will overcome Brockie's objections. I was forced to remind Aylmer that he owed a good deal to my efforts at the train – yours too, of course, Doctor.'

'Don't worry,' said the Doctor, hurriedly. 'You're welcome to any credit that's going!'

Like Peri, he noticed Winston Churchill's unscrupulous streak. No hesitation about moving in on someone else's escape plan – or about about trading upon an old friend's feelings of obligation. Just do whatever had to be done to achieve your aims. He smiled faintly. Perhaps it was a characteristic of all great men.

'How are your own plans progressing, Doctor?' asked Churchill.

'I'm not quite sure,' said the Doctor. 'It all depends upon my ward, Miss Brown.'

Winston Churchill gave him a disapproving look. 'Surely you are not proposing to entrust the hazards of an escape plan to a young lady? Even if she *is* an American.'

'Don't worry, I'll take care of any dangerous bits,' said the Doctor cheerfully. 'It's just that I need certain information first. And Peri's rather better equipped than I am to obtain it.'

'It seems such a little thing to ask,' said Peri.

She opened her eyes appealingly wide, fluttered her eyelashes, and sighed gustily.

On the other side of the railings, Field-Cornet Oosthuizen found himself hypnotised by the rise and fall of the white cotton blouse. He blushed and looked away.

A very young and inexperienced officer, Oosthuizen had distinguished himself by actually capturing the notorious Winston Churchill.

Now he had been retained at the prison, on temporary attachment to the squad of prison guards. He had soon noticed the beautiful young American girl who spent so much time peering sadly through the railings that barred her way to freedom, and they had fallen into the habit of having a little chat every evening after he had inspected the sentries.

'My poor guardian is *so* worried,' Peri went on. 'He's a scientist, you see.'

'A most distinguished one, I'm sure,' said young Oosthuizen gallantly.

'He's spent years travelling all over South Africa, collecting specimens, fossils, native art-work, all kinds of valuable things.

It's all stored in that box.'

'I see,' said Oosthuizen thoughtfully. 'The box is a kind of specimen case?'

'Exactly,' said Peri. 'His life's work is in that blue box!'

'Forgive me, but why does it have "Police Box" written on top?'

'Er – camouflage,' said Peri.

'Camouflage?'

Maybe the word hasn't been invented yet, thought Peri. 'It's an American expression,' she said hastily. 'It means "disguise". You see, my guardian thought that if the case had "Police Box" written on it, it would deter possible thieves. He's rather unworldly, I'm afraid.'

Oosthuizen nodded sympathetically. 'And what is it you want me to do?'

'If we could just *visit* the box,' pleaded Peri. 'He and I together. Just let us look inside, so my guardian can assure himself his specimens are unharmed. It would mean so much to him.' She sighed again. 'And to *me*.'

Reluctantly Oosthuizen looked away. Then he shook his head.

'I'm afraid I couldn't do that. Not without the permission of the Commandant.'

Peri sighed again, genuinely this time. She hadn't really expected that part of her scheme to work. Taking a deep breath she moved rapidly to Plan B.

'Then let me ask you something else. If you could take a look at the box yourself…'

Oosthuizen looked puzzled. 'That, perhaps, would be possible. But why? What could be the point?'

'If you could just tell me where the box is, and check that it's unharmed, I could reassure my guardian. He's making himself positively ill worrying about it. Once he knows the box is safe, he'll be able to stop fretting.'

Field-Cornet Oosthuizen bowed. 'I will see what I can do,

dear lady.'

'Thanks, you're a sweetie,' said Peri anachronistically. She stretched her hand through the bars.

Oosthuizen pressed it fervently to his lips, then turned and marched away.

'I think he fell for it,' Peri reported to the Doctor later. 'There's a good chance he may tell me tomorrow night.'

'Well done, Peri.' The Doctor squeezed her arm. 'I'm sure I can find a way of getting out of here. I've broken out of tougher jails than this. But it will be a great help if we can make straight for the TARDIS instead of having to search the whole place for it.'

'When do we go?' asked Peri.

'We'll go as soon as we know where the TARDIS is,' said the Doctor. 'Young Winston's planning some kind of breakout as well.'

He told her of Churchill's scheme to join Haldane and Brockie's escape plan.

'I think we'd better try and go first,' he concluded. 'After a successful escape they're sure to tighten up security, and that will add to our problems.'

'The same thing goes for Churchill and his friends if we go first,' Peri pointed out. 'We don't want to screw things up for them.' She paused. 'Do we? *Did* they escape from here so soon?'

The Doctor held up his hands hurriedly, obviously keen to avoid this conversation, or having to think of the possible ramifications. 'Maybe we should all go on the same night. Several escapes to handle at once will confuse the guards.'

'So when is he going?'

'He's not quite sure. But if we get the information we need and Winston persuades his friends – it could all be happening tomorrow night.'

* * *

41

The next evening the Doctor met Winston Churchill just after what passed for dinner. It was obvious that the man was in a state of high excitement. The Doctor assumed Haldane's escape plan was going ahead – but the reason for Churchill's excitement was quite different.

'Come with me, Doctor,' said Churchill excitedly. 'I have something extraordinary to show you.'

He led the Doctor to the cubicle, partitioned off from a school dormitory, that served as his bedroom. It contained an iron bedstead, a table with jug and wash basin, and a chair. Churchill dived under the bed and emerged with a large brown paper parcel.

'I found this on my bed just before dinner,' said Churchill. He opened the parcel, revealing folds of rough brown tweed. 'It contains a suit of civilian clothing, a leather bag holding one hundred sovereigns – and this!'

Churchill fished inside the parcel and produced a pistol – a Mauser automatic.

'Good grief!' said the Doctor.

'And there was this,' said Churchill. He produced a sheet of writing paper and passed it to the Doctor. 'The paper contains a sketch-map of the prison perimeter. One point on the perimeter, in fact the, er, latrines, is marked with an X. Beside the X is written a time. Eight pm!' He looked expectantly at the Doctor. 'Is it not splendid?'

'Perhaps. Personally I find it rather suspicious.'

'Suspicious, Doctor? Why so?'

'Don't you think it's all rather convenient? A little too good to be true?'

Churchill looked at him in outraged astonishment. 'I am somewhat at a loss to understand your meaning, Doctor.'

The Doctor's wave took in the parcel, the paper and the gun. 'How do *you* account for all this?'

'I have given the matter much thought,' said Churchill. 'My

conclusion, Doctor, is this. There exists in this prison a secret escape committee. Its task is to organise the escape of those prisoners our Government considers particularly valuable.'

'Such as you, I suppose? Of all the egotistical nonsense...'

In his turn, Churchill indicated the parcel. 'There is the proof, Doctor!'

'There is nothing of the kind!' spluttered the Doctor. 'Listen to me, young Winston. The day may come when the British Government will be ready to expend every effort to save your skin – but not yet, I assure you. Not for a very junior ex-officer, a failed politician and a new and inexperienced war correspondent!'

Churchill's under-lip came out in the characteristic pout. 'I see. You do not estimate my value highly, Doctor. May I ask how you account for my unexpected good fortune?'

'I think it's a trap,' said the Doctor simply. 'You refused to listen when I tried to warn you at the train.' He frowned, remembering. 'Come to think of it, I only got captured because I *tried* to warn you. Some unknown assassin was present at that train-wreck – determined upon killing you, and you alone.'

'Then why should this unknown enemy now come to my assistance?'

'He's not assisting you, you young idiot, he's luring you into a trap! Haven't you ever heard of the *ley del fuego*?'

'I'm afraid my knowledge of Spanish...'

'It means the "law of flight",' said the Doctor impatiently. 'In other words, "shot while trying to escape".' He looked meaningfully at Churchill. 'It's a very useful way of getting rid of inconvenient prisoners.'

Churchill frowned. 'If what you say is true, Doctor, this would-be assassin must enjoy the co-operation of the prison authorities.'

'Perhaps he does!'

Churchill shook his head. 'In my experience, the Boer is an honourable opponent. I cannot believe that the Commandant would enter a conspiracy to murder me.'

'Perhaps he has no choice,' said the Doctor. 'You heard him say the Boer Government regarded you as a dangerous prisoner, a hero. I don't think they'd dare to go as far as executing you, you have too many influential friends. But if you attempted an escape – an *armed* escape, mind you – and they were forced to shoot you… Well, who could blame them for that? They'd ship your body home with a note of regret, and that would be the end of quite a promising career, wouldn't you say?'

Churchill shuddered. 'You paint a depressing picture, Doctor, and one which I am loath to accept. Perhaps, as you say, I have an unknown enemy. But I choose to interpret this parcel as evidence of an unknown friend, and I intend to accept it as the gift of a benevolent fate – and to take full advantage of it.'

'What about your friends Haldane and Brockie?' asked the Doctor. 'Do you propose to share fate's bounty with them?'

Churchill shook his head. 'Fate's bounty, Doctor, is clearly intended for me alone. There are not three suits of clothes, three maps, nor three Mauser pistols. Haldane and Brockie were not over-eager to include me in their scheme. I feel no great obligation to make them part of mine.'

That streak of ruthlessness again, thought the Doctor. He sighed. 'Then I can only wish you luck, Winston. I've a feeling you're going to need it!'

The Doctor went to find Peri.

She had just come from her evening tryst with Field-Cornet Oosthuizen, and was almost as excited as Churchill.

'He came through, Doctor. I know where the TARDIS is.'

'Where?'

'There's a group of huts around the back of the prison, just outside the back gate. One of them stands a little apart from the others. It's made of stone, not wood, and it's used to store arms and explosives. That's where the TARDIS is, surrounded by bombs, shells and guns, and under constant guard.'

'You're sure of this?'

Peri nodded vigorously. 'My little Oosty persuaded the guard commander to open up and let him have a look. He says the TARDIS is fine. They've given up trying to open it, and are planning to ship it off to some scientific institute. We've got to move soon, Doctor.'

'We shall have to move tonight,' said the Doctor grimly. 'Someone's setting a trap for that young idiot Churchill, and he's going to walk right into it!'

'What are we going to do?' asked Peri.

'We're going to walk right into it with him!'

Chapter Six
Evil at Work

The Commandant didn't like being in charge of a prison.

It wasn't that he hated the British – although it was a British bullet that had given him a permanently stiff leg. He just didn't like being away from the fighting, especially when the war was going so well. Ladysmith besieged, the British harried and on the run – and he was stuck here. A headmaster, in charge of a school filled with sulky and discontented pupils.

But he had never disliked the job as much as he did at this present moment. And he had seldom disliked a man as much as he did the young Staff Officer on the other side of his desk. Immaculately uniformed, dark-eyed and olive-skinned, this Captain Reitz looked more Latin than Boer. Portuguese blood, probably, thought the Commandant. He'd never really trusted the Portuguese.

All the same, the fellow had a letter of authorisation from General Joubert. A vague but impressive document, it ordered the Commandant to give Captain Reitz 'the fullest co-operation'.

The Commandant fixed the young officer with a baleful glare.

'Your message is unclear, Captain Reitz,' he said coldly.

'Then let me make it plain for you, Commandant,' said Reitz. His tone was languid, almost insolent. 'Officially, I bring you word that an escape plot is being hatched, concerning the prisoner Winston Churchill. You are urged to show extra vigilance. Clear so far?'

'Completely clear, Captain – and your warning is completely unnecessary. Escape plots are being hatched all the time – it provides the prisoners with one of their few sources of amusement. My sentries always exercise maximum vigilance. It is the rest of your message that concerns me.'

Captain Reitz smiled. 'The unofficial part.'

'Precisely.'

'Well, unofficially, Commandant, I have been sent here to tell you that the Government does not wish Winston Churchill to survive this escape attempt. While he lives he is regarded as a danger to the Boer Republic. He has already become a popular hero to the English as a result of the events at the train, a powerful boost to their morale. He has far too much influence back in England, and he can do us much harm. He must never reach England alive.'

'You are asking me to commit murder, Captain.'

'Not officially,' said Captain Reitz, calmly.

'The order is unacceptable,' said the Commandant. 'A soldier can only be required to obey lawful commands. If General Joubert wishes Winston Churchill to be tried and shot, he has only to send me an official order in writing and I will assemble the court-martial and organise the firing squad.'

'I warn you, Commandant –'

'You will warn me of nothing Captain. Not unless you wish to be arrested for insubordination.' The Commandant rose stiffly. 'I thank you for your warning of an escape plot. I will order my sentries to exercise extreme vigilance. The rest of your message is unacceptable. Sentry!'

The sentry opened the door.

'The Captain is leaving. Escort him from the prison premises immediately.'

When Reitz had gone, the Commandant sat down again. Should he keep his word and order the sentries to be extra alert? Should he give them specific permission to open fire on any escaping prisoners? Or would even that compromise his military honour?

The Commandant sat brooding in his darkening office.

The man calling himself Captain Reitz had had many names in many places and many times. As he strode along behind the sentry he was seething with impotent rage. Had the Commandant been a weaker man with fewer scruples, the thing would have been as good as done.

Dusk was already falling as Reitz followed the sentry across the playground towards the main gate. Suddenly he caught sight of three familiar figures, huddled together talking.

One was Winston Churchill, who he had last seen through the sights of a rifle. The second was the fool who had interfered, and the third was the girl who had been with them.

Reitz's hand went to the holstered revolver in his belt – and immediately dropped away. He'd never get away with it. If the sentry didn't shoot him down on the spot, the Commandant would have him shot later.

Besides, it would be against the Rules.

Acknowledging the salutes of the sentries on the main gate, Reitz strode from the prison. There was still the chance of a trigger-happy sentry. Otherwise he would have to attend to matters himself.

He decided to patrol the prison perimeter from the outside. After all, the area wasn't all that large. There was a good chance that he would intercept the escaping Churchill. If he did – well, shooting someone while they were trying to escape was certainly fair enough...

In the exercise-yard a furious row was threatening to erupt.

'I'm sorry, Churchill, old chap,' said the Doctor. 'Like it or not, we're coming with you!'

'I cannot permit it, Doctor,' growled Churchill. 'The plan is for me alone. With the three of us involved it will inevitably fail.'

'Don't worry, Winston,' said the Doctor, cheerfully. 'We're only accompanying you over the wall, and after that we'll split up.' He gave Churchill a reproachful look. 'I am forced to remind you, Mr Churchill, that you owe a great deal to my efforts at the train.'

Recognising a personality fully as forceful as his own, Churchill gave in.

'Very well, Doctor. But we must act swiftly.' He indicated his well-worn outfit. 'And you must allow me a little time to get changed.'

Peri looked up and her eye was attracted by two figures marching across the yard. One was a sentry, the other a staff captain in an immaculate uniform.

She grabbed the Doctor's arm. 'Don't look now, Doctor, but there's an old friend just leaving,' she hissed. 'The man who tried to shoot Churchill, the one you had the tussle with.'

The Doctor glanced swiftly round and saw an elegant uniformed figure going through the gates.

'You're sure?'

'Positive.'

'Did he see us?'

'I don't think so – but I'm not really sure.'

The Doctor turned back to Churchill. 'That was the man who tried to kill you. It looks as if he's been talking to the Commandant. I don't know what he told him, but it isn't likely to be helpful. We must go now – at once.'

'But it is not yet time,' protested Churchill. 'And I haven't put on my civilian attire!'

'Well, quickly, man! Better too early than too late. Now, where's the spot marked X on your map?'

'Around to the rear of the prison,' said Churchill resignedly. 'By the men's latrines – my apologies, Miss Brown.'

'Just so long as we stay out of the sewers,' said Peri.

'Come *on*, you two,' said the Doctor impatiently. 'Winston, you can change in the latrines, it's safer.'

They hurried away.

The men's latrines consisted of a long low brick building, built close to the high railings that surrounded the school.

There was nobody about as they hurried towards it – otherwise the sight of Peri following the Doctor and Churchill inside might have caused some comment.

Churchill at least knew exactly why the spot had been chosen. There was a long low aperture, a kind of open, oblong glassless window, next to the row of urinals. It was close up against the railings – and on the other side of the railings was a belt of thick shrubbery. There were sentries patrolling on either side, but it was likely this particular area could be a blind spot between patrols.

Churchill changed quickly and scrambled up into the aperture. He reached out and swung himself over the railings.

The Doctor followed.

Peri came last, and the Doctor and Churchill reached up and helped to lift her over the railings. 'I can manage, thanks,' she muttered irritably.

'Portuguese Mozambique to the right, I think,' said the Doctor. 'We go left. Goodbye, Winston, and good luck.'

'Good fortune to you, Doctor,' said Winston Churchill. 'And to you, Miss Brown. I hope we may meet again in happier circumstances.'

'So do I,' said Peri.

There was something very engaging about young Winston.

They shook hands and went their separate ways.

Churchill made his way cautiously through the shrubbery. His only plan was to reach the road before dawn and then lie low. He intended to hide by day and travel by night.

He leaped back, reaching for his Mauser, as a cloaked and

hooded figure appeared from the shadows. A voice said, 'Mr Winston Churchill?'

The voice was female, cool and amused, with a slight trace of some exotic foreign accent.

'That is correct,' said Churchill. 'And who are you?'

'You are a little early,' said the voice. 'Still, better early than late. Come with me.'

'Where to, madam?'

'To the railway line of course. Surely you don't plan to walk three hundred miles?'

As they walked through the dusk, the cool voice issued a stream of instructions.

'There is an up-gradient just outside the station where the trains slow sufficiently to enable you to board. The next goods train will pass by in fifteen minutes. You will ride this train as far as a station called Witbank. Leave the train there, and make for a cluster of lights in the distance. They are those of a coal mine. The largest house in that area is that of the mine manager, a man called John Howard. He is English, and he will help you.'

As he crouched by the railway line, listening to the rumble of the approaching goods train, Winston Churchill felt a glow of self-satisfaction. He was in the hands of some powerful organisation, without doubt a branch of the British Secret Service. So much for the Doctor and his ridiculous theories about unseen enemies.

He wondered how the Doctor and his companion were getting on. He never had learned anything about their escape plan.

The goods train rumbled slowly past, and Winston Churchill ran and swung himself aboard.

It was the first step on the way to freedom, fame and fortune.

* * *

Under cover of darkness, the Doctor and Peri worked their way slowly and carefully around the perimeter of the prison, standing stock still from time to time to avoid patrolling sentries.

Not far from the back gate, illuminated by a solitary lamp, they found a little cluster of out-buildings, guarded by a field gun and its crew. One of the buildings, a low stone hut, stood some way from the rest. There was an armed sentry on the door.

'That's the one,' said Peri. 'Just as my little Oosty described it. How do we get in?'

Before the Doctor could reply, there came the sound of an alarm siren from somewhere behind them. They heard excited shouts.

'Alarums and excursions,' said the Doctor. 'Time to go, I think. Come on!' He marched straight up to the astonished sentry, Peri close behind him.

'I am Professor Erasmus Potgeiter from Pretoria Scientific Institute,' said the Doctor. 'This young lady is my assistant. I have been ordered to take charge of a certain blue box, which I believe is inside this hut.'

'That is so, Professor,' stammered the sentry. 'But I have received no orders.'

'No doubt they will arrive in due course,' said the Doctor impatiently. 'There seems to be a certain amount of panic and confusion back at the prison. Perhaps that is delaying things. A prisoner has escaped, an Englishman called Churchill.'

'Winston Churchill has escaped?'

'So your Commandant tells me. Now, open the door please.'

'Forgive me, Professor, but without written authority…'

'My dear man, I am not proposing to *take* the box anywhere! How could I until my transport arrives? By the time the ox-cart is present, the orders will be here also. Until then, you are welcome to stay on guard. And if that isn't enough, you can call in that field gun over there.' The Doctor put the snap of authority into his voice. '*Now, unlock that door, man!*'

The bemused sentry obeyed.

'On second thoughts, perhaps you had better report back to the prison,' said the Doctor. 'The Commandant mentioned something about a general alert. Every man is needed to hunt for the prisoner Churchill.'

As the guard lumbered off, the Doctor and Peri went inside.

They found themselves inside a low stone bunker. Racks of weapons lined the walls and ammunition and munition cases were piled high all around them. Standing in the middle of all this military clutter was the familiar blue shape of the TARDIS.

'There she is, bless her,' said the Doctor affectionately. 'Have you missed me, old girl?' He patted the blue box's side.

'Never mind the sentimental anthropomorphism, Doctor,' said Peri. 'Where's the key!'

'Key, key, key!' said the Doctor, searching through innumerable pockets. 'Where did I hide the key? Of course!'

He took off his left boot and shook it out. Nothing.

'Wrong boot,' said the Doctor. 'Hang on a minute, Peri.'

'Doctor, please, hurry…'

The crew of the field-gun snapped to attention as a smartly dressed officer strode up.

'I am Staff Captain Reitz, here on a tour of inspection. What's going on here? What's all that noise from the prison?'

'Not sure, sir,' said the corporal. 'I heard the siren.'

'What siren?'

'The one they sound when somebody escapes. I think I heard the man say it was the English hero, Churchill.'

'What man?'

'The one who got the sentry to let him into the armoury hut.'

'What man? What did he look like?'

54

'Thick-set, a gentleman. Very bossy type.'

'You fools,' exploded Reitz. 'That *was* Churchill. He's hiding in the armoury, right under your noses!' He looked around. 'Is this thing operational?'

'Sorry, sir?'

'The field-gun. Will it shoot? Do you have live ammunition?'

The corporal pointed to the pile of shells stacked by the gun. 'Of course, sir. We're guarding the rear gate.'

'Then open fire – on the armoury hut!'

'But sir, there was someone with him –'

'I don't care who was with him. Open fire, I said. I'll take full responsibility. There's a dangerous enemy of the Boer republic in there, with a massive supply of arms and ammunition. He could do untold damage. Now, open fire!'

Orders are orders. The corporal began shouting a stream of orders at his crew and the field-gun opened fire. The first shell merely dented the stone walls but, peering through the smoke, the corporal discerned that the second had made a hole. The third shell went through the hole made by the second and touched off the ammunition inside.

The hut disappeared in a column of smoke and flame.

Chapter Seven
Journeys

The Doctor was shaking his right boot when the first shell thudded into the side of the stone hut.

'Doctor, please, hurry!' urged Peri.

The Doctor frowned. 'Funny, I could have sworn...'

He shook the boot harder, and the key, which had been lodged in the toe, tinkled on to the stone floor.

The second shell blew a hole in the hut wall, showering the Doctor and Peri with dust and debris.

'Doctor!'

Coughing and spluttering, half-blinded by smoke and dust, the Doctor scrabbled on the floor for the key. He found it at last, opened the TARDIS door, thrust Peri inside and followed her, closing the door behind them.

Seconds later, the TARDIS dematerialised with a grating, grinding sound... just as the third shell whizzed through the hole made by the second, struck a crate of blasting powder and sent the hut and its contents sky-high...

Outside the hut, the corporal in charge of the field-gun detail regarded the result of his efforts with horror.

'Poor devils,' he muttered. 'And all the ammo gone up! There'll be trouble about this.'

He turned to the Staff Captain who'd ordered the attack. 'You did say you'd take full responsibility, sir?'

But the Captain was nowhere to be seen.

Roused from his brooding reverie by shouts and the sounds of shell-fire, the Commandant found all his worst fears realised.

Winston Churchill had escaped. So too, apparently, had the mysterious Doctor Smith and his ward.

The prison was filled with angry rumours, and the British officers were on the verge of revolt. It was whispered that Churchill had been killed in a mysterious explosion at the armoury, whilst attempting to steal weapons. The Boers had shut him up in there and deliberately blown the place up.

Things calmed down a little when the Commandant's inquiries, and his interrogation of the luckless corporal, established that it was almost certainly Doctor Smith and his ward who had died in the explosion. Churchill really *had* escaped and was on the loose somewhere outside Pretoria, heading, presumably for Portuguese Mozambique.

To the Commandant's relief, the uproar about Churchill's escape distracted attention from the explosion at the armoury and the death of two civilian prisoners. He made cautious inquiries about a certain Captain Reitz, and discovered that the officer was completely unknown.

Since Doctor Smith and his ward were civilians they had never been entered on the list of military prisoners. The Commandant discreetly removed all mention of them from his records, and hoped to hear no more about them. The explosion in the armoury was recorded as a freak accident. A case of gelignite had 'sweated', become unstable and exploded in the heat. The corporal and his men were sworn to secrecy – under threat of court-martial for killing innocent civilians and destroying government property.

The Boer Government in Pretoria instituted a massive search for the missing prisoner. They circulated posters, with a somewhat unflattering description, throughout the Transvaal:

'Englishman, 25 years old, about 5 feet 8 inches tall, average build, walks with a slight stoop, pale appearance, red brown

hair, almost invisible small moustache, speaks through the nose, cannot pronounce the letter "s", cannot speak Dutch, last seen in a suit of brown clothes.'

Churchill's capture, the authorities insisted, was only a matter of time. Reports flooded in from all over the Transvaal. Churchill had been spotted disguised as a Catholic priest, as a nun... but the man himself was nowhere to be found. In England the story of his daring escape filled all the newspapers. The whole country waited eagerly for news of him...

Meanwhile, Winston Churchill's escape was proceeding with almost unnatural smoothness. He had the feeling that he was aided every step of the way by invisible hands.

He jumped from the train at Witbank as instructed and found the house of John Howard, the mine manager. Howard hid him in the coal mine for several days and then smuggled him on to a railway wagon filled with bales of wool. The wagon was attached to a train heading for Portuguese territory.

Supplied with two roast chickens, a loaf of bread, several bottles of cold tea and his Mauser automatic, Churchill was slowly trundled towards the border.

Before crossing into Portuguese East Africa, the train was shunted into a siding for eighteen hours where it was searched by a party of Boer soldiers. Churchill burrowed deep into the bales of wool. The searchers pulled back the tarpaulin covering the wool bales and rooted around a little, but they didn't find him and the train was soon on its way over the border.

Emerging cautiously from his wool bales, Churchill saw the Portuguese station names flash by. He shouted and whooped for joy, firing his pistol in the air... He rode the train into Lourenço Marques, jumped down in the goods yard and made his way to the British consulate. There he found a hot bath, clean clothes, an excellent dinner and a hero's welcome. The news of his safe arrival was telegraphed to England and the whole country rejoiced.

Churchill took a ship for Durban that very night. On the boat, he wrote his despatch for the *Daily Mail*. To his surprise and delight, when he arrived in Durban there was a cheering crowd on the quayside.

The war was still going badly for the British. They needed a hero, and Churchill's escape gave them something to celebrate. Churchill found himself having dinner with the Governor of Natal, and going on by train to receive the congratulations of General Buller.

'I wish you were leading troops instead of writing for some rotten paper,' said the General. 'We're short of good men out here.'

Churchill was unable to resist such a flattering invitation. In January 1900, he took a commission in the South African Light Horse. To his delight, he was allowed to continue as a war correspondent as well.

There were to be more wars in the life of Winston Churchill… and in the lives of the Doctor as well.

Chapter Eight
Memories

Back in the TARDIS, Peri took yet another hot bath.

After a long, luxurious soak, abandoning any hope of elegance for the moment, she changed into jeans and a baggy T-shirt, dialled herself a cola and a hamburger, and went to look for the Doctor.

She found him in his shirt-sleeves in the control room. He had removed one of the panels from the control console and was tinkering delicately with the maze of complex circuitry inside.

'What are you doing, Doctor?'

'Just a few in-flight repairs. I'm sorting out the spatial circuits. The wrong place can be as embarrassing as the wrong time.'

'As we've just found out!' said Peri.

She watched him work for a moment or two and then asked, 'What was that war all about, Doctor?'

'The Boer War?' The Doctor considered. 'Oh, financial greed. Lust for territory. Racial tension. All those qualities that make you humans such a lovable little species.' He frowned at the hamburger and cola. 'How can you eat and drink that stuff?'

'It's my native cuisine,' said Peri defiantly. 'Accompanied by the wine of the country.'

'Well, don't drip any of it on to my circuits. Even the TARDIS has her limits.'

Peri never failed to be amazed by the way the Doctor could just switch off from an adventure the second it was over. Here he was, already preoccupied with some piece of extra-dimensional DIY or other, when they'd just helped save Winston Churchill for God's sake!

'Tell me more about the war,' she said.

'War?' repeated the Doctor. 'Which one?'

'The one we've just left behind, of course.'

The Doctor smiled archly, 'You're sure I wouldn't be too much of a *boer*?'

Peri groaned.

'Very well, then. The British and the Dutch were struggling over who got which bit of South Africa.'

'Nobody asked the Africans, I suppose?'

The Doctor shook his head. 'In the nineteenth century? Nobody even thought about it.'

'So what started the fighting?'

'The Boers had settled in an area called the Transvaal, which just happened to be rich in gold and diamonds. Hearing about this, many of the British flocked there to make their fortunes. Soon there were more British than Boers, but the Boers refused them any political rights. So the British used that as an excuse to take over the Transvaal – *and* its gold and diamond mines!'

'So much for that famous British reserve,' said Peri. 'The Boers seemed to be on top when we were there. Who won in the end?'

'The British did – eventually. But they found it a lot harder than they thought it would be.'

'I guess it often is, huh?'

'They underestimated the Boers. No proper army, you see, just a lot of irregulars dashing about on horseback. Never stand up to regular troops, they reckoned.' The Doctor sighed. 'One of your lot made the same mistake about Native Americans. Impulsive fellow called George Armstrong Custer. Mind you, I tried to warn him. "George," I said, "don't take your Seventh Cavalry over that ridge or you'll be in for a very nasty surprise." Would he listen?'

Peri swallowed the last of her hamburger. 'Something else I wanted to ask you...'

The Doctor huffed. 'Peri, I'm very busy. These spatial circuits are very complicated things…'

'You said something about meeting Winston Churchill before. In his future and your past.'

'That's right.'

'Tell me about it,' said Peri remorselessly.

'It was a *very* long time ago,' the Doctor protested.

'I'm interested,' Peri insisted. 'I thought I was here with you to learn!'

The Doctor gave in. 'All right… ' He gazed into the depths of the TARDIS console. 'I was very different in those days,' he said slowly.

Suddenly he jumped up, making Peri step back in surprise. 'Of course!' he cried, immediately starting to rummage through a large chest lying by the console. 'Now, it must be around here somewhere…'

Peri frowned. 'What are you doing? I thought you were going to tell me –'

'I can do better than just tell you!' exclaimed the Doctor. 'I can *show* you – at least, provided this thought scanner's still working.' Even as he spoke he was putting on an oddly-shaped metal headset that he connected to the console.

As he closed his eyes, the scanner screen whirred open and revealed a dark-haired little man illuminated brightly against thick blackness, arguing furiously with someone unseen.

'Who's that meant to be?'

'Me,' said the Doctor, simply. 'Told you I was different back then.'

'You're thinking that for me, aren't you!' Peri smiled. 'How does it work?'

'It's a neat trick, isn't it?' the Doctor said, a little smugly. 'I last used the thought scanner to show one of my companions an adventure I'd barely survived with the Daleks – an example of how dangerous travelling the universe can be.'

'And was your companion put off?' Peri asked.

'Not in the least.' The Doctor glared at her. 'An incorrigible lot, you humans.'

Peri snorted. 'That's rich coming from you!'

'In any case…' The Doctor closed his eyes again, and the little man on the screen span away into blackness.

'You've lost the picture!' said Peri.

'No. That's just what happened to me.' He sighed. 'I was captured by my own people and put on trial for interfering in the affairs of the universe.'

'I take it you pleaded guilty.'

'I conducted my own defence very eloquently.' He frowned. 'Then sentence was passed and I was exiled to Earth.'

Peri wasn't sure how to take this. 'Could've been worse, huh?'

'It was. *Before* they did that, a group of some of the… shall we say, less scrupulous Time Lords decided they had one or two other odd jobs for me to perform first.'

'Community service?'

The Doctor didn't smile. 'If you like. I certainly didn't have much say in the matter.'

Peri tried to stay patient. 'This is all fascinating, Doctor, but what about Churchill?'

The scanner showed the little man stepping out of the darkness into another ray of light. Three tall, shadowy figures – Time Lords, Peri assumed – were gathered around him.

'The reason I was captured,' the Doctor went on, 'was because I helped stop a series of war games. Thousands of soldiers were kidnapped from Earth's history and made to fight and die in a series of carefully controlled wars.'

Peri frowned. 'That's… that's awful.'

'Your talent for the understatement is considerable, Peri. I couldn't put things right alone. I had to ask… them. They put everyone back in their proper place and time, and took away my freedom for my trouble. But before I'd agree to do *anything* they asked, I insisted on seeing that they'd actually put things right with my own eyes.'

Peri watched as a silver bracelet formed round the little man's – around the *Doctor's* – arm.

'What's that?' she asked.

The Doctor smiled faintly. 'Wait, watch, and *learn!*'

The Doctor held up his arm and examined the bracelet. 'What the devil is this?' he demanded.

'That, Doctor, is a Time Ring,' said the first Time Lord. 'The technology, perhaps, is new to you.'

The Doctor tugged at the bracelet. There was, he noticed, no obvious point of closure. The thing appeared to have sealed itself.

'It cannot be removed,' said the second Time Lord. 'At least, not by you.'

'It will take you to the time zone you wish to visit,' said the third Time Lord. 'And return you to us here, at a time we decide, to perform as we would wish you to.'

'Anyone would think you didn't trust me!' said the Doctor indignantly.

The first Time Lord smiled thinly. 'Have you decided which time zone you wish to visit?'

The Doctor considered his options. Ancient Rome, the Mexican Revolution, the American Civil War…

There was only one possible choice.

'I have,' said the Doctor.

'Hold the time and place in your mind,' said the first Time Lord. 'The temporal transference beam will do the rest.'

A beam of light shone down from somewhere in the high ceiling. Slowly, the Doctor faded away…

Chapter Nine
No Man's Land

The Doctor found himself standing at the edge of a road. It wasn't much of a road, mind you. It was muddy and rutted and potholed, barely distinguishable from the surrounding landscape.

It wasn't much of a landscape either. An unending sea of mud, stretching in all directions, broken up only by the occasional glimpse of a shattered farmhouse or ruined barn. The land on either side of the road had once held houses and gardens and farms – fertile, cultivated fields. But it had been fought over so often, churned up again and again by advancing and retreating armies that it had become a wasteland.

He'd been here before, only recently. The soldiers of this war had a chilling name for the place: No Man's Land.

It was a dull and misty winter afternoon, with a hint of rain in the air. From somewhere in the distance came the dull rumble of heavy artillery.

The Doctor waited. Soon he heard the sound of an engine coming towards him. The sound was rasping, spluttering and uneven, suggesting that the vehicle was in a bad way. But somehow it laboured on.

The Doctor peered through the mist in the direction of the sound. He saw a square vehicle lurching along the road towards him. It was so caked with mud it was more or less impossible to discern what colour it might once have been.

As the vehicle came closer the Doctor jumped up and down waving his arms.

'Hey!' he yelled. 'Hey, huzzay, hullo!'

The vehicle came to a halt. Close up, it was just possible to make out the red cross printed wide and fat on the side.

Through the open window, the Doctor saw a woman in uniform at the wheel of the ambulance. She had the faintly horsey good looks typical of the female English aristocrat.

Beside her was a young man. He wore the uniform of a Lieutenant in the British Army.

'Sorry to be a nuisance,' said the Doctor. 'I wonder if you could possibly give me a lift.'

'A lift?' echoed the woman. 'Where to?'

'Oh, to anywhere at all. I seem to have got separated from my delegation.' The Doctor smiled in what he hoped was an appealing manner.

The woman smiled back. 'I don't see why not, sir, always room for a little one!' She had a high, clear upper-class voice.

'Splendid, splendid!' said the Doctor, rubbing his hands.

'Seems to be my day for picking up stray lambs,' she went on. 'I found the Lieutenant here wandering around just back down the road.' She held out her hand. 'Jennifer Buckingham – Lady Jennifer, actually, not that it matters a jot.'

The young man beside her said, 'Carstairs. Jeremy Carstairs.'

'Smith,' said the Doctor. 'Doctor John Smith.'

He studied the two young people thoughtfully. They were old friends, comrades-in-arms. The three of them had shared life-and-death adventures on the Planet of the War Games. But Lady Jennifer and Lieutenant Carstairs didn't know it. Not any more.

And they didn't recognise him. Which, thought the Doctor, was just as it should be.

Carstairs got out of the ambulance and held open the passenger door. 'Perhaps you'd care to sit in the middle, Doctor?'

The Doctor climbed onto the long front seat, and Carstairs got back in beside him and closed the door.

Lady Jennifer put the engine into gear and with a spluttering and coughing the ambulance lurched on its way.

The Doctor decided it was time for a little test. 'Have you been out here long?' he asked.

'Only about six months,' said Lady Jennifer. 'Though I must say it seems like forever.'

'I've been here for over a year,' said Carstairs. 'I came out near the beginning in '14. Had a couple of leaves, though.'

'I should imagine you lose track of time out here,' said the Doctor casually. 'I certainly do. What's the date exactly?'

Carstairs frowned. 'It's the 18th, I think. November the 18th.'

'Year?'

'1915 of course!' Carstairs smiled a little uncertainly. 'You can't be that confused already, Doctor!'

'November the 18th, 1915,' confirmed Lady Jennifer. 'How long have you been out here?'

The Doctor shrugged apologetically. 'Just long enough to get myself lost – and confused!'

'Medical delegation?'

The Doctor nodded.

'We get all sorts of groups out here,' said Carstairs. 'Politicians, doctors, actors, singers, the lot. There was some writer chap out here on a lecture tour the other day. Jolly old fellow.'

'G.K. Chesterton?' suggested Lady Jennifer.

Carstairs shook his head. 'That other one, great friend of Chesterton.'

'Belloc?'

'That's the one! Hilaire Belloc! The troops called him –' Carstairs broke off.

'That's right, Hilaire Belloc,' said Lady Jennifer. 'Go on.'

'I think perhaps I'd better not…'

'Come on, you've got to tell me now,' insisted Lady Jennifer. 'What did the Tommies call him?'

'Hilarious Bollocks!' said Carstairs, blushing furiously. 'Awfully sorry...'

Lady Jennifer gave a whoop of laughter. 'Don't worry, Lieutenant Carstairs, I've heard far worse than that out here.'

The Doctor watched the two humans closely, his eyes darting keenly between them as they engaged in their trivial banter. Time for one last test, he decided, peering out of the window. It was darker now, and the mist was thickening.

'Have you any idea where we are?' he asked.

'Well, I *hope* we're somewhere between Boulogne and St Omer,' said Lady Jennifer. 'But I wouldn't swear to it. Someone seems to have been mucking about with the signposts – or what's left of them!'

The Doctor nodded, satisfied at last. His two friends knew who they were and when they were. They even knew where they were – more or less – presumably near the point where they'd been interrupted.

Sadly, the Doctor reflected that he hadn't achieved all that much. All they'd done was swap one war for another. He looked at them both – cheerful, confident, ready to die for king and country. He'd thrown away a life of his own to enable them to perish here on earth instead of throwing away their lives in the service of some mad alien experiment.

The ambulance rolled on into the mists, and the Doctor looked ahead through the grimy windscreen. 'Evil must be fought,' he remembered himself saying. The other Time Lords could probably never understand. He smiled to himself. These two humans, cheerful in adversity, weren't so very different to himself.

It was a sobering thought.

'How did you get lost, Lieutenant Carstairs?' asked the Doctor.

'I'm serving as aide to General Sir John French at his Headquarters at St Omer,' said Carstairs. 'He sent me to

Boulogne with despatches. I got a lift back on a supply convoy and we got ambushed by a German patrol. There was a bit of a scrap, and the convoy crashed on through. I was fighting a bit of a rearguard action and somehow I got left behind.'

'Frightfully bad luck,' Lady Jennifer offered.

The Doctor suspected Carstairs had sacrificed himself so that the convoy could get away, and was too modest to say so.

'Well, Doctor, as Lieutenant Carstairs here knows, I'm making for St Omer too,' Lady Jennifer continued. 'I've been to Boulogne to pick up medical supplies from the supply depot. Is St Omer all right for you, Doctor Smith?'

'Fine, fine,' said the Doctor. 'If my party's not there, I'm sure someone will know where they are. Er, how long before we arrive?'

'It's a matter of "if" rather than "when", Doctor,' said Lady Jennifer. 'To be honest with you, we're pretty thoroughly lost. I've an idea we took a wrong turning some way back – the signposts have all been messed about with. We need someone with local knowledge, or a definite place-name so we can get our bearings. Until then, your guess is as good as mine.'

'Never mind,' said the Doctor cheerfully. 'What is it they say? To travel hopefully is better than to arrive!'

He beamed affectionately at them both.

Suddenly they heard a faint droning sound on the road ahead.

'There's a car in front of us,' said Lady Jennifer. 'Maybe we can catch them up and ask directions.'

She pushed the old ambulance forward, and soon a dark shape loomed into view.

'Looks like a staff car,' said Carstairs. 'Some bigwig on his way to see the General at St Omer, I expect. He'll know where we are – or at least his driver will.'

The road led past a clump of trees. Just as the staff car passed by it, there was a stuttering of machine-gun fire. The car lurched off the road, ran into the ditch and overturned. More shots came from the dark wood.

They saw a bulky uniformed figure struggle out of the wrecked vehicle, crouch down behind it and begin returning fire.

'It's another ruddy ambush!' said Carstairs indignantly. 'Better stop, Lady Jennifer, you don't want to drive right into the middle of it.'

The ambulance jolted to a halt and, drawing his revolver, Carstairs jumped out. 'You two wait here,' he instructed. 'I'll go and see if I can help.'

The Doctor was reminded of Jamie and his habit of heading straight for any promising fight, and felt a bitter pang of resentment at the Time Lords for taking away his old friend.

As Carstairs ran off, the Doctor turned to Lady Jennifer. 'I suppose I'd better go as well. He seems to be rather an impetuous young man, doesn't he!'

'I'm coming too,' said Lady Jennifer spiritedly. She began rooting about under the dashboard. 'I've got a service revolver here, somewhere. We're not supposed to carry arms, but I thought, just in case…'

'Please, do stay here,' said the Doctor. 'It's your duty to look after this ambulance – and don't forget, you're our way of getting out of here!'

Lady Jennifer leaned forward, peering anxiously into the gloom. Shots crackled between the wood and the wrecked staff-car as the Doctor and Carstairs ran towards danger.

Chapter Ten
Ambush

As Carstairs ran up, the man behind the car swung round, covering him with his revolver.

Carstairs got a quick impression of a thickset figure in army officer's uniform, of a round, pugnacious face with a jutting jaw, and eyes blazing with the light of battle.

'It's all right, Major, I'm on your side,' gasped Carstairs.

The Major took in Carstairs' uniform and relaxed. 'A welcome reinforcement,' he said solemnly. 'I don't suppose you happen to be accompanied by a platoon of infantry?'

'Afraid not, sir. Just me!'

'Well, we must contrive as best we can. The fellows attacking us are concealed in that wood. I think there are only two or three of them. Unfortunately, they appear to be in possession of a machine gun.'

There came another stuttering of fire from the wood. Bullets ricochetted off the upturned staff car and sang over their heads, as if to reinforce his words.

Carstairs and the Major returned fire with their revolvers, but it was hard for them to see who they were shooting at.

'The revolver is a weapon of limited use in modern warfare,' said the Major calmly, his words punctuated by gunfire. 'It served well enough against swords and spears in the Sudan, but even against the rifles of the Boers…'

He looked round as the Doctor came running up.

'And who is this?'

'This is Doctor Smith, sir,' said Carstairs. 'He's travelling with us in the ambulance back there. Oh, and I'm Lieutenant Jeremy Carstairs, sir.'

'Our little army grows apace,' said the Major, a gleam in his eye. 'We already have a Major and a Lieutenant – and now a medical officer and an ambulance!'

'And a WVS nurse sir,' said Carstairs. 'She's back in the ambulance.'

'Better and better! All we need now are some troops!' He turned to the Doctor. 'Would you oblige me by taking a look at my driver, Doctor? He was hit in the first burst of gunfire, and I fear the poor fellow is in a bad way.'

The Doctor nodded uncertainly. 'Well, I'm not… I'll do what I can, of course. Maybe we can get him back to the ambulance.'

Crouching low to avoid the hail of bullets from the woods, the Doctor worked his way to the front of the staff car.

The driver, an army private, lay sprawled half-out of the driving seat. The lower part of his body was pinioned under the over-turned car, and the front of his tunic was soaked with blood.

As the Doctor felt the faint pulse in his neck, the man's eyes fluttered open. He gazed unseeingly up at the Doctor.

'It's all right, old chap,' said the Doctor gently. 'We'll soon get you looked after.'

The man's eyes widened. '*Mutti*,' he gasped. '*Mutti*… '

His head fell back and the Doctor felt the pulse beneath his fingers die away. The Doctor looked down at him, both puzzled and sad. Then he dodged back to the others, who were still returning fire.

'Too late, I'm afraid, the poor fellow's gone.' He frowned. 'It's odd… he said… well, it doesn't matter now.'

'We must work out some plan for dealing with those fellows in the wood,' said the Major. He turned to Carstairs. 'If you hold them off while I work my way around behind them, we can catch them in a cross-fire. If we can dispose of that machine gun…'

'Good idea, sir,' said Carstairs. 'Only I'd better do the working around behind them part. I mean…' He broke off.

'You mean, Lieutenant, that you are not only younger and more agile, but will present a smaller target?' the Major inquired lightly. 'That is undeniable. Very well! Let us see if we can eliminate these fellows.'

'Do you have to kill them?' asked the Doctor, his face drawn in pained disapproval.

Lieutenant Carstairs looked shocked. 'Really, Doctor…'

'You are a man of peace, Doctor, as befits your profession,' said the Major. 'Believe me, I am no advocate of slaughter, I have seen too much of it. But I must confess, in the heat of battle I am perfectly prepared to kill anyone who is trying to kill me!'

'I'll go with Lieutenant Carstairs,' said the Doctor, dabbing his forehead with a handkerchief. 'If we get behind them and make enough noise, they may think they're outnumbered and run.'

'Their flight will serve our purposes equally well,' said the Major cheerfully. He took a handful of shells from his pocket and reloaded his revolver, then passed some to Carstairs who did the same.

'I wish you both good fortune,' he said. 'I'll give what covering fire I can.' Almost immediately, he began firing into the wood, one careful, aimed shot after another.

The Doctor and Carstairs slipped away into the gloom.

They made their way around to the edge of the wood, deliberately moving in a wide circle so as to come up behind their attackers.

Carstairs moved swiftly and silently. He had been on patrol in No Man's Land before. He was surprised at how quickly and quietly the Doctor moved beside him, slipping like a ghost between the trees. From time to time they had heard the stuttering roar of the machine gun. Now they heard it again – only this time it was somewhere ahead of them.

They moved cautiously forward.

At last, they came in sight of a little clearing in the wood. In it crouched a handful of men. One of them lay flat behind a machine gun on a tripod. The rest were clustered around him, firing an assortment of rifles and revolvers.

A narrow lane in the trees gave a clear field of fire to the wrecked staff car.

'That's a British machine gun!' whispered Carstairs indignantly. 'What's it doing firing at us?'

'Look at their uniforms,' said the Doctor quietly. 'Or rather, the lack of them. Look at their condition.'

The men were grimy and unshaven, wearing a tattered assortment of different uniforms. They looked wolfish and half-starved.

'They're not regular soldiers at all,' said Carstairs wonderingly. 'Some kind of renegades...'

He took careful aim at the man behind the machine gun.

'Wait!' whispered the Doctor. 'Aha! Here they are.' Searching frantically through the pockets of his shabby frock coat, he produced a handful of strange-looking objects.

Peering down at them, Carstairs saw long thin cardboard tubes, folded back on themselves in a kind of recurring Z-shaped pattern, each with a blue fuse at the end.

'What the devil...'

'Fireworks,' said the Doctor happily. 'Chinese firecrackers to be precise. I always carry a few about with me in case of emergency. They make a lot of noise and they don't really hurt anyone.'

The Doctor fished a large red-topped match from another pocket.

'Now, Lieutenant, when these things start to go off, fire your revolver in the air and yell as loudly as you can. With any luck they'll think we're the entire Brigade of Guards!'

'All right, Doctor, we'll try it,' said Carstairs dubiously. 'But I warn you, if anyone shoots at me, I'm shooting back!'

'It may not be necessary at all,' said the Doctor hopefully. 'I'll just light the blue touch paper – and, with any luck, our foes will retire immediately!'

Striking the match on his thumb-nail, the Doctor lit the first firecracker and tossed it close behind the men.

He lit and threw another, and then another...

Suddenly, with an amazingly loud bang, the first firecracker went off. It produced a whole series of astonishingly loud explosions. So did the second firecracker and the third, a whole fusillade of bangs, all merging with each other.

At the same time the Doctor bellowed, 'Up Guards and at 'em! Get 'em lads, we've got them surrounded!'

Carstairs joined in at the top of his voice. 'Number One Platoon here to me. Number Two Platoon enemy's left flank, Number Three take the right. Charge!' He fired his revolver in the air.

With shouted military orders and explosions all round, and the crack of Carstairs' revolver alarmingly close, the illusion of an attack in force was complete. The terrified renegades panicked and fled into the darkness of the woods, leaving the machine gun behind them.

Carstairs pointed to the abandoned weapon. 'Shall we take it with us?'

'Certainly not!' said the Doctor.

Carstairs reloaded his revolver and fired a couple of shots into the machine gun's loading mechanism, and then stamped on the barrel, bending it out of shape.

'Well, your scheme worked, Doctor!'

'A famous victory,' agreed the Doctor happily. 'And nobody dead!'

'Come along,' said Carstairs. 'We'd better go and tell the

Major it's all over.' Cupping his hands he shouted, 'Don't shoot, Major, it's only us! The Doctor has put the enemy to flight!'

They walked down the lane of trees towards the overturned staff car, and the Major rose from behind as they approached.

'Well done, gentlemen! How did you do it?'

Carstairs told him, and the Major roared with laughter.

'A brilliant tactical use of deception and the element of surprise, Doctor! You are a born general. Even from here, it sounded as if help had arrived in force.'

Suddenly they heard the click of a rifle bolt.

They turned and saw that one of the ragged renegades had followed them from the woods. He was standing only a few yards away, his rifle at his shoulder. Clearly, he had realised how he had been tricked and had come to take his revenge.

Carstairs and the Major raised their revolvers – but the rifle was already aimed and level, pointing directly at the Major.

The renegade bared yellow broken teeth in a mocking grin.

The crack of the two revolvers was joined by the deeper note of a rifle-shot... The renegade staggered and fell, his weapon firing harmlessly into the air.

Cautiously, Carstairs and the Major went over to the body. It lay face down, with a spreading stain between the shoulders.

'Shot in the back!' said Carstairs wonderingly. 'So it wasn't either of us who did for him.'

The Doctor came over to join them. 'The shot was fired from the forest,' he said quietly.

'Whoever fired it saved my life,' said the Major.

The Doctor said, 'It appears you have unknown friends, as well as unknown enemies, Major –' he broke off. 'I'm sorry, I don't think I know your name...'

'I'm afraid I find scant time for social formalities in the midst of battle,' said the Major. 'However, now that we have peace... permit me to introduce myself. My name is Churchill, Doctor. Major Winston Churchill.'

Chapter Eleven
The Chateau

For a moment, the three men stood silently by the wrecked car with its dead driver. Mist swirled eerily around them, and the dark wood with its unknown dangers loomed close behind.

Lieutenant Carstairs was staring at the Major with a mixture of amazement and awe. 'You're Churchill, sir? Winston Churchill?'

Churchill couldn't help but be flattered by the young soldier's tone of respect. 'I am.'

'We heard you were coming out here, sir,' said Carstairs. 'We could hardly believe it.'

The Doctor too was staring at Churchill in astonishment. 'Winston Churchill? What the devil are you doing out here – and in uniform?' he said, almost indignantly. 'Aren't you supposed to be, what is it, First Lord of the Admiralty?'

'I was, Doctor, until recently. Can it be you have not heard of my downfall?'

'I've been travelling,' said the Doctor hurriedly. 'Outer Mongolia, very little news reached...' He waved a finger. 'Though now that you mention it, I did hear something... ' He racked his brain for his memories of twentieth-century history. 'You came a cropper over that Dardanelles business, didn't you?'

'Really, Doctor,' said Carstairs, embarrassed.

Winston Churchill was quite unperturbed. 'I did indeed "come a cropper", Doctor, over my plan to attack Turkey via the Dardanelles. The plan failed, and I was blamed for its failure. My political enemies, of whom there are many, seized the opportunity to combine against me. I was dismissed from the Admiralty and given no further say in the conduct of the war.'

'I see. So you gave up politics, rejoined your regiment and came out here!'

'Exactly so. The wisest decision I ever made!'

The Doctor nodded, thoughtfully. 'Is it, now?' Churchill was now about 40, no longer a young man. For years he had led a life of privilege, comfort and luxury. He could have stayed in the safety of Westminster, seen out the war as an MP. Instead he had chosen to come to France and fight in the trenches.

'I feel released from a great burden of care,' Churchill was saying. 'But the soldiers who died in the Dardanelles will haunt me for the rest of my life. Now – well, I may still have to risk men's lives, but at least I can risk my own alongside them!'

'Well, there's no need to risk it unnecessarily, Major Churchill,' said the Doctor, bringing things back to earth. 'May I suggest we should all be on our way?'

'Quite so, Doctor.'

Churchill surveyed his wrecked staff car. 'Can this vehicle be righted and set in motion again?'

Carstairs went over and examined it. 'Looks like the petrol tank's shot to pieces. I'm afraid you'll have to join us in the ambulance, sir… '

'And my unfortunate driver?'

'His body's jammed in the wreckage, sir. We'll have to leave him.'

Churchill frowned. 'He served me faithfully, if only briefly. His is yet one more death upon my conscience. I do not care to leave his body to decay in this evil place.'

He went to the back of the car and heaved out two huge leather suitcases. 'Let me take those to the ambulance for you, sir,' said Carstairs, hefting them away.

'We shall provide my poor driver with a funeral pyre fit for a hero,' said Churchill.

Waving the Doctor back, he raised his revolver and fired deliberately into the shattered petrol tank.

The car exploded into flames, and for a moment Winston Churchill stood gazing into the blaze. Then he holstered his revolver.

'Come, Doctor,' he said, simply. Then he turned and trudged heavily away.

Once more the ambulance trundled on through the misshapen landscape. Introduced to their distinguished new passenger, Lady Jennifer had been delighted to take him on board. Particularly since, as is so often the way with English aristocrats, they were distantly related...

The front seat was long enough for three, but it wouldn't take four, especially when the fourth was someone of Churchill's considerable bulk. Carstairs had offered Churchill his place in the front, but the Major had been more than willing to travel inside. The curtain had been drawn back so they could all talk.

'I think the General plans to offer you the position of his Chief Aide de Camp,' Carstairs was saying.

They could hear Churchill's voice rumbling behind them, and the smell of cigar smoke wafted over them. 'I did not come to France to skulk in the safety of Headquarters,' he said heatedly.

'What do you want to do, sir?'

'In due course I shall ask General French to give me command of a Brigade. But first I must serve at the front and gain some experience of trench warfare.'

'The General was saying he wished he knew the precise time of your arrival,' said Carstairs. 'He wanted to send a car to meet you at Boulogne.'

There was a puzzled silence from the back of the ambulance.

'But he *did* know,' said Churchill. 'The car was sent.'

'There was a car waiting for you at Boulogne, sir?'

'Yes indeed. It was the vehicle in which I was travelling when we met.'

Carstairs shook his head. 'That's very strange.'

'I can tell you something even stranger,' said the Doctor, frowning. 'Just before he died, your driver said, "*Mutti*".'

Lady Jennifer said, 'But that's German – German for "mother" – well, more like "mummy" actually.' She paused. 'A dying man always goes back to his native tongue,' she said in a hushed tone. 'I've looked after enough French – and German – wounded to know that.'

'Precisely,' said the Doctor.

'What are you suggesting?' rumbled Churchill.

'A great man once said, "Never take the first cab that offers – nor yet the second."'

'Which great man?'

'Sherlock Holmes of course!'

'You believe the car was some kind of trap, Doctor? An attempt to kidnap me?'

'Well, if the driver was German... He drove you here, remember – straight into an ambush.'

'But the poor fellow was killed!'

'An accident, perhaps,' said the Doctor. 'Or more likely they just didn't care. After all, he'd served his turn by then – and dead men don't talk.'

'I hope you're wrong about all this, Doctor,' said Lieutenant Carstairs. 'But in case you're not – I think the sooner we get Major Churchill safely to St Omer the better.'

'That may be easier said than done,' said Lady Jennifer. 'I don't know if you've noticed but it's getting darker and foggier all the time. I still don't know if we're on the right road – and there's no sign at all of a – I say, hang on. There's one now!'

'One what?' asked Carstairs.

'A signpost! It seems to be pointing off to the right. I'll drive up to it.'

She drove up to the white post. Its single pointing finger was shrouded in mist.

Carstairs jumped down and studied it. After a moment he climbed back into the cab.

'It points up that narrow lane to the right. And it says, "*Au Chateau*".'

'*Au Chateau*,' said Churchill thoughtfully. 'What a graceful, musical phrase that is! And do you know the German for "To the castle"?' He paused. 'It is, "*Zum Schloss*"! Grace versus brutality! In those two phrases, my friends, is summed up the character of the two opposing nations!'

Lady Jennifer was in no mood for linguistic discussions. 'Is there any mention of *what* chateau?' she asked impatiently. 'Any kind of place name to give us our bearings?'

'Sorry, not a thing,' said Carstairs. 'Just those two words – "*Au Chateau*".'

Lady Jennifer looked around the crowded ambulance. 'Then I think we'd better go up there and ask where we are!' she said. 'Especially with our distinguished passenger on board. After all, I might be driving Major Churchill straight towards enemy lines. What does everyone think?'

'Might as well give it a try,' said Carstairs.

'Major Churchill? You're senior officer here.'

'To be honest, Lady Jennifer, I should be loath to fall into enemy hands on my first day in France. It would end my glorious military career before it had begun!' His eyes glinted in the gloom. 'And it occurs to me that if the owner of the chateau is hospitable, there may be a warm fire, a good meal and a decent bottle of champagne awaiting us. I'm for the chateau! What do you think, Doctor?'

'I think that signpost looks surprisingly new.'

Churchill frowned. 'You suspect another trap?'

The Doctor sighed, ruefully. 'It's always possible.'

'I take it you are against going to this chateau, Doctor?'

'No, I don't think so, all things considered,' said the Doctor thoughtfully. 'We can't go blundering on through night and fog forever.' His expression hardened, becoming almost sly. 'Besides, you can sometimes turn a trap to advantage, once you know it's a trap…'

'Well, that seems to make it unanimous,' said Lady Jennifer. She swung the wheel and drove up the narrow lane. It was long and winding, with high hedges on either side. Even with the ambulance headlights on full, it was hard to see anything but the few feet of road ahead.

It was all the more surprising, therefore, when the lane opened out onto a patch of gravel and they saw before them a huge pair of ornately decorated iron gates, giving on to a long gravel drive. At the end of the drive stood the chateau, a vast affair of towers and turrets, silhouetted starkly against the darkening sky.

They drove slowly up the drive and stopped on the broad stretch of gravel before the steps. The Doctor and his companions got out of the ambulance and assembled on the bottom step.

Churchill peered up at the chateau. 'Welcome to Castle Dracula!' he said. 'You are familiar with Mr Bram Stoker's celebrated romance, Doctor?'

'I used to be familiar with Count Dracula himself,' said the Doctor, apparently quite serious. 'A charming fellow – so long as you managed to avoid him at mealtimes.'

'Garlic with your stakes, everyone?' chortled Churchill. Nobody laughed.

Smiling broadly, Churchill led the way, marching up the stone steps to the massive door. He was just raising a fist to hammer at it when it swung open of its own accord.

On the other side stood a dark shadowy male figure holding

a candelabra in which burned several tall candles, their flames guttering in the night wind.

Before Churchill could speak he said, 'Come in, sir! Come in!' He raised the candelabra. 'And you, madam, and you, gentlemen. The Count is expecting you…'

Chapter Twelve
Gala Evening

They followed the man with the candelabra into a vast stone-flagged hall lit by blazing torches in wall-brackets.

By their light, he was revealed as a slim white-haired figure in the formal black uniform of a major-domo.

At the rear of the hall, a vast staircase led upwards to shadowy darkness. In front of it a row of maids and footmen stood motionless, waiting.

'Your rooms are prepared if you would care to change for dinner, lady and gentlemen,' said the major-domo. 'The Count and his lady invite you to meet them for cocktails in the library one hour from now.'

'My luggage is in our – conveyance,' said Churchill. 'But as for my companions, I fear…'

'Do not trouble yourself, sir,' said the major-domo smoothly. 'Everything is provided. If you will all come this way?'

They began climbing the great staircase, escorted by maids and footmen. Lady Jennifer and Carstairs went first, with Churchill and the Doctor bringing up the rear.

'You're taking all this very calmly,' muttered the Doctor, as he and Churchill climbed the stairs. 'Or is this sort of thing routine for you?'

Churchill chuckled. 'Scarcely, Doctor. It is true that I was born at Blenheim Palace, but that was only because my mother insisted on attending a shooting party there whilst in the last stages of an extremely delicate condition. Mind you, there are those who say she did it deliberately, to ensure a suitably impressive birthplace for me!'

They were led along an upper corridor and shown into a

series of luxurious bedrooms.

In the Doctor's room a fire blazed in the grate and a large porcelain hip-bath stood on the rug before it. Into it, relays of maids were pouring hot water from a series of jugs. Warming by the fire was a huge pile of white linen towels and on the four-poster bed a complete set of evening dress clothes, with all accessories, was carefully laid out. Intriguingly, it seemed to be exactly his size.

Combs and brushes, sponges, soaps, lotions and all kinds of elaborate toiletries were arranged on a nearby dressing table.

The footman bowed and waved a hand, indicating the contents of the room. 'If you require anything further, sir, or if the maids and myself can be of any service to you…'

'No thank you,' said the Doctor firmly. 'I'm quite capable of washing and dressing myself thank you!' He shooed the servants out of the room. 'All this bowing and scraping,' he muttered. 'Ridiculous.'

Once alone, the Doctor began a thorough search of the room. He looked under the bed, in cupboards and behind the curtains. He tried the window, and, as he expected, found it locked.

When he'd finished his search he stood gazing into the fire for a moment. Then he started taking off his coat…

An hour later, the Doctor, looking unusually elegant and somewhat uncomfortable in white tie and tails, came hurrying out of his room. A waiting footman escorted him to the library.

The Doctor was the last to arrive. It had taken him some time to transfer all the contents of his pockets, some of which came as a surprise even to him. He found Carstairs, Lady Jennifer and Winston Churchill assembled before yet another blazing fire, in a handsome book-lined room. In a corner, a footman stood beside a well-stocked drinks trolley.

'Ah, there you are, Doctor,' boomed Churchill. 'We are

drinking champagne. Will you join us? It's a very decent Veuve Clicquot '97.'

Sipping his champagne, the Doctor studied his companions. Lieutenant Carstairs was also dressed in white tie and tails, while Lady Jennifer wore a yellow satin evening gown. Most splendid of all was Churchill, who wore an elaborate dark-blue uniform with a high gold-laced collar and a scarlet-lined cloak.

He saw the Doctor studying him and smiled. 'How do I look, Doctor?'

'Like something out of a Viennese operetta, frankly.' The Doctor frowned. 'I keep expecting you to lead us in a rousing chorus.'

Lieutenant Carstairs looked shocked, but Churchill only laughed and drained his glass.

'An excellent idea, Doctor. I suggest the drinking song from *The Student Prince*!'

There was the pop of a champagne cork and a footman came forward to refill their glasses. When the footman withdrew, Churchill said quietly, 'This comic opera outfit, as you call it, Doctor, is the full mess kit of my regiment. It was waiting for me on my bed, correct in every detail, and a perfect fit. As was my favourite brand of champagne, and my favourite Romeo y Julietta cigars.'

The Doctor nodded. 'You, sir, were expected.'

'What about the rest of us?' asked Carstairs.

'For us, a supply of standard evening wear in assorted sizes would take care of things. What about you, Lady Jennifer, what did you find waiting for you?'

'An assortment of evening gowns, stockings and various – undergarments.'

'Did all of it fit? Was all of it suitable in style?'

'Well… no. But it was all of the highest quality and there was plenty to choose from.'

'Clear enough, then,' said the Doctor. 'Our unknown hosts

were catering specifically for Major Churchill and for an unspecified number of male and female companions.'

'You mean they bought all these things just to be prepared?' asked Lady Jennifer. 'It must have cost them a fortune.'

'Oh, nothing compared to the money that's been spent on this chateau,' said the Doctor, pushing his hands into his pockets and muttering in annoyance at their lack of volume.

Lieutenant Carstairs looked puzzled. 'Over the years, you mean?' The Doctor shook his head. 'Over the last few days. Not long ago, this chateau was derelict. Soon after we're gone it will be derelict again.'

There was a stunned pause.

'How can you tell, Doctor?' asked Lady Jennifer, at last.

'Oh, by looking about, poking into a corner or two. All the furnishing's brand new, but the chateau itself is ancient. It's been cleaned from top to bottom during the last few days. Some of the stonework in my room is still damp! They must have moved in an army of workers and servants.'

'But who?' demanded Churchill. 'And why?'

'That's what I hope to find out this evening,' said the Doctor. 'But I can tell you this. We're dealing with someone with virtually unlimited financial resources. Someone prepared to spend an entire fortune simply on a whim. This chateau, this whole evening, is no more than an elaborate practical joke!'

Footmen opened the double doors to the library, and two people were revealed on the threshold. One was a man of about sixty, with a high, forehead and hooded grey eyes. He wore immaculate evening dress, and leaned upon an ivory-handled stick. Beside him stood an extraordinarily beautiful woman with a cloud of black hair and, unusually for her dark colouring, deep blue eyes. She wore an elaborate red silk evening gown. A diamond necklace blazed around her long, slender neck, and there were more diamonds in her hair.

The man came forward. 'Good evening,' he said. 'I am Count

Ludwig Kroner. This lady is the Countess Malika Treszka. We are your hosts.' The voice was deep and cultured, with no trace of accent. 'It is a great honour to welcome you here, Major Churchill. We have been expecting you. Your companions however come as a surprise – a most pleasant one, of course. Won't you introduce them?'

'With the greatest of pleasure,' said Churchill. Accustomed to the very highest of society all his life, he spoke with an assured formality equal to that of his host.

'I have the honour to present Lady Jennifer Buckingham, Lieutenant Carstairs of my Staff, and Doctor John Smith, my personal physician!'

Lady Jennifer gave a stately inclination of her head, while the Doctor and Carstairs bowed stiffly.

The Doctor glanced at Churchill, and saw the mischievous twinkle in his eye. If their mysterious hosts wanted Ruritanian pomposity, they should have it.

'Allow me to add my welcome to that of my friend the Count,' said the Countess. Her accent was exotic, musical, utterly foreign. The accent of the beautiful spy on the Orient Express.

More charades? wondered the Doctor, shifting uneasily from foot to foot. Why do I feel everyone is playing a part? Playing games?

'We were expecting you earlier, Major Churchill,' the Countess went on. 'And, forgive me, alone and in a staff car rather than in an ambulance with your so-charming companions.'

Churchill bowed. 'Were it not for my companions, Countess, I should be unable to be here at all. I did indeed begin my journey in a somewhat mysteriously provided staff-car. Close to a wood, not far from this chateau, I was ambushed and my driver was killed.'

The Count looked at the Countess and spat out something

in a language that sounded, as Carstairs said later, like a cat-fight.

The Countess retorted with something equally spirited in the same tongue. The Doctor watched them with keen interest. Both had had their composure badly shaken.

'Forgive us,' said the Count, forcing a thin-lipped smile. 'We are shocked at your news. Ambushed, you say? By whom?'

'We're not sure,' said the Doctor.

'Did you not see them?' asked the Countess sharply. 'What nationality were they? What uniforms did they wear?'

'A mixture,' said the Doctor. 'They wore scraps of many different uniforms. They were hungry and half-starved.'

Again the Count and Countess exchanged glances, and there was another brief exchange in a foreign tongue. The Doctor got the distinct impression that his news came as a relief to them.

'Bandits,' said the Count scornfully. 'Renegades! There are quite a few of them, here in no man's land. Criminals and deserters from both armies. They form an unholy alliance and prey on anyone they can find. They would have killed you for your car, your luggage and your clothes.'

'They certainly endeavoured most earnestly to do so,' said Churchill, and the Countess gazed at him with her eyes flatteringly wide.

'Aren't these renegades a danger to the chateau?' asked the Doctor.

The Count smiled. 'Our defences are strong, Doctor. Perhaps you will see them later.'

'We are keeping our guests talking when they must be famished.' said the Countess. 'Major Churchill, will you take me in to dinner? We are dining in the *Petite Salle*. We are too few for the Great Hall, and it is always so cold and draughty. The table is so long that one is forced to shout, and food gets cold travelling from one end of the table to the other...'

Gallantly, Churchill gave her his arm, and led her, still chattering brightly, from the room.

The Count offered his arm to Lady Jennifer, and the Doctor and Carstairs followed.

While the *Petite Salle* was still somewhat large, the round table in the centre was small enough to make conversation possible.

Relays of servants brought course after course, and wine after wine to the table. The Doctor ate and drank little and spoke less, being content to observe. The others more than made up for him. Carstairs and Lady Jennifer sat together and seemed to find a great deal to talk about.

The Countess listened to Churchill's political anecdotes with flattering attention. Occasionally she would say something in a low voice that made him roar with laughter.

The meal ended but there was no move for the ladies to leave. Port and brandy and coffee were served at the table, and the Countess encouraged Churchill to light a cigar. Suddenly, the Count broke in on their conversation with an outburst in the foreign tongue he had used before. The Countess made a brief and angry reply in the same language.

The Count turned stiffly to Churchill. 'I was sorry to hear of your problems over the Dardanelles, Major Churchill. Your scheme was a good one and should have succeeded.'

Churchill, who unlike the Doctor had been eating and drinking – especially drinking – heartily, responded at once.

'It would have succeeded, Count, had it been properly executed. For a fraction of the effort that is being expended out here we could have disposed of Turkey and shortened the war. But General Kitchener had little faith in the scheme and refused to send sufficient troops until it was too late. Admiral Fisher too had doubts and was irresolute in pressing home the naval attack…' He broke off, shaking his head. 'Ah well!

Recriminations are useless, and all that is behind me now.'

'So, your political career is over, and you come out here in search of military glory.' There was a curious edge of malice in the Count's voice. 'How unfortunate that your military career is also over.'

Churchill laughed, uncertainly. 'Over, Count? It has scarcely begun.'

'It is over before it has begun,' said the Count. 'I hope you have enjoyed tonight's dinner, Major Churchill. Tomorrow night you dine with the Kaiser in Berlin!'

Chapter Thirteen
Flight

Winston Churchill leaped to his feet, his chair crashing to the stone floor. His hand went to the revolver – that was no longer at his belt.

'Revolvers are not worn with mess dress, Major Churchill,' said the Count mockingly.

Calmly, Churchill picked up his chair and sat down again. He took his cigar from the ashtray at his elbow and took a long meditative puff. The Countess watched him with bright, fascinated eyes.

'I am, of course, aware, Count, that it was you who sent the car to Boulogne for me,' said Churchill quietly. 'Indeed, your beautiful lady friend has already admitted as much. I was delayed by the ambush – and then walked, by chance and ill fortune, into the lion's den of my own accord. But if you think you and your attendant servants can keep me here, armed or not…'

'I have other servants,' said the Count. He clapped his hands and soldiers marched into the room. They carried rifles, and wore grey uniforms with spiked helmets. Effortlessly, they arranged themselves so that they formed a cordon about the dinner table.

'A detachment of the Imperial Guard,' said the Count. 'The Kaiser is most anxious to see you, Major Churchill. It was one of their patrols that saved your life in the wood, incidentally. They knew I wanted you alive. You have been in my power since you left Boulogne. If you had not come here of your own accord, you would have been captured and brought to me.'

'You can't hope to get away with this,' said Churchill

confidently. 'Without wishing to sound immodest, I am something of a public figure. My arrival in France is widely known. Indeed, General French is already expecting me at St Omer. When I fail to appear, inquiries will be made. When it is discovered that I have been kidnapped, there will be uproar and an extensive search will be mounted. Do you really think that you and your band of enemy soldiers can whisk me through No Man's Land unseen?'

'The soldiers are for my protection, not yours,' said the Count. 'Soon they will pass through No Man's Land and merge with the German army again. Yours is a swifter and surer means of travel.'

'Why are you doing this?' asked the Doctor suddenly. 'Are you of German blood?'

'I am Danish in origin,' said the Count coldly. 'My friend the Countess is Hungarian. But we are – internationalists. We have lived all over Europe, we have both been expatriates for many years. For many, many years…' He gazed off into the distance, then smiled faintly. 'We have no petty patriotic stake in this conflict.'

'For money then? You're mercenaries?'

The Count laughed. 'I hold high rank in the German Secret Service, but only because it suits me to do so. I accept no salary. I am one of the richest men in the world.'

'That still doesn't answer my question.'

'Why am I doing this, Doctor? Because I choose to!'

'Just for the fun of it, eh?' said the Doctor, rubbing his hands. 'To see what happens?'

'If you wish.' Losing patience with him, the Count turned to Churchill. 'It will be interesting to see what use the Kaiser makes of you.'

'What use can I possibly be, except as a captive to gloat over?' said Churchill scornfully.

'He might announce that you have joined him voluntarily,'

said the Count. 'A gesture to show that you disapprove of the war.' He nodded in approval. 'Yes, that would be of great help to the German cause.'

'Nobody would believe such a thing,' said Carstairs indignantly.

The Count smiled. 'Many would believe such a thing of a failed politician. Especially in the light of your singular presence in Berlin.'

'No one who knows me would credit such a vile suggestion for a single moment,' growled Churchill. 'And since I should make no statement to support it… '

'Captives can be persuaded to say practically anything, Major,' said the Count. 'There are many effective means of persuasion. My friends in the Secret Service are expert in them all… '

'At least let my companions go free,' pleaded Churchill. 'We met by chance today, they can have no interest for you.'

The Count shook his head. 'On the contrary, they form part of a fascinating mixed bag. The Doctor, in particular, interests me.'

'Oh, thank you!' said the Doctor, beaming with delight.

The Count ignored him. 'They will all go with you, and I shall follow at my leisure. Later on, we shall all have a happy reunion in Berlin…' He paused, holding up his hand for silence. 'Listen.'

They heard the low drone of an aircraft engine.

'Ah, at last…' The Count rose, and strode over to the window. He gestured to two of the soldiers who immediately drew back the long velvet curtains, revealing a long flat field next to the chateau.

The field was lined with two rows of the Count's servants, all carrying blazing torches.

As they watched, the dark shape of an aeroplane dropped out of the clouds, glided between the parallel lines of light, and landed in the field below them.

'Night landings are difficult, you see, but not impossible,' said the Count. 'Night take-offs, apparently, are another matter. I should advise you all to get some sleep. You leave at dawn.'

'Will there be room for us all?' asked the Doctor, airily.

'The plane is one of Germany's latest and largest designs. It is unmarked, and holds six passengers as well as the pilot. Room for you all, and two armed guards. I repeat, at dawn tomorrow you fly to Berlin.'

The captives were taken back to their bedrooms. The baths had been taken away, and their former garments, now sponged and pressed, were laid out on the bed.

Churchill, Carstairs and Lady Jennifer changed back into their everyday uniforms, but both Churchill and Carstairs discovered that their service revolvers had disappeared.

The Doctor changed back into his check trousers and frock coat with some relief, lost in thought as he carefully transferred all his miscellaneous possessions back again to their usual pockets. He failed to find anything that looked as if it might be useful – this didn't seem to be the sort of situation that called for a sonic screwdriver.

The prisoners discovered that while they had liberty of movement in the upper corridor, there were armed sentries at either end. Nobody felt much like sleep and, eventually, everybody ended up congregating in the Doctor's room.

'I'm sorry, everybody,' said the Doctor. 'I should've known better. I wanted to find out what was going on, but I didn't expect anything as elaborate as this.'

'It was a joint decision, Doctor,' growled Churchill. 'We are all equally to blame. Now we must concentrate on finding some way of escape. Windows, perhaps? Mine was locked, but –'

'I think you'll find they're all locked,' said the Doctor. 'Mine is, I know.'

'And mine,' said Lady Jennifer.

'Mine too,' said Carstairs.

'We could break one open,' suggested Churchill.

'Not without alerting those sentries out there,' said the Doctor. 'Besides, there are plenty more soldiers in the corridors and outside the house.'

'But we *must* form some plan of escape,' insisted Churchill.

'Oh, I've already done that,' said the Doctor.

Churchill stared at him. 'You have? Splendid, Doctor! What scheme have you devised? If it is as ingenious as your stratagem in the wood...'

The Doctor smiled disarmingly. 'There'll be just one moment when we may be able to seize our chance,' he said. 'I'll tell you all about it in a moment... There's a special part I'd like you to play, Major Churchill.'

'At your command, Doctor.' As he spoke, Churchill realised this was quite true. He wasn't a man who took anyone's orders easily, but there was something about this strange little fellow...

'I want you, when the time comes, to say a particularly affectionate farewell to the Countess,' said the Doctor solemnly. 'I rather think she's taken a shine to you.'

Churchill harrumphed as he thought on this. 'She is an extremely attractive woman, Doctor, and I admit to a brief flirtation at dinner. But at heart I am a happily married man. My dear wife Clementine...'

'She'll forgive you, I'm sure,' said the Doctor, looking a little flustered. 'It's all in a very good cause! Now listen carefully, all of you...'

In the chill of the dawn, the prisoners were marched out to the waiting plane. It was guarded by armed sentries and the engines were already turning over.

Beside the plane stood the Count and Countess, waiting to see them off. The Count wore a long cloak and the Countess was wrapped in furs.

'Farewell, dear lady,' said Churchill cheerfully as they approached. 'And thank you for a most pleasant evening.'

Before anyone could stop him, he stepped forward and embraced her. For a moment her fur-clad body pressed against him, and her hand found his... Then she pulled away, and slapped him hard on the face.

The Count smiled, and the sentries marched them to the plane.

As the Count had told them, the plane was an unusually large one. There were three rows of two seats behind the pilot. Churchill looked at the Doctor, nodded briefly and climbed into the front row.

Then instead of sitting down he stood up and presented an automatic to the pilot's head.

'*Raus, raus!*' he roared, heaving the startled pilot bodily from the plane and scrambling over to take his place at the controls.

The astonished sentries raised their rifles, but by that time Churchill had tossed the gun to Carstairs, who covered the Count with it and bellowed, 'Nobody move!'

The soldiers froze.

Suddenly the Doctor snatched the automatic from Carstairs and thrust it at arm's length into the Count's ear.

'I'm a terrible shot and guns make me nervous,' he said agitatedly, as if afraid the weapon would go off in his hand of its own volition. 'But I don't think even *I* could miss at this range! Lieutenant Carstairs, you and Lady Jennifer get onto the plane.'

'But Doctor –'

'Do as I tell you,' shouted the Doctor. 'And look after her, Carstairs. You two are made for each other, don't be too British to see it! Once you're aboard, tell Major Churchill to take off!'

'We can't leave you here, Doctor...' said Lady Jennifer.

'You must.' His voice became more gentle. 'Someone has to stay.'

'Why, Doctor?'

'Because we can't keep the Count covered properly from the plane, can we? The minute he's a free agent, his soldiers will riddle the plane with rifle-bullets before you leave the ground.' He glanced nervously at the Count, who was still standing stock still, then back at his friends. 'Now go!'

Carstairs helped Lady Jennifer into the plane, climbed in after her and leaned forward to speak to Churchill.

The Doctor saw Churchill shake his head. Cupping his free hand to his mouth, the Doctor raised his voice in a shout so loud it rose above the noise of the engine.

'I implore you, Winston, just go! Take off! Your country needs you, now and in years to come!'

He saw Winston Churchill touch the brim of his cap in salute.

The plane rolled forwards, and rose slowly into the dawn sky. The Doctor waited until it was out of rifle range. Then, ignoring the furious Count, he tossed the little automatic to the Countess.

'Yours, I think…'

As the plane soared upwards Lady Jennifer said, 'It feels so awful, leaving the Doctor.'

Churchill had grown fond of the Doctor during their brief friendship, but he had no intention of landing the plane until it was safely behind British lines.

'The Doctor made a noble gesture,' he said. 'We cannot save him by sacrificing ourselves.' He considered for a moment. 'Many years ago, I was helped in my hour of need by another Doctor…' Abruptly, he shook himself back to the present. 'Now, we must fly low and look for some familiar landmark. Inform me if you see anything useful, Lieutenant.'

'I didn't know you could fly a plane, sir,' shouted Carstairs.

'I had a number of lessons before the war. Pressure of work and the pleas of worried friends forced me to abandon the sport.'

'But you *are* a qualified pilot?' asked Lady Jennifer.

'I fear not. I never found time to take the qualifying tests.'

'Have you made a solo landing before, sir?' called Carstairs.

'Not yet!'

Carstairs took Lady Jennifer's hand. 'You heard what the Doctor said, back there?'

She smiled. 'About being made for each other?'

'I think we'd better not waste any more time,' said Lieutenant Carstairs. 'I'm not sure how much we've got left!'

'Is that St Omer down below?' called Major Churchill some little time later. Receiving no reply he glanced over his shoulder and saw that his passengers were staring deeply into one another's eyes. They kissed.

'Ah well,' thought Churchill. He saw a Union Jack flying above a parade ground and the familiar sight of marching British troops.

As he circled to find a suitable landing field, the Doctor's words echoed in his head.

'Your country needs you, now and in years to come…'

Outside the chateau, the Count and Countess were arguing furiously in the same fiery language that they'd used before.

At last the Count shook his head angrily and went to speak to the officer in charge of the soldiers.

'I'm sorry, Doctor,' said the Countess sadly. 'I tried to have you spared, but the Count insists –'

'Upon having me shot? Yes, I heard. Thank you for trying.' He smiled at her astonished face. 'My Hungarian is reasonably fluent.'

'I see. So that's why…'

'I heard the Count accuse you of betraying his plans last night, of being – unreliable. And of having taken what he called "one of your fancies" to Major Churchill. I thought you might have a sudden impulse to help us – as you did!' He looked suddenly crestfallen. 'Will it get you into any trouble!'

'The Count will not harm me, I know too much about him. But as for you, Doctor…'

'I know, the firing squad.' The Doctor sighed. 'It's quite astonishing how many people have that reaction to me!'

'He means it, you know. I'm afraid you hurt his pride.' She studied his face. 'You don't seem too worried.'

The Doctor smiled. 'I have an ace up my sleeve!'

The Countess stepped back. 'I have enjoyed our brief acquaintanceship, Doctor.'

A young officer came over and saluted stiffly. 'You will please come with me, *Herr Doktor*.'

The Doctor followed him.

Having overborne the objections of Lieutenant von Schultz, the young officer in charge of the Imperial Guard detachment, the Count had succeeded in setting up his firing squad. He watched happily as the officer marched the Doctor to the chosen section of chateau wall.

'Blindfold, Doctor?' he called. 'Last cigarette? We must do things properly.'

'No blindfold,' said the Doctor. 'Not on such a lovely morning. And I don't smoke, it's very bad for the health you know.'

Everything was ready. The Doctor and the firing squad were all in place.

'Ready,' called Lieutenant von Schultz. 'Aim…'

The soldiers raised their rifles.

Von Schultz, a sensitive soul, averted his eyes.

'Fire!' he shouted.

Nothing happened, and Lieutenant von Schultz looked up in surprise.

The firing squad was staring bemusedly at the section of wall where the odd little figure had been standing. They hadn't fired because there was nobody to shoot at.

The Doctor was no longer there.

Chapter Fourteen
Return

'You jolly well took your time!' said the Doctor indignantly, as he faded back into view in the Capitol ante-room on Gallifrey.

'You were only under intermittent surveillance,' said the second Time Lord irritably. 'Can't you go anywhere without getting into trouble, Doctor?'

He held out his hand.

The Doctor pushed back his sleeve and the time amulet dropped into the Time Lord's hand.

'Now, Doctor,' said the second Time Lord. 'We have indulged your whimsy. It is now time for your work to begin.'

'Just a moment before we start,' said the Doctor. 'There's something odd going on in Earth 1915. Some kind of historical interference. I'm not sure who's doing it or why, and it's all rather petty but it needs looking into. I'd be happy to…'

'No, Doctor!' said the first Time Lord firmly. 'No more delays, distractions or diversions. We have much to do.'

The Doctor sighed. 'Yes… I suppose *I* do, don't I…'

Interlude

'Treachery!' The deep voice was shaking with fury. 'The plan was complete, the Piece was in my hands and then… Betrayal, by one I believed I could trust.'

'"Trust nobody" is the first precept of the Game.' The woman's exotically accented voice was cool and amused. 'My Reversal was within my rights, and within the Rules.'

'Had it not been for the intervention of the Doctor –'

'This Doctor…' The third voice was much older, ancient, cold and dispassionate. 'Fifteen years ago, when this Piece was first brought into play, a certain Doctor Smith interfered. Describe the man who – vanished.'

'A clown! Small, black-haired, untidy, whimsical…'

'A clown of genius,' said the woman. 'He stole your Piece from the board, eluded your firing squad and vanished before your eyes!'

'It cannot be the same man,' said the old voice thoughtfully. 'Yet the name, the title… It is curious. Warn all Players everywhere to be alert for someone calling himself Doctor John Smith. He is clearly a random factor.'

'May I remount my operation?' asked the deep-voiced man.

'Not yet. This Piece has been in play too much of late. Remember, the hand of the Player must never be seen.

'I declare this Piece in balk. It must be out of bounds for the next twenty years…'

Chapter Fifteen
Interference

'Weird,' said Peri, as the Doctor concluded his story, and the images faded from the scanner screen. 'We meet Winston Churchill when he's young, but you've already met him before when he was older – and when you were younger! You could go to some guy's funeral and follow his life backwards until he was born!'

'The inevitable paradoxes of time travel, Peri,' said the Doctor dismissively, yawning as he removed the thought scanner's headset. 'That's not the point.'

'So what is?'

'Interference!' said the Doctor, suddenly bursting with renewed energy. 'Deliberate interference in human history!'

'Shocking!' said Peri, looking at him meaningfully.

The Doctor scowled. 'While I may have intervened myself from time to time, very occasionally, in a minor way, at moments of real crisis – my intentions are always for the best. This interference is wilful, malicious – malevolent even.'

'Do you think it was the same people both times?' asked Peri. 'That's quite a gap – 1899 to – when was it you met him again?'

'1915. Yes, I do. The technique is the same.' His eyes narrowed. 'Discreet, cunning interference. If Churchill had been killed in the Boer War, who in England would've suspected a third party at work? You can imagine the headlines, I'm sure: "Tragic End of Late Cabinet Minister's Son".'

Peri snorted. 'They're not always so discreet. "Churchill defects to Germany" would have been a real whammy!'

'Whammy?' echoed the Doctor, apparently appalled. '*Whammy?*'

Peri moved on quickly to avoid another lecture on linguistics.

'Don't forget there were people helping him as well,' she said. 'Someone sent him clothes, money – even a gun in the prison camp. And that snooty Countess in 1915…'

'That's the baffling bit,' said the Doctor irritably. 'It's as if they were playing some kind of game! Human history is a complex and finely-balanced system, Peri. Tinker with it and the consequences could be disastrous!'

'I know. I know. That whole web of time thing…' she sighed. 'Anyway, what *did* happen to Churchill once he'd flown home?'

'You can ask him yourself if you like!' said the Doctor, replacing a panel in the console.

'Huh? When?'

'When we get to London, of course. Elegance I promised you, and elegance you shall have.'

'Look, Doctor,' began Peri, 'I'm starting to go off the whole idea…'

The Doctor ignored her. 'It's just a matter of hitting the right time-period,' he went on. 'We don't want to arrive in the First World War – or the Blitz either, come to that. The trouble is, there's only about twenty years of peace between them!' He bent over the console and made a minute adjustment to the controls. 'I think the mid-30s would be the best time…'

'The mid 2030s knowing the TARDIS,' muttered Peri.

'What?' the Doctor asked, irritably.

'I – er – you told me I could ask Churchill what happened to him.'

The Doctor nodded. 'Well, we're bound to run in to him some time.'

Peri looked at him shrewdly. 'You're planning to investigate this business, aren't you?'

The Doctor seemed too preoccupied with the TARDIS controls to look up. 'What business?'

'This interference in history.'

Now the Doctor looked shocked. 'Oh, I couldn't do that, Peri. As you know, we Time Lords operate a strict non-interference policy. Although…'

Peri nodded, wearily. 'Although?'

'Well, if you interfere with interference, is it still interfering? You might say they cancel each other out. In a way, interfering with interference is a form of non-interference in itself!'

'You *are* going to investigate it!'

'Not at all.' He flicked some switches with a flourish. 'Of course, if I happen to stumble across anything, purely by chance… Meanwhile, you'd better get out of your barbarous native costume and into something more ladylike. Come along, I'll help you to pick something out. I have a keen eye for such things.'

Peri shuddered. 'What makes you think these people will still be active, twenty years later?' she asked as they left the control room.

'Why shouldn't they be? If they were busy tinkering with history in 1899 and in 1915… I think our unknown friends are playing the long game, Peri. Tweaking here, adjusting there. Somebody dead, somebody ruined, somebody else suddenly rising to power. There are all sorts of odd little anomalies in human history. Maybe this accounts for some of them.'

'But who are these people?' demanded Peri. 'What are they up to?'

'I've no idea,' said the Doctor broodingly. 'But take it from me, Peri, somewhere, somehow they're still out there. And still plotting…'

The Chancellor signed the last of the documents and handed it to the thick-set little man hovering deferentially at his side.

Martin Bormann took it and added it to the sheaf of files under his arm.

'Thank you, my Fuehrer.'

'Is that the last?' asked Adolf Hitler petulantly.

'It is, my Fuehrer.'

Hitler's mood improved. 'That is good. What would I do without you, my faithful Bormann? With you I can work through a pile of papers in ten minutes. With anyone else – ten hours!'

Bormann bowed his head deferentially.

When Hitler seized the post of Chancellor, the Nazi Party had only 33 per cent of the vote. Now, just three years later, he held Germany in an iron grip. All his political enemies were dead or in concentration camps.

There was only one party in Germany now.

Despite his amazing achievements, and his public image as an untiring superman toiling endlessly for his people, Adolf Hitler wasn't fond of hard work. He liked sleeping late, and he liked long lunches, haranguing his deferential subordinates over world affairs. He liked inspecting factories and newly-built autobahns.

Best of all, he liked addressing thousands of the faithful at torch-lit rallies, whipping them up to a hysterical frenzy with long ranting speeches denouncing the enemies of the Reich.

But work, real work, memos and meetings and committees, the nuts and bolts of running a business, or a country, bored him.

He had other people to take care of that. Goering for the ruthless policing. Goebbels for the propaganda – newspapers, radio, films, everything under Nazi control. Himmler for ruthless terror and repression – the night and fog policy, under which enemies of the Reich vanished silently and without trace, and Bormann for administration and paperwork.

Hitler yawned. 'Is there anything else?' He was ready for tea.

'Only one matter, my Fuehrer, but it can easily be postponed if you wish. Von Ribbentrop is here. He requests an immediate audience. The matter, he says, is urgent.'

Hitler brightened. 'You know, Bormann, it always cheers me up to see Joachim.'

'Indeed, my Fuehrer?'

'I like his enthusiasm. I have to spend my time inspiring my other colleagues, trying to put some heart, some guts into them.' He held a hand to his head. 'Very tiring, Bormann. But with von Ribbentrop, I have to hold him back! Much better! Send him in.'

Bormann's face was sour as he turned away. He knew exactly why the Fuehrer was so fond of von Ribbentrop. The man's only principle, his only policy, was whatever Hitler wanted – only more so.

'If the Fuehrer says grey,' thought Bormann, 'von Ribbentrop says, black, black, black! I wonder what mad scheme he's come up with now?'

None of the Nazi party officials cared for von Ribbentrop. Goering, in particular, detested him and had nicknamed him Ribbensnob. Then again, there might have been a certain amount of rivalry involved. Apart from Goering himself, von Ribbentrop was one of the few party chiefs with any claim to being a gentleman. The son of an army officer, von Ribbentrop came of an old military family. As a young man he had travelled to Canada and Holland before the First World War. During the war he had served in a decent regiment as a Lieutenant of Hussars.

After the war, a young man on the make, he had married the plain and sickly daughter of a wealthy champagne-making family. Perhaps unsurprisingly, he had subsequently done well as a champagne salesman. He had visited Rome and Paris and, particularly, London.

Ribbentrop and his wife had been well-known society

figures in the Berlin of the 1920s. It was at this time that Ribbentrop had awarded himself the 'von' that denoted nobility.

Coming under Hitler's spell in the early thirties, von Ribbentrop had joined the Nazi Party in 1932. The Fuehrer was convinced that von Ribbentrop had the entrée to English high society, and was determined to make him Ambassador to Britain.

'He knows them all over there, you know,' Hitler had once said, admiringly.

'True, my Fuehrer,' Goering had replied. 'Unfortunately, they all know him!'

But Hitler wouldn't listen. Von Ribbentrop was high in the Fuehrer's favour, and for the moment at least his position was assured. He came in now, tall and thin and elegant, an almost-handsome man with a beaky nose that held the attention over a weak mouth and chin. He wore the uniform of a General in the SS, an honorary rank awarded to him by the Fuehrer.

Von Ribbentrop came to attention and delivered a theatrical salute.

'My Fuehrer!'

'You can leave us now, Bormann,' said Hitler carelessly. 'Oh, and get them to send in some tea for us, will you? And some of those little cream cakes.'

Von Ribbentrop gave a curt nod to Bormann as the man stomped sulkily away. Then Hitler gave his favourite one of his rare smiles. 'Well, Joachim, what's so urgent this time? What have you got for me?'

'My Fuehrer,' said von Ribbentrop emotionally. 'I bring you – England!'

Chapter Sixteen
Consortium

Adolf Hitler sat back and looked thoughtfully at his excitable diplomat, then waved him to a chair.

'That is a considerable claim, my dear Joachim. Explain!'

Von Ribbentrop's explanation was delayed by the arrival of an SS waiter with tea and cakes on a silver tray. When they were both served and the waiter had withdrawn. Hitler bit into a cream cake and gestured to von Ribbentrop to continue.

'I have long been aware, my Fuehrer,' said von Ribbentrop earnestly, 'that it is your dearest wish to achieve a closer rapprochement with England.'

Hitler nodded. 'That is so. Look at the way the British rule India,' he said. 'A whole continent held down by a handful of troops. Why? Because they are of the superior Aryan race. One day that is how we Germans will rule Russia and all the barbarous lands to the east.'

'During my many diplomatic missions to England on your behalf, my Fuehrer,' Ribbentrop went on, 'I have done my utmost to promote this cause. I have spoken, publicly and privately, to many of the most influential figures in English society. I think I can say that at last my words have begun to bear fruit.' He paused impressively. 'I have received – an approach.'

Hitler leaned forward eagerly. 'From the English Government?'

'From those who speak for someone higher still.'

Hitler scowled. 'Damn you, talk plainly, Joachim.'

'The approach came from a group calling itself the

Consortium,' said von Ribbentrop. 'Their members include many international financiers, men of vast power and wealth. Also among them are leading members of the English aristocracy. These men wish you well, my Fuehrer, and support your aims. They recognise in you a force for law and order and decency, someone to hold back the Bolshevik hordes. For the moment, however, their names must remain a secret.'

Hitler nodded his understanding.

'And have the unknown members of this Consortium anything specific to propose?' he asked sceptically.

'They have indeed, my Fuehrer.' Von Ribbentrop paused impressively. 'They refer to it simply as the Plan.'

Over tea and cream cakes, von Ribbentrop proceeded to outline the Consortium's scheme. A smile flitted over Hitler's face at the sheer audacity of it.

'The Plan will give you England, my Fuehrer, without a shot being fired. At the very least, the English will become your staunchest allies. In time England will become a province of Germany, in actuality if not in name. The advantages to the Reich –'

'The advantages to the Reich are quite clear,' snapped Hitler, '*if* the plan succeeds. Remember, even with allies in England, we have many enemies. That gangster Churchill and his friends continue to conspire against me.'

'I am assured that Churchill and those like him will be suitably dealt with, my Fuehrer. Plans are already under way.'

Hitler brooded for a moment, As always, when important decisions had to be taken, he was racked by doubts and fears. 'It is a daring plan… and if it succeeds…' he swallowed hard. 'The members of this Consortium, Joachim, can they carry out their Plan successfully?'

'I believe they can, my Fuehrer – with our help. But we must act soon. The next few weeks are vital. If the opportunity is lost, it will never return.'

Caught up in von Ribbentrop's enthusiasm, Adolf Hitler made up his mind.

'Very well. We will back this Plan. Give these Consortium people any help they need to carry it out. The resources of the Reich are at your command. I wish you to take personal charge of this operation, Joachim.'

'I shall be honoured, my Fuehrer, and most glad to do so. Fortunately, I am due to return to London to prepare to take up my appointment as your Ambassador. Under cover of that office I can assist the Consortium.'

'Excellent,' Hitler beamed. 'You have done well, Joachim. Keep me informed.'

'At your orders, my Fuehrer.' Von Ribbentrop rose, gave the Nazi salute, and marched out.

Left alone, Hitler considered further. With England as his ally, he need have no fear of European or American intervention. He had already re-occupied the Rhineland. Austria, Poland and Czechoslovakia would fall next, and then Russia. A German Empire of the East.

Hitler sat back, dreaming of world conquest. Absently, he reached for another cream cake...

Peri surveyed himself in her bedroom mirror.

Now she was wearing a black coat and skirt, a grey silk blouse and a wide-brimmed hat. It was more comfortable than her 1899 outfit – the skirt was a lot shorter for a start – but she still felt strange and overdressed. God only knew what the Doctor would've chosen for her if she'd let him.

She adjusted the angle of the hat-brim and went to find the Doctor.

She found him in his study, a cosy oak-panelled book-lined room in which a coal fire burned perpetually in an old-fashioned grate. He was sitting behind a massive mahogany desk, cramming a variety of documents, papers and parchments into a big leather briefcase.

Looking up, he gave Peri a nod of approval. 'The glass of fashion and the mould of form,' he said.

'Thanks.' Peri grinned. 'You don't look too bad yourself.'

The Doctor was wearing a dark-blue three-piece suit with a faint pinstripe, a white shirt and regimental tie. On a side table she saw yellow kid gloves, a walking stick, and a grey Homburg hat with a black band. It struck her that the Doctor's outfit wasn't so different from his 1899 costume. As before, he looked both dignified and impressive in the dark formal clothes.

Peri nodded towards the pile of papers. 'What's all this?'

'We'll be arriving in an age of bureaucracy and documentation,' said the Doctor with a grimace. 'And we may be staying a while this time. All this will help us to establish an identity.' He shoved the last few papers into the briefcase and closed it with a snap. 'Come along, Peri, we must be nearly there by now.' With that, he jumped up and headed for the door.

'Yes, but nearly *where*?' muttered Peri.

She followed him back to the control room.

For once, the Doctor – and the TARDIS – had got it right. With a discreet murmuring and humming sound, the TARDIS materialised in a quiet corner of Green Park.

The Doctor came out, Peri close behind him. He took a gold watch from his waistcoat pocket, opened the back and touched a control.

The TARDIS disappeared.

Peri looked alarmed. 'Where's it gone?'

'*She* is now in a parking orbit in the space-time continuum.' The Doctor smiled a little smugly. 'I think it's a bit early for her to blend in properly with the police boxes of the period, and we don't want to have to go chasing after her again, do we?'

'Can you get it – *her* – back?'

'Of course! Providing the recall circuit works.'

'And if it doesn't?'

'We'll just have to settle down here.' He sniffed dismissively. 'There's a war due in a few years. At least things won't be boring!'

'That'll be World War Two? When the Germans dropped lots of bombs on London?'

'That's the one.'

Peri gave him a look. He was treating this like one big game. Peri remembered the bullets flying back in the veldt, the noise, the bodies. Perhaps the Doctor did, too – now he was smiling at her, apologetically.

'Come along, Peri,' he said.

They strolled out of the park and walked along Piccadilly. Peri couldn't help feeling a thrill at being here some thirty years before she was even born. Looking around, she had to admit they fitted in pretty well with the crowds moving along under the overcast sky.

She thought how different things must be in this time.

There was radio, of course and the cinema – but no television. No pop music, either, no raves, no clubbing – not as she knew it. There'd be night-clubs of course, and jazz and big band music… Then there was travel. You could fly to Paris and New York by now, if you were part of the jet set… Otherwise, it was long trips by boats… a more leisurely time.

She was still mulling all this over when the Doctor came to an abrupt halt before a plain-fronted corner building with an ornately-carved entrance.

'Why've we stopped?' asked Peri.

The Doctor pointed with his stick to the faded letters carved above the door.

Peri tried to read them. 'Chol… Cholm…'

'Chumley's,' said the Doctor. 'Spelt Cholmondeley's,

119

pronounced Chumley's!'

'Just another little Brit joke to confuse the Yanks, huh?'

'I don't suppose they've ever had a "Yank" in Cholmondeley's,' said the Doctor. 'You'll be a first for them.'

'What is the place anyway?'

'It's a bank – *the* bank in many ways.' He smiled. 'Not the biggest, but one of the oldest and by far the most prestigious.'

Peri looked at the single word carved above the door. 'Why doesn't it say it's a bank?'

'Because,' said the Doctor, 'if you don't know it's a bank you've no business going in there.'

'So why are we going in?'

'To reclaim my family fortune of course.' He gave her a mock-dignified look. 'I shall expect a bit more respect from you, young lady. As it happens, I'm a very wealthy man!'

The Doctor pushed open the heavy door and ushered Peri inside.

Chapter Seventeen
The Bank

The door opened to reveal a surprisingly large and luxurious hall with a high ceiling and a marble floor. There was a long mahogany counter, lots of highly polished brass and a hushed cathedral-like atmosphere. Peri sniffed. 'What's that smell?'

'Money,' said the Doctor. 'Lots and lots of very old money!' Just then, a suave-looking type in morning-dress glided towards them. 'May I be of assistance?' he asked in languid tones.

'Hope so,' drawled the Doctor in tones more languid still. 'Believe I have an account here.'

The assistant's eyebrows rose. 'You – *believe*, sir?'

'My great, great – forget quite how many greats – grandfather set it up years ago. Went off to South America and forgot all about it. Account's never really been used.'

'I see, sir. And this ancestor's name, sir?'

'Smith. Doctor John Smith.'

'And your name?'

'The same,' said the Doctor blandly. 'Family name, you see.'

By now the assistant was looking distinctly sceptical. 'And the year in which the account was set up, sir?'

'Ah, hang on a minute.' The Doctor made a great show of thinking hard, then snapped his fingers. 'Got it! Year they founded the bank!'

The assistant's eyebrows shot up even higher. '1816, sir?'

'Sounds about right.'

'You have – documentation?'

'Lord, yes, masses of it.'

The Doctor opened the leather briefcase and produced an

enormous bundle of papers and parchments. The assistant drew a deep breath. 'I think you'd better come and see Mr Cholmondeley. The manager, sir…'

Half an hour later, the Doctor and Peri were sitting in a luxurious oak-panelled office sipping sherry.

Mr Cholmondeley, a round Pickwickian type in gold-rimmed half-moon glasses, looked up from the Doctor's pile of parchments.

'Well, everything seems to be in order. The account was set up by a Doctor John Smith, for the use of himself and his direct descendants in perpetuity. Your proofs of identity are more than satisfactory. We are at your service, sir.'

The Doctor nodded graciously.

Mr Cholmondeley turned back to the Doctor and lowered his voice.

'I don't know if you realise, sir, but the balance of your account is now extremely large. There was a substantial deposit to begin with, of course, and with cumulative interest for 120 years…'

He wrote something on a slip of paper with a gold pen and handed it to the Doctor.

The Doctor glanced carelessly at it for a moment and then showed it to Peri. The figure seemed to have an awful lot of zeros on the end of it.

'How much is that in dollars?'

The Doctor laughed. 'I know, I know! It probably seems like small change to you!' He turned to the manager. 'Miss Brown is the daughter of old Capability Brown, the American railway tycoon. I'm an old family friend, keeping an eye on her while she tours Europe.'

'Indeed, sir?' said the manager politely. 'Well, tell me, how may the Bank be of service to you both?'

The Doctor drew a deep breath. 'I'll need some ready cash,

of course – five hundred should do for now. I'd like a cheque book… Oh, and we'd better open a drawing account for Miss Brown as well. And one more thing.'

Cholmondeley smiled obsequiously. 'You have only to name it, sir.'

'The P&O Line lost all our luggage, it's on the way to Penang or somewhere. Only got what we stand up in. We'll need to buy some replacements till our stuff turns up… Meanwhile my ward and I need a hotel. Looks a bit off, y'know, turning up with no luggage and a young lady in tow. Wonder if you could vouch for us, until everything's sorted out?'

'A pleasure, sir.' Cholmondeley rubbed his hands together. 'Where would you like to stay?'

'We passed a decent looking little place on the way. Just down the road, in Piccadilly. Think you could fix us up there?'

'Many of our clients patronise the establishment you mention, sir. I shall… fix you up without delay.' The manager raised his voice. 'Miss Farquharson?'

A severe-looking grey-haired woman appeared at the door. 'Yes, sir?'

'Miss Farquharson, get me the manager of the Ritz Hotel on the telephone, will you, please?'

Peri and the Doctor were sipping champagne cocktails in the chandeliered sitting-room of the most luxurious hotel suite Peri had ever seen in her life. Somewhere below, the traffic of Piccadilly was muted to a low background murmur.

'Well!' said Peri. 'I can't believe this is happening, Doctor. All this opulence! How come you've got so much loot at this Cholthingummies place?'

'Just chance, really. I'd dropped in to congratulate the Duke after Waterloo, and we had a bit of a night on the town. Went to some gambling den or other and I cleaned up at faro. I went to see Prinny down at Brighton the next day and told him the story. I didn't have much use for the money at the time, and Prinny suggested I deposit it with some crony of his who'd just founded a bank.' The Doctor laughed. 'Knowing how dodgy Prinny's finances were I was lucky not to lose the lot, but it seems to have worked out all right.'

'Slow down,' said Peri. 'I need a cast list. The Duke? Prinny?'

'Sorry. The Duke of Wellington and the Prince Regent.'

'And all this happened a hundred years ago?'

'One hundred and twenty to be precise. It's one of the fringe benefits of being a Time Lord – the investment opportunities are enormous!'

'But how come we're going in for all this conspicuous consumption? I thought you didn't approve of this sort of thing.'

The Doctor looked a little embarrassed. 'Because we want to enter London society in a hurry.'

'Why?'

The Doctor looked surprised. 'To show you some of the elegance you're after, of course.'

'And to help you find the movers and shakers tinkering with history?'

The Doctor winced. 'If you insist!'

'I thought you needed background and breeding and all that sort of thing to get into high society?'

'Don't you believe it, Peri. Money's the key, always has been. Wealthy Americans have been sending their daughters over here for years. You'd be surprised how many ended up marrying into the aristocracy.' He looked at her thoughtfully, much to Peri's alarm.

'You're not expecting *me* to marry anyone?'

'Oh, it won't come to that,' said the Doctor. Then he sniffed. 'Well, probably not, anyway.'

'So what *is* the great plan for introducing ourselves into society?'

'The manager of Cholmondeley's Bank and the manager of the Ritz know absolutely everybody between them. And then there's their respective staff. It won't take long for news to get round that a rich and mysterious stranger, and an even richer American heiress, have arrived in town.'

'So we start networking, making a few social contacts?'

'Not a bit of it. We sit back and let them come to us.'

'Why?'

'Because you can't get into society if you let them see you *want* to get into society. They'll only accept you if you make it clear you couldn't care less!'

Peri finished her cocktail, and looked round the luxurious suite. Then she sighed theatrically.

'I guess I can handle staying here for a few days,' she said.

The Doctor looked pleased. 'Just until I can hire a house, of course. We'll rent somewhere furnished in a good part of town. Then there are servants to be hired... Oh, and we'll both be needing several new outfits. It'll mean a good deal of shopping, I'm afraid, especially for you...'

Peri sighed again and stretched luxuriously. 'In a good cause, Doctor, I'm prepared to make any sacrifice! How about another of these champagne cocktails?'

The phone rang and a long white hand lifted the receiver from its stand.

The deep voice said, 'Yes?'

'I am sorry to trouble you, Count, and indeed, the matter may be trivial...' The voice from the phone was male, upper class, yet humble and deferential. 'I was at the bank earlier and I overheard two of the cashiers gossiping. Some mystery customer has turned up and reactivated a dormant account. A very *large* account.'

'Why do you tell me this?'

'Because of the Alert. He gave his name as Smith, Doctor

John Smith. Had a pretty American girl with him.' The voice sniggered. 'Said she was his ward... They took a two-bedroomed suite, keeping up appearances, I suppose.'

'Thank you for letting me know.'

The receiver was replaced, and, almost immediately, the telephone rang again.

'Yes?'

The voice had a strong French accent.

'It's Antoine, under-manager at the Ritz.'

'Well?'

'I thought it might interest you to know that we have two new customers, a man and a girl. They arrived without luggage but the manager seemed to be expecting them. They have taken one of the best suites and appear to have unlimited funds. The man's name is –'

The deep voice cut in. 'Would the name be Smith, Antoine? Doctor John Smith? Accompanied by a Miss Brown, an attractive American girl?'

There was a long silence before Antoine continued.

'You know already.' It was a statement, not a question.

'Thank you for calling, Antoine.'

'Do you wish me to take any further action?'

'Not yet. Keep an eye on them. Let me know of any visitors, and inform me at once if they leave the hotel.'

'That is all?'

'That is all, for the moment.' The knuckles of the long hand grew whiter as the man gripped the phone more tightly. 'I intend to deal with them myself.'

Chapter Eighteen
Explosion

News of the arrival of the wealthy Doctor Smith and his even wealthier American ward soon spread around fashionable London. They dined in the best and most expensive restaurants and took boxes at the opera and the theatre.

They hired horses and went riding in Rotten Row, then hired a Rolls Royce and chauffeur, and paid brief visits to all the obvious tourist sights.

It became known that the Doctor was looking for a house to rent. Only the most expensive and exclusive properties were being considered.

He also wrote formal letters to several of the most exclusive clubs in London, presenting documents that gave him associate and travelling members' rights.

Curiosity rose to fever pitch when the Doctor, immaculate in top hat and tails, paid a call at Buckingham Palace and presented certain documents, credentials and letters of introduction.

At the Palace the Doctor encountered a tall good-looking man with a weak chin. They were both kept waiting in the same ornate ante-room for a time. A suave young Foreign Office aide introduced them.

'Herr von Ribbentrop, may I present Doctor Smith, Honorary Consul for the Republic of Santa Esmerelda? Doctor Smith, allow me to introduce Herr von Ribbentrop, the new German Ambassador.'

The two men exchanged dignified bows.

'Like yours, Herr von Ribbentrop's is in a sense an informal visit,' the aide went on, 'since His Majesty has not yet been crowned. There will, of course, be formal presentation ceremonies for both of you after the Coronation.'

As both the Doctor and von Ribbentrop knew perfectly well, King Edward VIII, formerly the fantastically popular Prince of Wales, had only recently succeeded to the throne. Even so, the crowning ceremony had been mysteriously delayed.

It was rumoured that the reasons were not unconnected with the King's long-standing attachment to a twice-divorced American woman called Wallis Simpson, although nobody in society could understand what all the fuss was about. Royal mistresses, after all, were part of a long and honourable tradition. All the new King had to do was marry some understanding European princess and produce the necessary two sons, the 'heir and spare', and he and his Wallis could go on as before...

As befitted his superior rank, von Ribbentrop was granted his audience first.

Patiently the Doctor awaited his turn. He didn't expect to be kept hanging around for long. The new King was rumoured to be bored by his formal constitutional duties, and liked to get them over with as quickly as possible.

Sure enough, von Ribbentrop emerged from the throne room only a few minutes later. He paused before the Doctor, as if compelled to explain the shortness of his time with the King.

'Not the formal visit,' he said. 'One wouldn't wish to intrude at a time of mourning. Nor, of course, to appear to be remiss in introducing oneself.'

The Doctor bowed. 'My own dilemma exactly. I am glad to see, by Your Excellency's presence, that I took the correct decision.'

Von Ribbentrop visibly glowed under the Doctor's flattery. The Doctor guessed he knew little of South America, but was always anxious to befriend any potential ally of the Reich.

He bowed stiffly in return. 'A great pleasure to meet you, Doctor. I hope you will attend one of my little soirées at the German Embassy?'

'I should be honoured, Excellency. I am currently residing at the Ritz, as I am between abodes. My ward, Miss Brown, is staying with me at present. I wonder if she might also…?'

'I will arrange invitations for you both.'

Von Ribbentrop bowed again and left.

'The King will see you in just a moment, sir,' said the aide. He paused. 'I feel I should point out that His Majesty is new to his royal duties, and has many obligations.'

'My dear chap,' said the Doctor cheerfully. 'If the German Ambassador only gets three minutes, I should imagine I probably rate about thirty seconds!'

The Doctor walked forward into the throne room, where a slight, fair-haired figure stood by the throne, dwarfed by a group of tall, uniformed court officials.

'Ah, Doctor Smith…' said a husky, pleasant voice.

A handshake, a charming smile, a few kind words, and the Doctor was out in well under his thirty seconds…

While the Doctor went about his business, Peri went about hers – shopping! She'd been told not to stint herself, but to draw freely upon his apparently limitless credit. After all, she was supposed to be a millionaire heiress, he reminded her. She had an image to keep up!

Now, thoroughly shopped out, Peri lay stretched out on an enormous sofa, surrounded by boxes, bags and parcels of all shapes and sizes, listening to the sound of running water from the adjoining bathroom.

Lazily, she reminded herself to get up soon and check if the bath was full. Not that there was any great hurry. The baths at the Ritz were enormous, you could practically swim in them…

She had just kicked off her shoes and was wriggling her

aching feet in the air when the Doctor returned. It was so odd seeing him dolled up in tail coat and top hat, the multi-coloured nightmare of his usual attire safely locked away in the TARDIS wardrobe.

'Where've you been?' she said idly. 'Buckingham Palace?'

The Doctor tossed his topper onto a table and sprawled into an enormous armchair. 'That's right! Is that my bath you're running?'

'No way!' She sat up, taking in what he'd said. 'You haven't *really* been to the Palace, have you?'

The Doctor nodded. 'Presenting my credentials to the King as Honorary Consul for Santa Esmerelda.'

'The *King*?' Peri stared at him.

'That's right. Charming man, Edward.'

'Well, what's an Honorary Consul?'

'A sort of low-grade, cut-price ambassador.' He smiled.

'I gave the President of Santa Esmerelda some help a few years ago. The revolutionaries were about to shoot him and I persuaded him to liberalise his programme. Lower taxes, a health service, that sort of thing...'

'Flush sanitation?' Peri cheekily inquired.

The Doctor ignored her. 'He's very popular now. He was so grateful he made me Honorary Consul to Great Britain for life. You never know when that sort of thing will come in handy!'

The Doctor stood up.

'I'll just go and have that bath, then.'

'You'll do no such thing, go and run your own!'

The Doctor pouted. 'Is this the thanks I get for offering you opulence the like of which you've never seen?'

'Yes!' said Peri, throwing a cushion at him. 'If you *will* go to see the King and not take me!'

'It was protocol, Peri! A semi-official visit!' He smiled benignly. 'Don't worry, we'll be on the official diplomat list now. I imagine we'll be invited to a reception or a royal garden party before long. Oh, and by the way, I've found us a house, nice little place in Mayfair.'

Peri wasn't listening. 'A royal garden party? I don't think I've got anything to wear!'

The Doctor waved a hand at the boxes and parcels. 'You amaze me!'

Peri looked at the boxes and parcels too, trying to remember what was inside them. 'I haven't even unpacked half this stuff yet. But I really don't think –'

'Don't worry,' said the Doctor, dismissively. 'You can always go shopping again tomorrow.'

Peri was staring at a green striped hat-box beside the door. 'That's odd!'

'What is?'

'That box – it's from Harrods.'

'So?'

'I went to Harrods yesterday. I thought they'd delivered everything the same day.'

The Doctor shrugged. 'Perhaps that one got left behind and has only just caught up!'

'And it's a hat box,' Peri went on. 'I didn't buy any hats at Harrods. I must've picked up someone else's –'

The Doctor got up waving a hand for silence. He went slowly over to the hat box and knelt beside it, putting his ear up against it, listening.

'Did you buy any clocks at Harrods by any chance?' he asked Peri, his face grave.

Peri shook her head.

Suddenly the Doctor stood up, picked up the hat-box very carefully, and strode rapidly through the bathroom door.

Seconds later, Peri heard a loud splash, and gave a startled yelp as the Doctor hurtled back into the room and took a flying leap at her on the sofa. It toppled over, and the Doctor and Peri went backwards, ending up on the floor behind it.

Peri disentangled herself from the Doctor. 'What the hell are you –'

'Sssh!' said the Doctor imperatively, peering over the back of the upturned sofa.

Cautiously Peri did the same.

Nothing happened.

'You see?' said Peri. 'There's no need to panic, Doctor. It was probably just –'

There was a muffled boom from the bathroom, and the Doctor grabbed her shoulder and pulled her down.

Steam and smoke gushed into the room, followed by a miniature tidal wave as the contents of Peri's enormous bathtub flooded across the floor. Alarm bells started ringing somewhere in the hotel, and there were shouts and the sound of running footsteps.

The Doctor stood up, righted the sofa with a single heave, and sat on it cross-legged, beckoning to Peri to join him.

She looked at him in alarm.

'Shouldn't we get out of here?'

'Don't panic,' said the Doctor gently. 'I don't think there's any danger of fire, not with all this water about. And we're scarcely likely to drown!'

They sat and watched the water rippling across the carpet.

'Quite a pretty effect, really,' said the Doctor.

Suddenly the door to the suite was flung open, revealing the sallow figure of Antoine the under-manager, with what looked like half the hotel staff crowding the corridor behind him.

'What is it, Doctor Smith?' gasped Antoine. 'What has happened?'

The Doctor waved towards the flooded carpet.

'Antoine,' he said sadly, 'I'm afraid we shall have to leave your hotel. The suite is comfortable, the beds are excellent, and the cuisine superb. The plumbing, however, leaves a lot to be desired…'

Chapter Nineteen
Invitation

Winston Spencer Churchill was building a wall.

He was in the garden of his country house, Chartwell Manor in Kent. What he liked to do most of the time was to eat and drink, to smoke his cigars, and talk – about politics, history, art, literature, any of the hundred-and-one subjects that interested him. He liked to write. He already had a formidable number of books to his credit. When he felt tired and drained, he liked to paint, here at Chartwell or in the south of France.

But when things were going badly, when he felt tired and angry and despairing, he built walls. Something about the mixing of the mortar, the careful and laborious placing of the bricks, the steady rising of the wall itself, brought him a kind of solace.

As he worked, Churchill's mind drifted back over his life. Sometimes it seemed a very long life indeed.

He was sixty-one.

He thought of his escape from prison in the Boer War, of his flight from that mysterious chateau in the Great War.

He had served for a year on the Western Front, fighting in the trenches with the Scots Fusiliers and ending up as a Lieutenant-Colonel.

A year later he had returned to Parliament, feeling that by risking his own life in battle he had, at least to some extent, purged the shame of the failed Dardanelles attack. Moreover, his friends told him, and he knew in his heart that it was true, that he could make a far greater contribution to the war effort in the Government than in the trenches.

He had helped to pioneer the development of the tank, the

war-winning weapon that eventually freed the troops from the hell of the trenches, and ended the war as Minister of Munitions.

After the war, for many years, his political career had prospered. He had held most of the important Cabinet posts, including that of Chancellor of the Exchequer. Now, however, in the mid-1930s, Winston Churchill's career was in decline. He had quarrelled with his party leaders, and had been out of the Cabinet for many years. His unpopularity with the Conservative party, and in particular with its leaders, was made worse by the fact that Winston Churchill had found a cause.

Ever since Adolf Hitler's rise to power in 1933, Churchill, and Churchill alone, had raised his voice in repeated warnings about the Nazi menace, about the dangers of German rearmament. But nobody wanted to know. The only result had been the virtual end of his political career.

Perhaps it was time he accepted the inevitable and retired. He could write and paint – and build walls.

He sighed, and put another brick in place.

A slim, beautiful woman in her early fifties came down the long path from the house towards him. She was Clementine Churchill, Winston Churchill's beloved Clemmie. They had married in 1908 and, as Churchill said, lived happily ever after. Clemmie was strong-minded enough to manage him, and intelligent enough not to let it show.

She was also the only one who dared to disturb him when he was in this kind of mood.

As her shadow fell over him, he looked up and grunted. 'Well?' Despite his gruffness, his eyes were twinkling. As always, the mere sight of Clemmie made him feel better.

'Colonel Carstairs is here, dear,' she said.

'Bringing me more disastrous news, no doubt. I don't think I want to see him!'

After their escape from the chateau, Carstairs had joined Churchill's staff. He had remained in the Army after the war, transferring to Military Intelligence. Now he was one of the many unofficial helpers who kept Churchill informed about the state of England's defences.

'You and Jeremy are having drinks on the terrace,' said Clemmie placidly. 'Come along!'

Churchill came along.

Churchill put down the sheaf of documents, his face bleak. He took a long swig of brandy, drew hard on his cigar, and sent a cloud of blue smoke into the afternoon air.

'You are sure of these figures?'

The tall, lean man on the other side of the little table gathered up the papers and put them back in his briefcase. He was in civilian clothes, in *mufti* as soldiers called it. His visit to Chartwell was unofficial, possibly even illegal.

'Absolutely sure, sir,' Carstairs said in answer to Churchill's question. 'I checked with Anderson at Air Ministry and Wigram at the Foreign Office, and all our sources agree.'

Churchill thumped the table with his fist, making the ashtray jump.

'Already we begin to lose our advantage. In a year, two years at most, their air force will be superior to ours, in both number and quality of aeroplanes. Their army too is expanding... We have the Navy to hold them in check, but if they gain superiority in the air... I tell you, Carstairs, step by step that madman Hitler is preparing for war.'

'I know, sir,' said Carstairs quietly. 'So do most of the leaders of the Armed Forces. It seems that the only ones who *don't* know are the Prime Minister and the Cabinet. If only they'd make you Minister of Defence...'

'Baldwin is a fool,' growled Churchill. 'He is determined to keep me out of the cabinet at all costs. Few are willing even to contemplate the possibility of war.' He sighed. 'It is understandable. The horrors of the last conflict are still too close, but dangers are not overcome by ignoring them. And all the time we do nothing, our enemies are plotting against us…'

The Doctor and Peri left the Ritz within hours of the explosion. By a good deal of fast talking, and an offer to pay the cost of repairing the shattered bathroom, the Doctor persuaded the manager not to call the police.

'No point in attracting a lot of bad publicity for the hotel,' he pointed out. 'Or for Santa Esmerelda. Far better to tell the guests an old boiler exploded and hush the whole thing up.'

The manager agreed. He expressed great regret at losing two of his most distinguished guests – but Peri had the distinct impression that he was relieved to see them go. So too was Antoine the under-manager, who seemed to have been badly shaken by the explosion.

The hired Rolls was big enough to take the Doctor and Peri and all their newly-acquired possessions to their new home. It was a short enough trip, up to the far end of Piccadilly and a sharp right turn into Mayfair. The Doctor had hired an elegant little town house in Hill Street.

'Belongs to a rather impoverished Duke,' he explained as the Rolls Royce turned off Piccadilly. 'Went shooting on his country estate and shot himself in the foot. He's staying down in the country till his foot gets better and everybody stops laughing at him. He was glad to let the place out, servants and all.'

'He wouldn't be if he knew his new tenants were prime terrorist targets all of a sudden,' said Peri. 'I still can't believe they slipped a bomb in our room. What *was* that all about, Doctor?'

'As I keep saying Peri, I'm not sure,' said the Doctor a little irritably. 'Still, suffice it to say, it was certainly a reaction of some kind.'

'To what?' asked Peri, snorting. 'My shopping?'

'Doubtful, I agree,' said the Doctor. 'So it must be me. What have I done since we arrived? I've been to the bank, and I've been to Buckingham Palace and met old Ribbentrop and the King. Why should that make anyone want to blow me up?'

'Perhaps someone who doesn't care for name droppers?' Peri inquired sweetly. Then she sighed. 'In any case, are you sure that's what they wanted? If that bomb was meant for you, it was a bit misplaced. I'm the one who would have opened that hat box, and that makes me far more likely to be the target!'

'That's a very good point,' said the Doctor thoughtfully. 'I don't think it was a terribly serious assassination attempt, not really. It wasn't even a very big bomb. I think it was meant as a warning to me – a warning not to interfere.'

Peri shuddered. 'So they were prepared to risk killing me, just to warn you?'

'Apparently.'

'Charming,' said Peri broodingly. 'What a gentle world you've brought me to. Do you think they'll send any more warnings?'

'It's possible,' said the Doctor, brightly. 'In any case, I've taken a few precautions.'

The Rolls turned into Hill Street and and drew up outside an elegant house. A silver-haired butler appeared on the steps to welcome them, and showed them inside.

In the small but well-appointed hall, a line-up of servants stood ready for their inspection.

'My name is Rye, sir and madam,' said the butler. He nodded towards a round-faced older woman in a black gown. 'This is Mrs Danvers, the cook-housekeeper, and these two girls are Emily and Martha, the maids. The gentleman from the agency arrived a short time ago. I hope everything is satisfactory? His Grace only keeps a very small staff here in town.'

The Doctor glanced quizzically at Peri. 'What do you think?

Will we be able to manage?'

'I'm sure we'll be fine,' said Peri. In theory she disapproved of people having servants. But it was surprising, and rather worrying, how soon you got used to people looking after you.

The maids took them upstairs to their rooms, which were as quietly luxurious as the rest of the house. The chauffeur brought up Peri's luggage, and one of the maids began unpacking her things. Watch out for any stray hat boxes, Peri thought.

She wandered over to her bedroom window and looked out into a small, high-walled garden. There was a flash of movement in the corner of her eye. Peri caught a glimpse of somebody moving in the dense shrubbery.

'Doctor!'

The Doctor came out of a room further down the hallway. 'What's up, Peri?'

'There's someone in the garden. I caught sight of him lurking in the bushes.'

The Doctor seemed quite unperturbed. 'Ah yes, the butler said he was here. This way, Peri.' He led the way downstairs and into a small sitting-room that looked out on to the garden.

Opening the French windows, the Doctor called, 'We're in here!'

'Look out, Doctor,' warned Peri. 'He's probably got a bazooka or something.'

The Doctor laughed. 'I doubt it, Peri. Don't worry, he's on our side.'

A very large man appeared from the shadows of the overgrown garden. He wore a trenchcoat and a soft hat and he had what Peri thought of as a nicely ugly face.

He touched the brim of his hat. 'Doctor Smith? Miss Brown?' The deep gravelly voice was unmistakably American.

'That's right,' said the Doctor. 'You'll be the man from the Pinkerton Detective Agency, I take it?'

'That's right, sir. The name's Dekker. Tom Dekker.'

'What's a fellow Yank doing over here?' asked Peri.

'I used to run a one-man agency back in Chicago,' said Dekker. 'Back in the old Capone days.'

Peri grinned. 'Wow! That must have been exciting!'

'It had its moments. But then my friend Ness got the Big Fellow sent to Alcatraz, and they repealed Prohibition and things kinda slowed down in Chicago. Got so whole weeks went by without a decent shootout.'

'Frustrating for you,' said Peri sympathetically.

Dekker grinned. 'Terrible. Anyway, what with the Depression and all, things got pretty tough. So when the Pinks offered me a job I was glad to take it. I worked for them for a while all over the USA, and then they put me in charge of their London office.'

'And very glad we are to have you,' said the Doctor briskly. 'I hate to interrupt a meeting of compatriots, but can we talk business for a moment? What do you think of the set-up here, Mr Dekker?'

'Could be worse. Nice compact secure front entrance, good visibility. Plenty of servants about, so the place is never empty. The back garden wall is a bit of a worry, gives on to some kinda alley, whaddya call it over here?'

'A mews?' suggested the Doctor.

'That's right, a mews. Anyway, the wall's pretty high but we could do with some spikes or some barbed wire. And you need some alarms. I can see to all that for you.'

'Please do. Anything else?'

'I'll have someone keeping an eye on the place, day and night. If you're going anywhere special, let me know and I'll send someone, or come myself. That's about it, really.'

The Doctor nodded, sagely. 'It all sounds very reassuring.'

'Can you give me any idea what kind of opposition we're up against, Doctor Smith?' Dekker asked.

'Not really. It's just that I seem to have annoyed some very powerful and ruthless people.'

'Political? Criminal?'

'I'm not sure yet. Possibly both.'

'These guys heeled – armed?'

'It wouldn't surprise me. Are you?'

Suddenly there was an enormous automatic in Dekker's hand.

'I told you he had a bazooka,' said Peri. She turned to Dekker. 'You may need that. Somebody put a bomb in our hotel room!'

The big automatic disappeared. 'Pineapple?' said Dekker. 'That's pretty rare over here. We better take these guys seriously. OK, Doctor Smith, I'll get right on to things.' He paused. 'I used to know a guy called Smith back in Chicago. Everyone called him Doc. Ran a speakeasy – a saloon – during Prohibition.'

'Wasn't me,' said the Doctor. 'You may have noticed that Smith is a somewhat common name.'

'Hell no, he was nothing like you. Doc was a funny little guy. Very tough though, very shrewd. Had a girl with him…' He broke off. 'Hell, here I go again, talking about the old days. Must be getting old myself. Nice to meet you, Dr Smith, Miss Brown. I'll be in touch.'

He touched the brim of his hat and went out of the room. They heard him talking to the butler for a moment, and then the slam of the front door.

Peri touched the Doctor's arm. 'You must be really worried, Doctor, hiring a bodyguard.'

'Not a bodyguard,' said the Doctor. 'A security consultant! I can't be around all the time, and it will be nice to think someone's keeping an eye out for suspicious strangers and ticking parcels.'

'So he's really *my* minder?'

'If you like.'

'I don't mind,' said Peri. 'I think he's cute. Doctor…'

'What is it?'

'That Doc he knew in Chicago?'

'Yes?'

'Do you think it *could* be you? Another you, sometime in your future.'

'Don't be ridiculous, Peri,' said the Doctor disdainfully. 'I don't know what my future holds, any more than you do. But I very much doubt that it includes being a funny little "guy" running a speakeasy in Chicago during Prohibition!'

There was a knock on the front door and the sound of low voices. Rye the butler came in carrying a large white envelope with an embossed gold crest.

'This has just arrived by special messenger, sir.'

The Doctor took the envelope, ripped it open and extracted a big white card with embossed gold lettering.

He beamed at Peri. 'Looks like you'll be buying a hat after all. We're invited to a garden party. At Buckingham Palace!'

Chapter Twenty
Encounters

'An invitation to a Buckingham Palace garden party is an honour in itself,' remarked the Doctor, steepling his fingers. 'Attending one can even be quite enjoyable, if you're fond of weak tea, thin cucumber sandwiches and packed crowds. Getting there, however –'

'– is hell,' Peri concluded for him. 'What an honour. You spend ages travelling slowly along a jam-packed Pall Mall, then ages more waiting to get through this stupid visitors' gate.'

She sighed, and grumbled some more.

'You don't even get any extra prestige for being in a party frock and a Rolls Royce. *Everybody's* in a party frock and a Rolls Royce – or a Bentley, or a Daimler – or a Merc,' she added, noticing a car a little ahead of them in the slow moving queue.

It was quite a sight, an outsize Mercedes-Benz, with a swastika flag on the bonnet.

'Looks as if von Ribbentrop's turned up,' said the Doctor.

'That's Ribbentrop all right,' confirmed Dekker from the driver's seat. 'That car's famous. That's the *grossen* seven-litre supercharged model. Your Londoners don't reckon much to old Ribby, but they sure love his Mercedes. It draws bigger crowds than he does!'

Peri nodded. 'I can believe it!'

'Not too practical, though,' Dekker added, pulling on the handbrake as they came to a standstill once again. 'It does about three miles to the gallon. Every time they try to go further than around the block they run out of gas!'

The chauffeur's uniform jacket was tight across Dekker's broad shoulders, and the cap was jammed precariously on the back of his head. He'd insisted on driving them when the Doctor told him where they were going. 'Big crowds, public places, maximum danger,' he'd said. 'We lose a lot of politicians that way in the States.'

Peri wasn't buying that statement. 'You don't really think anything's going to happen, Dekker, do you? You're just another nosy American tourist, like me, keen to check out the King of England.'

'Sure,' agreed Dekker cheerfully. 'It's this Simpson dame *I* want to get a look at though, the one that's got her hooks into him so hard. She must be some piece of work.' He grinned at Peri. 'Mind you, I always say you can't beat American women for looks!'

They crawled through the visitors' gate at last, had their names and invitations checked and, guided by a fussy Palace official, made their way to the assigned parking place.

'Sorry to have to leave you, Dekker,' said Peri. 'Looks like we're going to have *all* the fun!'

'Don't worry about me,' said Dekker. 'I'm working, remember. I'll be around. You may not see me, but I'll be around.'

The Doctor and Peri followed the crowd to the part of the Palace gardens where the party was taking place. There were marquees, white-coated waiters scurrying to and fro, and, on the main lawn, a swirling fashionably-dressed crowd circulated around a slight, fair-haired figure – the new King.

The Doctor and Peri stood on the edge of the crowd and accepted tea and sandwiches from a hovering waiter. The crockery was bone china with the royal crest. Peri considered slipping her cup into her handbag, but decided it would be unworthy of her republican principles.

'I suppose we ought to go and pay our respects to the King,' said the Doctor. 'Come on, Peri, I said I'd present you at Court! This is almost as good, isn't it?'

Suddenly, Peri's attention was caught by a solitary figure standing alone on the fringe of the crowd. Solid, slightly rotund, with a massive head thrust forward and a smouldering cigar in the mouth, the figure was strangely familiar.

Peri tugged at the Doctor's arm. 'Look, Doctor, isn't that –'

'It is indeed,' said the Doctor. 'The man himself!'

Immediately, Peri hurried across to him. 'Mr Churchill! It's so nice to see you again!'

Churchill stared at her blankly. 'It is always pleasant to be warmly greeted by a pretty girl,' he rumbled. 'But I'm afraid you have the advantage of me, young lady.'

All at once, Peri realised a number of things. Firstly, that although it seemed no time at all to her since they'd met in South Africa, for Winston Churchill it was, what, thirty-seven years? Secondly, the years had left their mark on Churchill. The wispy moustache had gone, and so had most of the reddish hair on Churchill's head. And thirdly, since only a few days had passed in their subjective time, she and the Doctor hadn't altered at all.

It was going to be a hard one to explain away.

She heard the Doctor saying, 'Please forgive my ward, Mr Churchill. It's just that we've heard so much about you, we feel we actually know you! My father sends his regards.'

Churchill frowned. 'Your father, sir?'

'Doctor Smith. Doctor John Smith. You were captured together by the Boers in South Africa, on an armoured train.'

Churchill stared at him, looking through him into the distant past. 'Doctor Smith!' he breathed. 'Yes, he helped me to clear the track and free the engine. We were captured together, and escaped together!' He looked hard at the Doctor. 'Your father, eh? You're very like him, you know.'

The Doctor smiled. 'So they tell me, sir.'

'How is he? Did he succeed in making his escape?' Churchill was smiling broadly back at him. 'I made inquiries, but I never

145

did learn anything of his fate. There was a rumour that he'd been killed in an explosion, murdered by the Boers.'

'Not a bit of it, sir. He blew up the ammunition store for a diversion, stole a car, and made his escape in comfort!'

Churchill roared with laughter. 'I always knew he was a resourceful fellow. Indeed, he told me that he had made alternative arrangements.' He looked at Peri. 'And this young lady? She looks…'

'A descendant of the original Miss Brown, my father's ward,' said the Doctor smoothly. 'Again, I believe there is a strong family resemblance.'

'Extraordinary!' said Churchill. 'And what became of your father? Is he still alive?'

'Yes indeed, sir, he's quite unstoppable.'

Peri sighed inwardly. The Doctor was really enjoying himself, now.

'After he left South Africa, he settled in South America, and did very well. I myself am here as Honorary Consul for the Republic of Santa Esmerelda, where my father settled and made his fortune.'

'A fantastic and colourful story,' said Winston Churchill. 'I only wish my own life had been crowned with such success. Mine is a more melancholy tale. You see me now an extinct volcano, a spent force.'

'I don't believe it, sir,' said the Doctor. 'And neither should you. I believe that fate still has great things in store for you.'

'Like your father, sir, you lift my spirits and fill me with hope,' said Churchill. 'May I ask your full name?'

'It is the same as his,' said the Doctor. 'Smith. Doctor John Smith.'

'Doctor Smith and Miss Brown,' said Churchill, surveying them benignly. 'Extraordinary. I could almost believe that the years had rolled back and your ancestors stood once again before me, untouched by the passage of time. Tell me, have either of you met His Majesty?'

'Briefly,' said the Doctor. 'When I presented my credentials.'

'No,' said Peri. 'I'd love to meet him, but I think everyone has the same idea.'

'Come with me,' said Churchill, striding off. 'Has-been I may be, but a few shreds of my former glory still cling about me. Moreover, I have known young David since his youth. He's a reckless boy and very much spoiled, but he has a good heart.'

The crowd parted before Churchill and his small company as he marched up to the King and bowed.

'Your Majesty, may I present – I am tempted to say two old friends, but they are in fact the descendants of two old friends – Doctor Smith and Miss Brown.'

'Winston!' said the King warmly. 'Why do *I* never see you any more?'

'Your Majesty has new responsibilities, and new friends.'

'Does that mean *I* must forget *my* old ones?' The King turned to the Doctor. 'We have already met, I believe?'

The Doctor bowed. 'When I presented my credentials. May I present my ward, Miss Brown?'

Peri managed a very creditable curtsey. 'A great honour, Your Majesty.'

'You're an American,' said the King, looking around. 'Wallis, where are you? Here's a fellow countrywoman of yours.'

A small, extraordinarily thin woman, with a helmet of shining black hair, stepped forward from the group close to the King.

'Another one?' she said in a southern drawl. 'Well, I declare. I sometimes think poor old America must be empty, there are so many of us over here!'

Peri studied her with interest, and a sudden instinctive rivalry. Wallis Simpson was no beauty but the force of her personality, her will, burned inside that slim body like a flame. Her dark eyes seemed to blaze with life.

'I like American women,' said the King. 'They have spirit! Do you know what Wallis said to me when first we met, Miss Brown?'

'No, Your Majesty. Do tell me.'

'I asked her some banal question about her missing central heating. She said, "That's what everyone says to American visitors. I expected something more original from the Prince of Wales!"'

Wallis Simpson laughed, a little shrilly.

'How many times have I asked you to stop telling that story, David – Your Majesty?' She smiled at Peri. 'The fact is I was so nervous I blurted out the first thing that came into my head.'

They chatted for a moment or two longer, but it soon became apparent that Wallis Simpson felt they had taken up quite enough of the King's time. It was equally apparent that as far as the King was concerned, Wallis's will was law.

The Doctor, Peri and Churchill fell back, allowing other eager figures to surround the King.

Still, the Doctor and Peri had been touched by the royal favour. As the garden party wore on, other guests showed a flattering eagerness to speak to them. Several impressively bejewelled ladies made themselves known, promising future invitations.

Churchill looked on with sardonic approval. 'I have launched you upon the seas of society,' he growled. 'It is all I can do for you. Whether you sink or swim is now up to you.'

Finally von Ribbentrop himself made an appearance, greeting the Doctor and Peri warmly, and nodding coldly to Churchill.

'You must come to see us at the Embassy,' he insisted. 'I will take no refusal.' He looked pointedly at Churchill. 'With so many enemies around, my poor Germany needs all the friends she can get!'

'Buffoon,' growled Churchill, as von Ribbentrop moved away. 'The man is a diplomatic disaster, the laughing-stock of London society.'

They drifted to the edge of the lawn, under the shade of some towering trees. Von Ribbentrop made his way over to Wallis Simpson, and engaged her in what looked like an intimate conversation.

'An extraordinary woman!' said Churchill.

'With an extraordinary amount of influence upon the King?' suggested the Doctor.

Churchill nodded gloomily. 'I fear that is so, Doctor. And, as you can see, she is also close to von Ribbentrop. Some say very close indeed. She is said to dine frequently at the German Embassy, and Ribbentrop sends her red roses...' He sighed. 'His Majesty already inclines far too much towards Germany. He speaks German like a native, has many German relatives... Now, with the influence of von Ribbentrop, exercised through Mrs Simpson...' He shook his head in dismay. 'I fear we may soon have a monarch upon the throne of whose loyalty we cannot be entirely assured.'

Peri was shocked. 'You mean you can't trust the King?'

Even the Doctor was taken aback. 'Surely it can't be as bad as all that, sir?'

'Indeed it can,' said Churchill solemnly. He lowered his voice. 'Recently, vital diplomatic information was leaked to Germany. The leaks were traced to Fort Belvedere, His Majesty's private residence.' He spread out his hands in a gesture of despair. 'Who knows what the King tells Wallis Simpson, and what *she* passes on to von Ribbentrop? Things have come to such a pass that certain vital state papers have had to be *withheld* from the King!' Churchill checked himself. 'I am indiscreet. Yet it is a relief to speak of these matters. And somehow I feel I can trust you, Doctor, as I trusted your father.'

'Nothing you say to us will go any further,' said the Doctor quietly. 'Isn't that so, Peri?'

Peri nodded, and Churchill signalled a passing waiter, who offered a tray filled with cups of tea.

'Take that muck away,' growled Churchill. 'Bring a bottle of champagne and three glasses – now!'

The waiter scurried off.

Now that he had started unburdening himself, Churchill seemed eager to go on. 'To make matters worse, the King seems intent upon marrying the woman,' he growled.

'Why shouldn't he?' asked Peri. 'If he loves her…'

Churchill looked at her in outrage. 'An American?'

Peri frowned at him. 'What's wrong with Americans?'

'I mean no disrespect, my dear,' said Churchill hurriedly. 'My own mother is American. And indeed if that were all, that obstacle might be overcome. But a foreign woman of dubious reputation, twice-divorced, to be Queen of England? Inconceivable!'

'He's right, you know, Peri,' said the Doctor gently. 'In years to come, things might be different. But right now, in 1936…'

The waiter came back with the champagne. Churchill poured for them all and took a hearty swig.

'The boy has always had everything he wanted,' he muttered. 'He has been spoiled and cosseted since birth. He was the darling of the people as Prince of Wales. He cannot tolerate frustration or denial, and with his feelings for Mrs Simpson being what they are… I fear he is now meditating some desperate scheme.'

The Doctor nodded, glancing around the busy scene. Suddenly, a glint of light caught his eye. He looked upwards and saw the reflection of sunlight on metal high in one of the trees.

He threw himself at Peri and Churchill, sweeping them bodily out of the way.

There was the boom of a heavy automatic…

Chapter Twenty-One
Conspiracy

The branches of the tree shivered and crackled and something soft and heavy crashed to the ground. It was the body of a man in a greenish-brown tweed suit, still clutching a high-powered sporting rifle.

The Doctor swung round and saw the massive figure of Dekker some way away, a big automatic still in his hands.

The garden party crowd, stunned for a moment by the sound of the shot, began shouting and screaming and milling around. One or two elderly dowagers had hysterics, while large men in blue suits converged around the slight figure of the King and bustled him away.

'Sound security procedure,' muttered the Doctor approvingly. 'If the target's still unharmed, get him off the scene as soon as possible and sort things out later.'

But was the King the target?

The Doctor turned his attention to Peri and Churchill. 'Sorry about the shove.'

'No apologies are needed, sir,' growled Churchill, gesturing towards the body. 'The justification for your somewhat precipitate action lies there before us. Who is the large gentleman with the automatic, I wonder?'

'My chauffeur,' said the Doctor.

'A private detective, here to keep an eye on us,' said Peri.

The Doctor saw Churchill's baffled expression and said, 'Well, as a matter of fact he's both.'

As they were talking, all three were instinctively heading for the body at the foot of the tree. So too was Dekker, although his progress was being impeded by several more men in blue suits who seemed to be trying to arrest him. One of them grabbed Dekker's arm and tried to put it in an arm-lock. Another tried to take his gun. Dekker shook them off with an irritated shrug.

'Can it, you guys, I'm on your side.'

As the angry plain-clothes policemen closed in again, Churchill bore down on the struggling group, the Doctor and Peri close behind.

'Desist!' boomed Churchill. 'This gentleman has done us a great service. We owe him gratitude, not harassment.'

'He's carrying a gun on palace grounds,' protested one of the struggling blue suits.

'So was the assassin now lying beneath the tree,' thundered Churchill. 'An assassin who seems to have eluded *your* security arrangements, Chief Inspector Harris. Had it not been for this gentleman's prompt action, he might well have carried out his fell purpose.'

'All the same, sir, we have to know who he is,' said Harris, shooting a look at Dekker that was murderous in itself. 'We'll need a full statement.'

'He is in my employ,' said Churchill dismissively. 'Which is to say, in the employ of government. That is all you need to know for the present. If necessary, *I* will make a statement later. Meanwhile, you had better make a search of the grounds to ensure that no more of these villains are lurking unseen. You may permit the guests to depart, but advise them not to speak of what has happened here today. And I want a full press embargo. Not one word of this is to appear in any newspaper. Now go!'

Churchill might be out of office and out of favour, but the rasp of authority in his voice was unmistakable.

The Chief Inspector went.

Dekker looked at Churchill. 'Thanks.'

'Thank *you*, sir.' Churchill nodded towards the gun in

Dekker's hand. 'A 1911 Model Army Colt point-45, if I'm not mistaken? Heavy, noisy and not too accurate – except in the hands of an expert marksman such as yourself. And a definite man-stopper.'

'You know your guns, sir,' said Dekker, holstering the automatic.

They all went over to the body which was being guarded by more plain-clothes policemen. It lay face down, the exit wound forming a massive red-seeping hole between the shoulder blades.

Peri shuddered and looked away.

'Turn him over,' muttered Churchill to one of the policemen.

'Not supposed to move the body till the forensic people arrive, sir.'

'We *know* who killed him,' rumbled Churchill. 'Our current concern is with who he is. Now, turn him over.'

Two of the policemen turned the body over.

Peri heard an intake of breath from the Doctor, and risked another look.

The body's front presented a less gory sight. The tweed coat had flapped open and the entrance wound made a patch of red on the dark green shirt, just over the heart.

'Right through the pump,' murmured Dekker. He caught sight of Churchill nodding approvingly, and felt impelled to add, 'Sheer dumb luck. I was just depending on hitting him somewhere, knocking him outta the tree before he could use that rifle.'

Churchill studied the rifle, still clutched in a death-grip. 'A sporting Mannlicher. Old-fashioned, but still a fine gun.'

The Doctor and Peri looked at each other. It wasn't the wound that held their fascinated attention, but the dead man himself – thin and dark, with a pencil-line moustache. He looked Spanish, or perhaps South American.

He was the man they had seen trying to assassinate Winston

Churchill, thirty-seven years ago, in the Boer War.

The same man, with the same gun.

Churchill noticed their reaction. 'This man is familiar to you?'

Peri looked at the Doctor, wondering what to say. Slowly, the Doctor shook his head.

'I'm not sure. For a moment I thought he looked like someone I'd seen before, long ago...'

'We must endeavour to establish his identity,' said Churchill. 'We need to know his employers and his associates – and why they should wish to strike at the King.'

'If it's the King they're after,' said Peri.

Churchill looked puzzled. 'But surely –'

'Mr Dekker, were you able to see who the man with the rifle was aiming at?' asked the Doctor.

Dekker shook his head. 'From where I was standing it looked like any one of you would've been in his line of fire. And beyond you was the little fair guy with the crowd round him – the King, right? I guess he'd have been on the same eyeline too.'

'Which takes us no further,' said Churchill. 'Surely His Majesty must have been the intended victim. Who else?'

The Doctor said, 'You, perhaps.'

'My dear sir, I'm scarcely worth the trouble. A failed politician...'

'Don't be too sure,' said Dekker. 'You're that Churchill guy, right?'

Churchill's eyes twinkled. 'I am indeed that Churchill guy. And you, sir?'

'Dekker. Tom Dekker.'

The two shook hands.

'I've been over here about a year now,' Dekker went on. 'I read your London *Times* to keep up with things here, to get to know the territory.'

'You'll be buying a bowler hat and a rolled umbrella next,' said Peri.

154

Dekker ignored her. 'I've seen quite a few reports of your speeches, Mr Churchill, attacking Hitler and the Nazis. That Italian fatso too – Mussolini.'

'What of it?'

'Strikes me these dictators are like the old gang bosses, back in Chicago. They've got big egos, they don't mind killing and they don't like being slanged in public.'

Churchill nodded thoughtfully. 'It is a possibility, I suppose. A remote one in my view, but a possibility all the same. What about you, Doctor? Is there any reason why someone should wish to put an end to your existence?'

'I can't think of one,' said the Doctor.

'Indeed? Then why did you find it necessary to hire the services of Mr Dekker?'

The old boy didn't miss much, thought the Doctor. Winston Churchill was a hard man to deceive.

Peri said, 'Someone put a bomb in our hotel room.'

'Aha!' said Churchill. He looked down at the body. 'Our assassin has a Latin appearance, Doctor, and you did think he looked familiar. Can it be that the rather volatile politics of your South American homeland are involved?'

'It's a possibility,' said the Doctor. 'But like you I feel it is a remote one. I beg you to be careful, sir. I'm pretty convinced that rifle was aimed at you.'

'And what of your bomb?'

'Perhaps that's an entirely different story.'

'Or another part of the same wide-reaching conspiracy?' Churchill studied the Doctor for a moment. 'I have the feeling that you are not being entirely frank with me, Doctor.' He smiled. 'But then, to be honest, I am not being entirely frank with you. I propose a conference.'

'By all means,' said the Doctor. 'When and where do you suggest?'

'Not here,' said Churchill. 'Perhaps not in London at all.

Tomorrow I am returning home to Chartwell. There at least we shall be safe from listening ears and prying eyes. Will you do me the honour of lunching with me there tomorrow? It is a pleasant spot, and the journey from London is not arduous.'

The Doctor beamed. 'With the greatest of pleasure.'

'I will take your address and furnish you with directions and a map. And now, perhaps, I had better escort you all from the palace. The sooner you remove yourself from this place the better – particularly you, Mr Dekker. It will not suit your purposes or mine, Doctor, to have your party detained by our over-zealous constabulary...'

Under Churchill's protection, their Rolls was allowed to jump the exit queue. Soon Dekker was driving them back down the Mall.

'Will they be able to hush everything up the way Churchill said?' asked Peri. 'I would have thought an attempt to kill the King would have been on every front page.'

'Me too,' said Dekker from the driving seat. 'In Chicago they'd have the press and radio boys climbing all over them by now. And what about all those folks at the garden party? Bet your life they're gonna talk.'

'They'll talk to their friends,' said the Doctor. 'London will be buzzing with rumours by now. Some of them may even talk to journalists. But nothing will appear in the newspapers. The British government still keeps the press on a pretty tight leash.'

'I guess you're right at that, Doctor,' said Dekker. 'Look at all this business of the King and Wallis Simpson.'

'What about it?' asked Peri.

'It's been going on for what, four or five years now. Started back when he was the Prince of Wales. Wallis came over here with her husband, some rich American businessman.'

Despite herself, Peri couldn't help being fascinated by a bit of royal gossip. 'Go on. What happened next?'

'Seems the Prince was knocked out by Wallis as soon as they met. Pretty soon he'd ditched all his English upper-class dames and it was just her.'

'What English dames?'

'His other mistresses,' said the Doctor.

'Hold it,' said Peri. 'Are you telling me that the Prince of Wales had *lots* of mistresses, and everybody *knew*?'

'Everybody in the *know* knew,' said the Doctor. 'Court circles, upper-class society…'

'And nobody *minded*?'

The Doctor shrugged a little sadly. 'Why should they? Kings and princes have always had lots of mistresses, it goes with the job. I remember old Charles was always knee-deep in ladies.'

'Charles?'

'King Charles the Second…' The Doctor glanced at Dekker and added hurriedly, 'Well, according to the history books.'

'And Joe Public?' asked Peri. 'What do they think about the King and Wallis?'

'They don't know anything about it.'

'The press is *that* controlled?'

'Not back home,' said Dekker. 'Papers back there are full of it.'

'French ones, too,' said the Doctor 'Ever since the French decapitated their own royals, they've taken an obsessive interest in the English variety.'

'Mind you,' said Dekker, 'I think the story's gonna break pretty soon. Ever since Mrs Simpson's divorce came through…'

'What's that got to do with it?' asked Peri.

'Nobody minded much about Wallis while she was still married,' said the Doctor.

'Wait a minute,' said Peri. 'It was OK for Wallis to be the King's mistress *because* she was married?'

'All his mistresses were married,' said the Doctor, as if this was blindingly obvious. 'Part of the convention.'

'Besides,' said Dekker, 'while she was safely married to good old Simpson there was no chance of her marrying the King. Now that she's free again, for the second time...'

Peri nodded, remembering their earlier conversation with Churchill. 'So now the government's all stirred up,' she said. 'Well, I think it's romantic.'

The Doctor sighed, 'The King's attitude may be romantic, but it's not realistic.'

'What do you think he should do?' challenged Peri.

The Doctor shrugged. 'Not for me to say.'

'The lordly observer, huh,' said Peri. 'This society is too weird! It's a mixture of social formality and rampant immorality!' Dekker took a sharp corner, feeding the wheel through his big hands.

'What you gotta remember is, the people on top make their own rules to suit themselves,' he said. 'Same thing back in Chicago. If Big Al fancied some doll from the chorus line, he set her up in a fancy apartment somewhere. Same way as if he had to bribe a juror, or corrupt a cop, or rub out a rival mobster – he just went ahead and did it. Right and wrong don't come into it!'

By now they were outside the house in Hill Street. Rye, the butler, had seen the car arrive, and was waiting at the door to greet them.

'You make a very good point, Mr Dekker,' said the Doctor, as they got out of the car. 'Ruling elites always think that laws, rules and regulations – morals even – are only for lesser mortals. That can be a very dangerous attitude.'

With the Rolls parked, and out of his chauffeur's uniform, Dekker joined Peri and the Doctor in the little sitting-room for drinks. He poured himself a bourbon, and the Doctor poured

Peri a glass of the Duke's claret.

'I don't know how you feel about things, Doctor Smith,' said Dekker a little awkwardly. 'Or how much money you want to spend. I'm not touting for business, but... well, in view of what's going on, it might be better if I stuck around for a while.'

'Please do, Mr Dekker,' said the Doctor. 'And take any other measures you feel are necessary.'

Dekker nodded. 'The alarm systems and other security measures are already in place, and I'll keep up the outside surveillance.'

'I didn't see anybody,' said Peri.

'You're not supposed to!' said Dekker. 'The thing is, Doctor, all this is going to cost you a bundle. The agency is good, but it ain't cheap.'

'Expense is no object,' said the Doctor grandly. 'Is it, Peri?'

'Not when it comes to stopping mad tree-climbing assassins it isn't!'

Dekker nodded and sipped his bourbon. 'That's good to know!'

It was pleasant in the little sitting-room and they were still chatting idly an hour later. Then they heard a knock at the door and low voices. Upon the Doctor's command, Rye came into the room carrying two envelopes.

'Two communications have arrived, sir.'

One envelope was large, white and official looking with some kind of official seal. The other was smaller, violet in colour.

'Looks like business and pleasure,' said the Doctor, rubbing his hands together. 'Business first!' He opened the larger envelope and studied the contents.

'An invitation to lunch at Chartwell tomorrow, complete with map.' He passed the envelope to Dekker. 'Good old Churchill, efficient as ever. Perhaps you'll drive us down there,

Mr Dekker?'

'That is, if you can squeeze back into your chauffeur's uniform?' teased Peri.

Dekker studied the map. 'Sure thing.'

The Doctor opened the second envelope which held a handwritten note on expensive notepaper.

'Ah. This is just a little awkward…'

He passed it to Peri. It was a note inviting them both to lunch next day at a flat in Bryanston Court. Peri read the ending aloud. '"Do please come, I have a most distinguished guest who is longing to meet you again…" Wow, Doctor, it's from Wallis Simpson!' She grinned at him. 'What's so awkward about it?'

'Conflicting invitations,' said the Doctor. 'We're going to have lunch with Churchill.'

'*You* are,' said Peri.

'What do you mean?'

'We'll just have to divide our forces. You and Dekker drive down to Chartwell and talk politics with Winston, and I'll take a taxi round to this Bryanston Court and get the latest scoop on the royal scandal from Wallis.'

'Peri, I'm not sure…'

'Come off it, Doctor. You couldn't keep me away. Don't you realise who that mystery guest is?'

'It could be anyone,' he protested.

'Don't you believe it, Doctor,' said Peri. 'Don't you see? It's just got to be the King!'

Interlude

'Killed!' The deep voice shook with fury. 'One of Us! Butchered!'

'Marcos was a fool,' said the exotic female voice. 'He brought it upon himself. Twenty-one years he waited, until the Piece was out of balk – then this stupid, flamboyant gesture!'

'It was an audacious move –'

'Audacious?' said the female voice scornfully. 'Disastrous, you mean. What if he had succeeded? Would not the hand of the Player have been clearly seen? The scandal would have been enormous, the Game unbalanced. What if he had been caught? He endangered us all!'

'Marcos was rash,' said the deep voice. 'But he had past humiliation to avenge – as I have myself. Humiliation at the hands of this Doctor. And now he has died because of him.'

'The Doctor was not his executioner!'

'It may have been one of his minions, but the true guilt lies on the Doctor's head!'

A cold, detached old voice cut in, silencing them both.

'Let us not pile folly upon folly. Who is this Doctor who interferes in our Game and disappears? Who reappears sixteen years later, in a different form and defeats us again? Then reappears as first we saw him, as if not a moment has passed since 1899 – and meddles once more! A time traveller and a shape-shifter, some rogue Player... We must certainly destroy him, but we must move with caution – and always, always, act through others...'

Chapter Twenty-Two
The Guest

It took quite a lot of arguing before the Doctor agreed to Peri's proposition, but she got her own way in the end. He had no intention of missing his meeting with Churchill, but had to admit he was intrigued by the invitation from Wallis Simpson. What was behind it? Who was the mysterious guest she wanted them to meet – or rather, to meet again?

As Peri pointed out, there was only one way to find out…

They had their last discussion on the subject outside the front door the next morning, while the Doctor was waiting for Dekker to come round with the Rolls.

'Consider the implications of what happened yesterday,' he said, holding her by the shoulders.

'The mystery assassin?'

'The *same* mystery assassin,' corrected the Doctor. 'The man we saw trying to shoot Churchill in South Africa in 1899 – trying again in the grounds of Buckingham Palace, *with the same gun* thirty-seven years later. Untouched by time, Peri, not a day older.'

'Like us,' said Peri quietly.

'Exactly. A time traveller of some kind, has to be. And therefore someone not of this period, perhaps not even from this planet.'

'Like you?'

The Doctor frowned. 'Another Time Lord? No, I don't think so.'

'Why not? Could be another renegade Time Lord like you!'

'I am not a renegade!' said the Doctor indignantly. 'Not any more, anyway. I'm just a bit – semi-detached, that's all. No, this just doesn't feel like a Time Lord operation somehow. It's all too localised, too petty. We Time Lords think big. We hijack whole planets, not individual politicians.' He pondered. 'All the same, I think we may be dealing with something that isn't entirely human.'

'Some kind of alien conspiracy?'

'And not quite that either,' said the Doctor distantly. 'There seems to be a perfectly good *human* conspiracy going on. That's what Churchill thinks anyway. But there's something I'm not getting, something just out of sight...'

'A hidden tentacle, you mean?'

The Doctor scowled at her facetiousness. 'Something like that. In fact...'

His train of thought was interrupted by the arrival of Dekker with the car. Peri waved them both off, and went back into the house. She checked the clock – since she had far less distance to travel, she had plenty of time in hand. She decided a long, luxurious bath was in order, and a leisurely sort through her new wardrobe for the perfect outfit. She'd show that Simpson woman – and the King as well – something about glamour.

Toying for a moment with a vision of herself as Queen Perpugilliam, she went back inside the house.

The Doctor was still worrying as the Rolls Royce sped through the outer London suburbs on the journey out to Kent. He was wearing a comfortable tweed suit in a reasonably subdued green-grey heather-mixture, sitting in the front seat next to Dekker and watching the pleasant countryside flow by.

He reflected sadly on the really jolly suit in the nice bright tartan check he'd worn to breakfast. Peri had winced and sent him upstairs to change, claiming he was reverting to type.

Thinking about Peri brought back his worries about her safety. 'She'll be all right,' he said suddenly out loud.

'Sorry?' said Dekker.

'Peri,' said the Doctor. 'She'll be all right.'

'Sure she will.'

'I mean, even if Wallis Simpson *is* involved in some kind of conspiracy, her main value is in her influence over the King.'

'Right.'

'So they'd never let her become involved in any kind of overt violence – kidnapping, murder, anything like that.'

'Absolutely not.'

'And if the King himself *is* going to be there, well, that makes things doubly safe. Nothing untoward would happen with the King there.'

'Right.'

'So, there's really nothing to worry about!'

'Not a thing.'

'So why am I so worried?'

'Look, I told you earlier, Doctor, don't worry about Peri, I'm taking care of her.'

'Are you, indeed?' said the Doctor, a little huffily. 'May one inquire how, exactly?'

'I've got my eye on her,' Dekker said, unperturbed. 'The eye that never closes... If you want something to worry about, Doctor Smith, worry about us – and about that car behind us.'

The Doctor craned his neck and looked over his shoulder.

'Black Mercedes-Benz, keeping two or three cars behind,' added Dekker.

'What about it?'

'It's been tailing us ever since we left London.'

Dressed in a simple little black suit by Coco Chanel, Peri stepped out of the taxi, paid off the driver, and went inside Bryanston Court. Checking the invitation, she made her way up to Flat Five.

A maid opened the door and ushered her in.

Words like 'flat' or 'apartment' seemed inadequate to describe what she found on the other side of the door. It was a kind of miniature mansion inside the main building.

Wallis Simpson was waiting to greet her in a small but luxurious entrance hall. She was wearing a simple black dress, and a collar of diamonds blazed around her neck. Peri knew instinctively that both dress and diamonds had cost a fortune.

Wallis's welcoming smile froze when she saw that Peri was alone. 'Oh, my dear – but where's Doctor Smith?'

'He sends his apologies – a prior engagement. I was free, so I decided to come alone. I do hope you don't mind me coming by myself.'

'Of course not,' said Wallis a little mechanically. 'I'm delighted you could come.'

'I so wanted to meet you – and your special guest, of course,' Peri went on. She despised herself for gushing, but reminded herself it was all in a good cause.

'He's not here yet,' said Wallis. 'In fact nobody is. You're the first to arrive.'

For a moment, the two women stood summing each other up. It struck Peri once again, that Wallis Simpson was no beauty. She was undeniably elegant, though, her glossy black hair drawn back to emphasise her high forehead and her big, dark eyes. It was personality, thought Peri, sheer personality and a ferociously strong will, the determination to dominate.

Maybe that was what turned the King on.

At the same moment, Wallis's eyes flicked over Peri.

'You shouldn't have dressed up, my dear,' she murmured.

Peri's eyes widened for a fraction of a second. 'But I didn't,' she insisted sweetly. 'How kind of you to think I had.'

Wallis smiled frostily.

'I do love your diamonds,' Peri went on. 'So striking – and so daring at this time of day.'

Wallis's eyes flashed dangerously, but she remained brittly

polite. 'Come inside, my dear,' she said. 'Let me show you the apartment while we're waiting for the others.'

Honours more or less even, the two women went inside.

The large, luxuriously-furnished drawing room was a match for Wallis and her diamonds. Like the woman herself, thought Peri, it was expensive, and elegant, but somehow overdone.

Peri's eyes took in a jumble of overstuffed brocade sofas and armchairs, a mahogany table with an ornate Chinese vase, a Chippendale cabinet filled with Chinese ornaments. There was a Regency mirror over the fireplace, a Queen Anne chair, and a large, silk-covered sofa. Built-in bookshelves held a row of Dickens first editions, and a collection of *Winnie-the-Pooh* books by A.A. Milne.

'I guess this room is a kind of marital museum,' said Wallis dryly. 'The Chinese stuff comes from my first husband, Winfield Spencer. He was in the Navy, we went out to China together.'

'That must have been interesting,' said Peri politely.

'Fascinating,' said Wallis, airily. 'There was a war on, and Win turned out to be a part-time homosexual and a full-time drunk. It's kind of confusing being a new bride when your husband is having affairs with both your male *and* female acquaintances.'

The sudden brutal frankness was both shocking and engaging, and Peri found herself liking the woman better.

'The books belong to my second husband, Ernest,' Wallis went on. She laughed. 'He's kind of a Winnie-the-Pooh type himself.'

'Sounds like quite a contrast to your first husband,' said Peri.

'Oh he was.' Wallis Simpson sighed theatrically. 'One husband too wild, the other too dull. I make poor choices when it comes to men.'

'I hear things are going better these days,' said Peri, casually.

Wallis smiled – like a cat who's just got the cream jug,

thought Peri – and her hand stroked the diamond collar. 'Why don't I show you the rest of the apartment?'

Peri was impressed. There was a dining room large enough to seat fourteen, three bedrooms, two bathrooms, an enormous kitchen... The guest bedroom had a huge round bed with pink sheets and pillows. Peri had a good idea who was the most frequent guest.

'Not bad for a little girl from Baltimore, eh?' said Wallis.

'Not bad at all,' said Peri.

'I can't stay here, though,' the older woman sighed heavily. 'Too many unhappy memories. I'm moving to a Regency house in Cumberland Terrace soon. It's Crown property, David – the *King* – is fixing it for me.'

She was, thought Peri, quite shameless in her triumph. No wonder she was getting up aristocratic noses all over London.

By the time they got back to the drawing room, two more guests were just arriving.

One was a man of about sixty, with a high forehead and hooded grey eyes. He wore a grey tweed suit and leaned upon an ivory-handled stick. Beside him was an extraordinarily beautiful woman with a cloud of dark hair and, unusually for her dark colouring, deep blue eyes. She wore a red velvet day-dress, simple but elegant.

The man came forward.

'Good afternoon, Wallis my dear. I trust we are not too unforgivably late?' The voice was deep and cultured, with no trace of accent.

'Allow me to introduce two very dear friends of mine,' said Mrs Simpson. 'The Countess Andrea Razetki and Count Ludwig Praetorius. Ludwig, Andrea, this is Doctor Smith's... companion. Miss Perp... Perpug –' she stumbled over the name.

'Perpugilliam,' said Peri, feeling herself flush a little. 'It's an

168

old family name and a terrible tongue-twister. Please, call me Peri.'

'How do you do?' said the Countess. 'It is a great pleasure to meet you.' Her accent was exotic, musical, utterly foreign.

'For me also,' said Count Praetorius, with a stately bow.

Peri stared at the two newcomers, feeling the hairs on the back of her neck rising.

She'd seen them before, on the TARDIS scanner screen when the Doctor had used the thought scanner to show her his adventure in the First World War.

The names were different, but here before her were the mysterious couple from the chateau.

Wallis had noticed Peri's reaction. 'Is something the matter, my dear?'

'I'm sorry,' said Peri. She decided to try a random shot. 'It's just that – I have the strangest feeling that I've seen your two friends before. In France, perhaps?'

It was obvious that the Count and Countess were as interested in Peri as she was in them. She could feel their eyes upon her. The Count's icy-grey eyes gave a feeling of physical cold, while the dark blue eyes of the Countess felt warm and glowing.

'I do not think we have had the pleasure of meeting *you*,' said the Countess. 'But I think we may have a mutual friend – someone who met both you and the Doctor in South Africa, many years ago.'

'That would've been our... well, our parents,' Peri said, lamely.

The Countess smiled thinly. 'As you say, my dear.'

'You must introduce your friend, anyway,' said Peri brightly, soldiering on.

'I fear that will not be possible,' said Count Praetorius. The cold anger in his voice made Peri shiver.

'Our friend met with a most unfortunate accident,' said the

Countess. 'He was an extremely rash young man.'

She sounded almost amused. The Count shot her an angry glance.

They were an odd pair, these two, thought Peri. Allies and enemies at the same time, just as before. Peri decided she wouldn't trust either one of them the proverbial inch.

Wallis Simpson had been watching all this byplay with some irritation. Peri got the feeling the woman wasn't accustomed to standing at the sidelines. 'The Doctor is unable to join us,' she said. 'A prior engagement, apparently.'

'We know,' said the Countess. 'The Doctor is having lunch with Winston Churchill.' She smiled, as if at some secret joke.

'We must hope he will not be late,' said the Count.

'Why should he be?' asked Peri sharply. 'He set off in plenty of time.'

'Chartwell is some way out of London,' said Count Praetorius. 'And the roads can be dangerous. So much traffic, these days.'

Peri felt a sudden pang of alarm, and wished that there was some way she could warn the Doctor. He had Dekker to look after him, but even so...

The Countess smiled at her, as if enjoying her anxiety. 'Believe me, Peri, you are much better off with us here.'

Wallis snapped her fingers, and servants appeared with trays of drinks. The drinks seemed mostly to consist of cocktails, odd mixtures of liqueurs with names like Manhattans, Sidecars and Snowballs.

Peri asked for orange juice. She felt this was an occasion when she was going to need a very clear head.

'It was a real dilemma when both invitations arrived at once,' she said to Wallis when they all had their drinks. 'I would have loved to have lunched with Mr Churchill, but I so wanted to get to know you better – and to meet your mysterious guest!'

Wallis looked at an ormulu wall clock. 'He might be a little late. Diplomatic duties, that sort of thing… We'll give him a little longer and then start lunch without him.'

It seemed a pretty casual way to treat a King, thought Peri. Just then they heard the sound of a big car in the street below.

Wallis went over to the window and looked down.

'Talk of the devil!' she smiled lasciviously. 'Here he is!'

A few minutes later, the special visitor strode into the room, flourishing a bunch of red roses. He bowed, clicked his heels, and presented the roses to Wallis Simpson.

The special visitor wasn't the King of England after all. It was Joachim von Ribbentrop, the German Ambassador.

Chapter Twenty-Three
Lunch Party

'I reckon they'll make their move before long,' said the Doctor.

They had left London behind by now and were driving through quiet country lanes, but the black Mercedes was still maintaining a steady distance behind them. There was no other traffic on the road.

'Maybe they just want to know where we're going,' said Dekker.

'I think they already know where we're going,' said the Doctor. 'What they want is to stop us getting there. Can we outrun them?'

'Not a chance,' said Dekker. 'The Rolls is a good car, but it doesn't have the speed of the Merc.'

The Doctor nodded. 'Well, if we can't run…'

'We'll have to fight,' said Dekker. 'And attack is the best form of defence. What do you want to do, Doctor, drive or shoot?'

'I'd like to avoid violence if we can,' said the Doctor. 'Perhaps we could try talking to them?'

'If we're close enough to do that we're close enough to get shot,' stated Dekker. The Doctor frowned, clearly unhappy.

'We'd better change places,' said Dekker. 'We'll do it at the next gas station, it won't look so obvious.' A thought seemed to strike him then. 'You can handle a car, can't you?'

The Doctor glanced at him irritably. 'I think you'll find, Mr Dekker, I'm qualified to drive practically anything!'

Dekker nodded. 'OK'.

A few miles further on they came to a little village with a garage and a petrol pump. As the awed attendant pumped petrol into the Rolls Royce, the Doctor said hopefully, 'There'll be a telephone here. We could call the police.'

'And tell them what?' asked Dekker. 'That there's another car using the road behind us?'

The Doctor looked over his shoulder. The black Mercedes was parked some way back, waiting patiently for them to go on. 'Hmm. Yes, you may have a point.'

'Besides,' said Dekker, 'what are they going to send? A bobby on a bicycle? The cops here don't even carry guns.'

The Doctor nodded, accepting the inevitable. All they'd achieve by calling the police was to risk getting some unarmed English policeman killed.

The Doctor assumed an expression of exaggerated interest. 'So, what do *you* suggest we do?'

Dekker was studying the map. 'We're getting close to Chartwell now. If they're going to make a move it'll have to be soon. The road's narrower and twistier up ahead... Right, let's go.'

The Doctor got out of the car and paid the attendant, while Dekker slid over to the passenger seat and the Doctor went round to the driver's side and got behind the wheel. They pulled out of the garage and drove on their way. In his driving mirror, the Doctor saw the Mercedes start moving again.

'What do you reckon we're up against, Doctor?' asked Dekker.

'In what sense?'

'Numbers, arms, experience, that kinda thing.'

The Doctor considered. 'I'm more or less convinced that that Mercedes is a German Embassy car. Not Ribbentrop's monster model, but an Embassy car all the same. And *that* indicates it's probably packed with German Embassy domestic staff – in other words, armed SS men, trained killers, all of them.'

Dekker nodded grimly. 'How many?'

'Say about half-a-dozen.'

The Doctor's tone was breezy, but Dekker noticed the

concern in his eyes.

'What do you think they'll do?'

'Well, any sensible assassins would try to force us off the road, to make our deaths look like an accident. I imagine they'll try that first. If that doesn't work then they'll just riddle us with bullets and take refuge in their diplomatic immunity.'

'OK,' said Dekker. 'So what we need is some kind of edge. Something to give us an unexpected advantage. Luckily I brought a few souvenirs of Chicago over here with me. For purely sentimental reasons, you understand.'

He bent down, reached behind the driver's seat and came up with a gun. It was short, almost stubby, with a round drum-magazine at the centre.

The Doctor glanced quickly at it. 'Is that what I think it is?'

'A Chicago piano,' nodded Dekker.

'Strictly speaking, it's a Thompson sub-machine gun,' said the Doctor, sighing. 'Point-45 calibre shells in a fifty-round drum.'

'Used to be very popular in my neck of the woods,' Dekker grinned. 'It's what I *call* an edge. Right, here's what you do. Step on the gas, as if you're trying to lose them. If you take them by surprise we can pull ahead for a while.' He paused. 'As soon as you see a sharp bend, swing round it, drive on a while, then slew the car across the road and stop.'

'And then?' ventured the Doctor, smiling with exaggerated bonhomie.

'Then leave the rest to me.'

'Very well,' said the Doctor. 'This may seem a foolish request under the circumstances, Mr Dekker – but please, try not to kill anybody!'

'Let's leave it this way,' said Dekker grimly. 'I won't kill anyone I don't have to! Fair enough?'

The Doctor remained silent. Soon, they came to a long straight stretch of road with a sharp bend to the left at the far end.

'This looks like the place, Doctor,' said Dekker. 'Let her go!'
The Rolls Royce surged forward...

It took the SS driver at the wheel of the Mercedes a few seconds to realise that the Rolls Royce was drawing away from him. By that time the car was disappearing around the bend.

The SS man smiled, confident in his car's superior speed and his own driving skills. His quarry had no chance of escape.

'All right,' he snapped in German. 'We'll take them now.'

The five other SS men crowded into the car drew their guns as the Mercedes streaked down the straight stretch of road and made a racing turn to the right.

The driver saw the Rolls barring the road ahead, and tried desperately to slow down. At the same time he saw a very large man in a trenchcoat step out from behind the Rolls. The SS driver was a great admirer of American gangster films, a devoted fan of James Cagney and Edward G. Robinson.

The weapon in the big man's hands was dreadfully familiar.

'Tommy-gun!' screamed the SS driver – and the world exploded in nerve-shattering noise. Dekker's first burst raked across the windscreen of the Mercedes. As he'd half-expected, its glass was bullet proof.

The windscreen didn't shatter but it starred and clouded under the impact of the hail of bullets.

Dekker's second burst raked the Mercedes' tyres, two of which immediately exploded. The big car plunged off the road, crashing through the hedge and bogging down in the muddy ploughed field beyond.

Dekker took a metal sphere from his trenchcoat pocket, pulled the pin and tossed it not at, but close to, the stranded Mercedes.

Seconds later an explosion rocked the car, sending up a shower of mud.

* * *

The SS men in the car had carried out many ambushes and assassinations back in Hitler's Germany. But their targets had mostly been afraid and unarmed – politicians, intellectuals, trade-unionists and the like. None of their previous victims had ever fought back with such instant ferocity, and such devastating fire-power.

Terrified, they scrambled out of the car and fled across the ploughed field – six burly, crop-headed men in ill-fitting navy-blue suits.

Dekker raised the tommy-gun.

The Doctor grabbed him by the shoulder. 'Mr Dekker…'

Dekker laughed. 'Don't worry, Doctor, these tommys are mostly for effect. You couldn't hit a barn with one if you were standing inside it!' With an accuracy that belied his words, he sent a burst over the heads of the fleeing men.

A second burst sent up an enormous spray of mud at their heels.

Cradling the tommy-gun, Dekker took a second grenade from his pocket and tossed it some way behind the fast-disappearing group.

The explosion sent them haring across the field even faster. One by one they vanished through the hedge on the other side.

Dekker levelled the tommy-gun and went cautiously up to the Mercedes. Checking that it was empty, he tossed a third grenade just under the petrol tank and jumped back as the car exploded in smoke and flames.

He tossed the tommy-gun into the back of the Rolls and turned to the Doctor, a broad grin on his face.

'OK, Doctor? They'll have a long trip home and a very expensive chunk of Embassy equipment to account for!'

The Doctor sighed. 'Very efficient, Mr Dekker. But don't you think we might perhaps have searched that vehicle for clues?'

Dekker grinned. 'Everyone told me that England was gonna be peaceful,' he said. 'But what I say is, it don't do no harm to be prepared!' He got back behind the wheel of the car. 'We'd better get a move on, Doctor, or we'll be late for lunch.'

To Peri's relief, lunch didn't take place in the big dining room. Wallis had obviously realised that four guests would be lost in its grandeur. Instead, a lavish buffet was served in the sitting-room.

But why were there only three other guests? wondered Peri. She'd have expected Wallis to entertain on a much grander scale.

The uneasy feeling was rising in her that this lunch had been arranged so that she and the Doctor could meet the Count, the Countess and von Ribbentrop.

And now it was all for her benefit.

As a social occasion the lunch was heavy going. The food itself was excellent. White-coated waiters served canapés, caviare, smoked salmon, chicken, cold meats, all accompanied by champagne – or in Peri's case, by more orange juice. Von Ribbentrop and Wallis did most of the talking, sitting close together on one of the overstuffed sofas. It was clear that the two of them were close friends – very close friends in Peri's estimation. Much of their conversation was malicious gossip about people of whom Peri had never heard.

The Count and Countess listened to this gossip with benign indifference for a while. Then, politely but persistently, they began questioning Peri – confirming her growing suspicions that it was the Doctor they were really interested in, and that she was here merely as a source of information.

'Such a fascinating man,' purred the Countess. 'Have you known him long?'

'Since I was a child,' said Peri. 'Our families have been friends for years.'

'And how do you come to be travelling together?' asked the Count.

'Well, the Doctor arrived suddenly from Santa Esmerelda, and announced he was coming to London to be their Honorary Consul. I'd always wanted to come to Europe so I begged him to let me come with him, at least for a while,' She smiled. 'He was kind enough to agree.'

'And your family did not see anything improper in this?' asked the Countess. 'Such a thing would have been considered scandalous in the extreme when I was a girl. A beautiful young girl, travelling alone with such a very attractive man!'

These people are all obsessed with sex, thought Peri. But there was something gently mocking in the Countess's tone. Peri knew that the question wasn't really serious – she was being teased. It was hard not to like the Countess.

She answered with an air of wide-eyed innocence.

'Improper? Good heavens no. The Doctor is like a second father to me. He bounced me on his knee when I was a baby.'

'Indeed?' said the Count sceptically. 'Yet he scarcely appears old enough to be your father!'

'I thought you'd never met,' said Peri innocently.

'We're not sure if we have encountered your friend the Doctor before,' said the Count. 'If we did it was many years ago. Perhaps he is greatly changed.'

'The Doctor is a very changeable man,' said Peri with feeling. 'And he's much older than he looks!'

'Yes,' said the Count. 'I am sure he is.'

Feeling things were getting too close to home, Peri decided to go on the attack. 'And how about you two?' she asked sweetly. 'Have you known each other long? Are you related? Or are you just good friends?'

The Count wasn't happy with this turn in the conversation. 'Really, young lady! Such questions border upon the impertinent…'

'My dear Ludwig,' said the Countess. 'You are being unreasonable. We have asked questions and we must be prepared to answer them – as honestly as Miss Brown herself has answered us.' She gave Peri a mocking smile. 'The Count and I have been friends for many years,' she said. 'Not family friends, like you and the Doctor. We have no family, alas. Except for a few others like us, we are alone in your world.'

Peri's eyes narrowed. 'In *my* world?'

The Countess's eyes widened in innocence. 'Is that not the expression? Forgive my English.'

'Yeah. That's a point. Where do you really come from?' asked Peri. 'Originally?'

'I come from Hungary, the Count from Scandinavia. But for many years we have been exiles from our homelands. We are international. Citizens of Europe – of the world!'

Von Ribbentrop joined in the conversation.

'Today we must all be citizens of the world,' he said. 'The Fuehrer himself recognises this. It is particularly important for the Aryan races to stand together. We Germans, the British, the Americans… Already Germany has many friends in England. With America too we we are forging bonds of friendship. The German-American Bund for instance.'

Peri was puzzled. 'What's a Bund?'

'Bruderbund,' said von Ribbentrop. 'The bonds of brotherhood. It is an organisation of Americans with German origins.'

'People who come to America become Americans,' said Peri. 'That's the whole idea!'

'The Fatherland is hard to forget,' said von Ribbentrop.

'And here? In England?' asked Peri. 'Not so many German immigrants here.'

'Here the link is spiritual,' said von Ribbentrop. 'There are many who think as we do, in the Government, in the aristocracy…'

There was the ring of a telephone. Moments later a waiter came up to von Ribbentrop and whispered in his ear.

Von Ribbentrop rose. 'If you will forgive me?'

They heard his voice speaking in German coming from the hall.

Suddenly it rose to a scream. *Was? Feigling! Dummkopf! Ich komme!*

The Count and Countess were listening with keen interest.

'"Everybody fled",' murmured the Countess. '"Cowards and fools!" It sounds as if our friend von Ribbentrop has suffered some kind of setback!'

Von Ribbentrop marched back into the room, practically shaking with anger. 'I am afraid I must leave you. A problem back at the Embassy.'

'Something is wrong?' asked the Countess.

'An operation has failed…' He scowled.

'I see,' said the Count. 'Badly?'

'Total failure. I really must be going.' He took Wallis's hand and kissed it. 'Forgive me, dear lady.'

Seizing the opportunity, Peri rose to her feet. 'I must be going too.' She turned to Wallis. 'If you could possibly arrange a taxi for me?'

The Count said, 'Why don't you give our young friend a lift, Herr von Ribbentrop?'

Von Ribbentrop turned to Peri and bowed. 'But of course! With the greatest of pleasure.'

'Oh, I wouldn't dream of troubling you,' said Peri, quickly.

'Please, you *must* allow me,' said von Ribbentrop. 'Believe me, it is no trouble. No trouble at all.'

He led Peri to the window, and pointed to the huge black limousine in the street below. 'My car is waiting – it is always waiting. One of the privileges of a diplomat's life. Taking you home means only the smallest of detours on my way back to the Embassy.'

He tapped on the window and beckoned to the black-uniformed driver who stood waiting by the car.

Peri was feeling increasingly uneasy.

'Thank you, but no,' she said firmly. 'The Doctor insists I always take a taxi.'

'I am afraid we can accept no refusal,' said the Count. He rose to his feet, and he and von Ribbentrop came closer.

Peri prepared to fight.

There was a tap on the door and Wallis went to open it. Two burly black-uniformed men came into the room.

Peri looked round for help.

The servants had all disappeared.

'Let us not have an undignified struggle,' said the Count. 'We may have lost the Doctor – but we most certainly have you!'

Wallis and the Countess both stood motionless as the Count, von Ribbentrop, and the two SS men closed in on Peri.

Chapter Twenty-Four
Conference

When the Rolls Royce drove down the drive and drew up outside Chartwell Manor, Winston Churchill, cigar in mouth, was waiting on the steps to greet his guests.

He gave them an expansive wave of welcome. 'Drive your vehicle around to the back, gentlemen,' he called. 'There is adequate parking space there, and it will be better concealed from the road. No point in making life easier for our enemies if we are observed.'

They drove around to a little yard at the back of the old house. Puffing contentedly upon his huge cigar, Churchill strolled round after them.

'The old boy really loves it here,' the Doctor muttered. 'He's very much the Lord of the Manor!'

The Doctor and Dekker got out of the car, and stood gazing around them. The view was well worth looking at. The old red-brick manor house stood in its own rolling grounds, surrounded by trees. Here at the back, steps led down to a huge sunken lawn, at the bottom of which was a reed-fringed lake.

Even Tom Dekker, a big city man if ever there was one, was impressed. 'Genuine old-world English charm,' he said. 'Just like a picture book!'

Churchill smiled, pleased by their enthusiasm. 'I bought it sixteen years ago, for five thousand pounds,' he rumbled. 'A substantial sum in those days. And it was a ruin! Still, enough of my domestic concerns. Did you have a good journey, gentlemen?'

'It was a little over-eventful,' said the Doctor, smiling grimly.

He gave a brief account of the way they had been followed and eventually attacked by the SS thugs in their Mercedes-Benz.

Churchill was outraged. 'The scoundrels! To attempt a villainous and brutal act in the quiet Kentish countryside, so close to my home! Yet you are here, gentlemen, and apparently safe and sound. What was the outcome of this dastardly attempt to destroy you?'

The Doctor told him the rest of the story, much to Churchill's delight.

'And so you beat the rascals off? Splendid! That will make them think twice before essaying more such villainy. Doctor Smith, Mr Dekker, I congratulate you both upon a most notable victory!'

He insisted on seeing and handling Dekker's tommy-gun, waving it dangerously to and fro, shooting down legions of imaginary SS men. 'You should've mown the rascals down!' growled Churchill.

The Doctor winced. 'Mr Dekker, perhaps…'

Gently Dekker removed the weapon from Churchill's grasp and put it back in the car. 'The Doctor was against the mowing-down approach,' he said, covering the gun with his trench-coat and locking the car door.

'I thought it might be rather tactless to litter your peaceful Kentish countryside with Nazi corpses,' explained the Doctor.

Churchill frowned. 'This countryside may well be littered with Nazi corpses soon enough,' he said. 'And English ones too, unless we are very fortunate…' He broke off. 'Still, enough of such matters for now. Drinks first and then lunch. Clemmie is away for the day, but I have asked an old friend of mine to meet you…'

He led them into the house, along a corridor and into a comfortable study, a pleasant, old-fashioned room with a huge oak beam running across the ceiling.

A tall man with greying hair was standing by the mantelpiece, a glass of whisky in his hand.

He turned eagerly as they came into the room. 'Doctor!' he said. 'I'm very – ' He broke off in some confusion, clearly not seeing the man he was expecting to meet.

The Doctor recognised him at once. It was Carstairs, an older version of the keen young Lieutenant he'd first met during the War Games. Now, the man was looking at Churchill in some puzzlement.

'I'm sorry, sir, I must have misunderstood you. Your message said you wanted me to come down and meet Doctor Smith, so I naturally assumed…'

Churchill looked puzzled. 'What?'

'Well, that it was *the* Doctor Smith, sir. The one who helped us to foil your would-be kidnappers in 1915.'

'Good heavens, no! This Doctor is the son of an old friend of mine. His father and I were fellow prisoners of the Boers. This, quite evidently, is not the same man!' Churchill turned to make the introductions.

'Doctor, this is my old friend Colonel Carstairs, of Military Intelligence. Colonel Carstairs, this is Doctor John Smith, and his associate Mr Dekker.'

They all shook hands.

'Colonel, eh?' said the Doctor. 'Splendid. Well deserved, I'm sure.'

Churchill went over to a well-loaded drinks trolley.

'Now then, gentlemen… Carstairs, you're catered for, but Doctor, Mr Dekker… Whisky, brandy, gin? I can offer you an excellent claret… Or shall we go directly to the champagne?' Without waiting for an answer, he took the bottle from the ice bucket, popped the cork with casual expertise, poured four foaming glasses and handed them round.

'Confusion to our enemies – and especially to those currently trudging dejectedly back to London!'

They drank the toast, although Carstairs was clearly baffled. Churchill gave him a highly-coloured account of the Doctor's and Dekker's heroic victory.

'They're getting very bold,' said Carstairs angrily. 'Carloads of armed thugs on English soil? Anyone would think they had occupied us already.'

'Our enemies grow over-confident,' growled Churchill. 'They know they have powerful friends. Still, they have been defeated and for the moment at least we can rejoice.' He poured more champagne. 'Be seated, gentlemen,' he boomed, and they all sat down.

'Perhaps I should explain, Doctor,' Churchill went on, 'that Colonel Carstairs is one of a number of unofficial advisers, who supply me with vital information – information that concerns the security of this country.'

The Doctor nodded, wondering what his part was in all this. What did Churchill want from him?

'I am, as you know, out of office and out of favour,' Churchill said. 'The Prime Minister is determined to keep me out of the Cabinet. Recently, the post of Minister of Defence was denied me. I must work from the sidelines, and unofficially. Nevertheless, I have gathered about me a group of those who are concerned with England's fate.' He paused. 'I feel we are at a time of crisis, Doctor.'

'What kind of crisis?'

'We currently face the menace of Nazi Germany,' began Churchill. 'All my sources tell me they are steadily rearming, particularly in the field of air power. Hitler has already defied the Versailles treaty by re-occupying the Rhineland. I am convinced he aims to conquer Czechoslovakia, Poland – and, in time, all Europe.'

And indeed he will, reflected the Doctor, suddenly uncomfortable in the knowledge.

'Unfortunately, my warnings go unheeded,' Churchill went

on. 'The policy of this government is to appease Herr Hitler, by handing to him whatever he wants.'

'It will never work,' said the Doctor. 'Hitler will never be satisfied.'

'Precisely so, Doctor.' Churchill paused. 'And this madman offers us an alliance. He wishes us to ally with him, to become part of his evil schemes. I am ashamed to say that there are many in England who wish to accept this shameful offer.'

'I take it you believe there exists some kind of conspiracy of Nazi sympathisers?' asked the Doctor. 'And that perhaps they are planning some kind of action?'

'As to their plans, I cannot yet be sure,' rumbled Churchill. 'But in parliament, in public life, in society and amongst the aristocracy, there are many who support closer ties with Nazi Germany.'

'Including the King,' said Carstairs.

Churchill nodded his agreement. 'Tragically, he too is among them. His emotional problems make him particularly vulnerable at this time.'

'And Wallis Simpson is a close friend of von Ribbentrop,' said Carstairs. 'MI5 have been watching her for some time. According to their reports she spends occasional nights at the German Embassy.'

'All very interesting, but what has it got to do with me?' asked the Doctor, pointedly. 'Why am I here?'

Winston Churchill looked keenly at him. 'Recent events confirm my opinion that you are involved with these occurences, Doctor. Is there anything, anything at all you know about all this? If so, I beg you to disclose it.'

The Doctor considered for a moment. 'I believe you're right about the conspiracy,' he said at last. 'Moreover, I think it may go back further than you realise – and that it is directed, at least in part, against you.'

'Against me?' Churchill laughed. 'You exaggerate my

importance, Doctor.'

'Do I? I think the only reason I was attacked today was in an attempt to prevent my talking to you.'

'Go on.'

Again the Doctor paused, choosing his words very carefully. How could he tell Winston Churchill that he was one of the hinges upon which history turned? Unless the British defied Hitler, and, eventually, with American help, defeated Germany, Europe would descend into an age of darkness.

And that England would not, could not, stand up against Hitler without Churchill's future leadership.

'My father was convinced that someone was trying to assassinate you, even before you were captured by the Boers,' the Doctor said. 'Is it so very hard to believe that the assassination attempt at the palace garden party was directed not at the King but at you?'

Churchill looked at him in amazement. 'Doctor, you postulate a conspiracy stretching back thirty-seven years!'

Unexpectedly, Dekker joined in the conversation. 'There's an organisation, a conspiracy if you like, back in the States,' he said. 'Got a lot of different names – the Camorra, the Black Hand, the Mafia. Came over to America with the immigrants. Started in Sicily hundreds of years ago, still going strong today.'

'I take your point, sir,' said Churchill. 'Men die – but organisations can be immortal! Pray continue, Doctor.'

'I think the people who tried to kill you and to kidnap you are still operating today. I think they're manipulating the Germans, using them as tools, just as they did in 1915. But as for who they are and what their agenda is, I simply don't know. I may have a better idea when I've talked to my ward.'

'How so?'

The Doctor steepled his fingers. 'Miss Brown is having lunch with Wallis Simpson today. I imagine they'll try to get information out of her. But Peri's no fool. She won't give anything away, and she may well learn something.'

Churchill rose.

'These are deep waters, Doctor. Let us discuss matters further over lunch. Gentlemen, a cold collation awaits us in the dining room…'

Peri awoke to find herself leaning back on soft leather upholstery. Her head was throbbing and there seemed to be a sore spot behind her ear. She touched it and winced.

The air was filled with a mixture of exotic smells; there was leather, new car, and some very expensive cologne.

She opened her eyes and realised that the cologne belonged to von Ribbentrop, who was sitting next to her.

'Feeling better, Miss Smith?' he inquired solicitously.

'I'd imagined how much fun it would be to ride in your car, Herr von Ribbentrop,' she said. 'But I had hoped to be conscious at the time.'

'Believe me, Miss Brown, nobody regrets the necessity for this unpleasantness more than I do. But you would insist on struggling.'

'Yes, I did, didn't I?' said Peri.

She remembered the brief scuffle in Wallis Simpson's drawing room. She'd grabbed a Chinese vase – a priceless one, she hoped – and chucked it at one of the two advancing SS men. She'd missed and it had smashed against the wall. One of the SS men had grabbed her wrists and she'd kicked him hard on the shins, but the other one had slipped round behind her and tapped her behind the ear with something hard.

She touched the sore place again and winced.

'You will not feel the ill effects of the blow for long,' said von Ribbentrop. 'Sergeant Schultz is an expert.'

'I'm so glad,' said Peri. 'I'd hate to think I'd been knocked out by some clumsy amateur.'

'You joke, but it is a serious matter,' said von Ribbentrop

reprovingly. 'Too much force can result in coma or even death. The subject becomes useless.'

'What I want to know is why do it at all?' demanded Peri. 'I suppose you must have felt rejected when I didn't want a ride in your nice new car, but aren't you over-reacting a bit?'

'I assure you, Miss Brown, my motives are not personal but professional. You know very well why you have been taken into custody.'

'I do?'

'Of course you do,' said von Ribbentrop. 'You have been arrested because you are an enemy of the Reich. I am reliably informed, by my friends the Count and Countess, that you, Miss Brown, are an agent of the American Secret Service!'

Chapter Twenty-Five
Kidnap

The Doctor, Churchill, Dekker and Carstairs had discussed their concerns over a simple but excellent lunch – cold roast beef and salad with apple pie and cream to follow – washed down with several bottles of Churchill's 'respectable claret'.

Now they were back in the study with coffee, brandy and, for Churchill, another cigar. But for all their talking, nothing new had emerged, and the Doctor was beginning to feel that they were going round in circles.

They were discussing the King now, and the crisis caused by his determination to marry Wallis Simpson.

'They say he spoke of her to Baldwin as "my future wife" said Carstairs. 'Nearly gave the old boy a fit. He's been lavishing expensive gifts upon her as well, white fox furs, jewels worth thousands of pounds…'

'Some of them the property of the Crown, and not his to give,' said Churchill gloomily. 'The boy is besotted, and Baldwin is handling him badly. He should leave His Majesty alone and untroubled for a time, allow him to reflect upon the situation.'

'Do you think that would work, sir?' asked Carstairs, doubtfully.

'I know that badgering by bishops and prime ministers will not,' stated Churchill.

'But surely the King must be recalled to a sense of his duty,' argued Carstairs.

'Duty?' growled Churchill. 'He *has* no sense of duty! David has been spoiled since childhood. He was adored by the entire country when he was Prince of Wales. He has always had everything he wanted, the moment he asked for it.'

'So why not Wallis Simpson – especially now that he's King?' suggested the Doctor.

'Exactly so. And he will not respond to bullying. He has all the obstinacy of the weak. The more he is pressured to give the woman up, the more he will insist on marrying her. They will drive him to it!'

Carstairs was horrified.'But – Queen Wallis, sir?'

'Never!' said Churchill. 'There lies our dilemma.'

'You know,' said the Doctor thoughtfully,'I have a feeling that the King is the key to this whole business…'

They heard the ringing of a telephone from the hall, and Churchill went to answer it. After a moment he returned.

'It appears that the call is for you, Doctor!'

The Doctor rose.'That's odd. Who would know I was here?'

Churchill shrugged. 'The instrument is on the table in the hall.'

The Doctor went out into the hall and picked up the telephone.'Yes?'

'You would do well to leave Chartwell at once, Doctor,' said a strangely familiar voice. 'Do not return, have no further dealings with Winston Churchill, and cease meddling with matters that do not concern you. Return to London and make arrangements to leave for South America immediately.'

The Doctor looked at the receiver in outrage 'And why exactly should I do any of those things?' he stormed.

'Unless you do all of them, Doctor, you will never see Miss Brown alive again. Obey my instructions and she will be released, unharmed, in time to join you upon your departure from these shores.You will find the climate so much healthier in South America, Doctor!'

There was a click as whoever was at the other end of the line put down the phone.

The Doctor replaced the telephone receiver and strode back into the study. 'We must leave at once, I'm afraid,' he told

Dekker. 'Something's happened to Peri. I rather fear she's been kidnapped.'

Winston Churchill jumped up. 'Kidnapped?'

The Doctor gave them a brief version of the unknown caller's message.

'We must summon the police,' said Churchill. 'If you wish, I will make the call for you, Doctor.'

'I'll get on to MI5,' said Carstairs. 'And the Special Branch –'

'No!' said Dekker.

Churchill glared at him. 'I beg your pardon, sir?'

'Thanks but no thanks,' said Dekker. 'Doctor, we'll handle this ourselves.'

'Yes… you could be right,' murmured the Doctor.

'Damn right,' said Dekker firmly, turning to Carstairs and Churchill. 'If we need any help later we'll get in touch. If you two gentlemen would give the Doctor your telephone numbers?'

'I am not sure that this course of action is wise, Doctor,' rumbled Churchill, handing the Doctor his card while Carstairs did the same. 'Colonel Carstairs and I are prepared to mobilise all the resources of the state to assist you. With all due respect to Mr Dekker and his undoubted abilities…'

The Doctor glanced briefly at Dekker, then turned to Churchill.

'Thank you for your offers of help, gentlemen,' he said. 'As Mr Dekker says, we'll call upon you if we need you.'

Minutes later the Doctor and Dekker were on the way back to London.

'You've done right, Doctor,' said Dekker. 'A lot of cops and secret service guys rushing around isn't going to achieve anything. Even if they get close, there's a risk they'll panic the kidnappers – and kidnappers tend to destroy the evidence!'

'We have to find her,' stated the Doctor, his fury rising. 'Of all the despicable, deplorable –'

'Pipe down and let me drive, will you please, Doctor? It's hard enough having to keep this heap on the wrong side of the road, without you yelling in my ear!'

The Doctor subsided fuming onto his seat and Dekker drove the Rolls along the narrow lanes towards London.

After a while the Doctor muttered, 'Can't we go any faster?'

'No,' said Dekker.

The man drove, the Doctor noticed with reluctant admiration, exactly as fast as was safe and no faster. All the same, the Doctor was close to exploding when they drew up outside the house in Hill Street. As always, Rye the butler came out to greet them.

The Doctor leaped from the car and bounded up the steps. 'Have you seen or heard from Miss Brown?'

'No, sir. She went out for her luncheon engagement in a taxi this morning and has not yet returned.'

The Doctor turned back to Dekker, who was standing on the pavement looking up and down the street.

'She's not going to come wandering along the pavement you know!' thundered the Doctor.

Ignoring him, Dekker turned up his trenchcoat collar and scratched his nose. A tubby little man in a shabby grey suit appeared, apparently from nowhere, and he and Dekker had a brief, low-voiced conversation. The little man turned and was soon gone again.

'What was all that about?' demanded the Doctor.

'17 Carlton House Terrace,' said Dekker.

'What?'

'That's where they took her. Temporary German Embassy. Apparently Ribby's having the proper one gutted and redecorated by some Nazi architect guy called Speer, so they've hired this Carlton House Terrace place till it's ready.'

The Doctor stared at him. 'How can you –' He stopped himself. 'So simple. You had a man watching the house. This house. A man with a car.'

'Told you I had an eye on her!' Dekker allowed himself a small smile.

'He followed Peri to Wallis Simpson's flat?'

'That's right,' said Dekker.

'So, what happened?'

'Miss Brown gets outta her taxi and goes in. Not long after that two more people arrive by taxi, an old guy and a classy-looking dame. They go in. Some time later, good old Ribby turns up in his monster, leaves it parked outside and he goes in.'

The Doctor took several deep breaths before inquiring sweetly, 'And then?'

'In the end, Ribby signals his driver, and him and another guy rush inside. A few minutes later they come out, with Miss Brown between them, looking kinda dazed. They all get in the big Merc and it drives off – to 17 Carlton House Terrace.'

'Well, let's go and get her!' said the Doctor.

'Take it easy, Doctor. We'll go round and case the joint. Reconnoitre. If it looks like we can handle it, we get her out. If we can't, we call your pals Churchill and Carstairs, and surround the place with the Household Cavalry.'

'That might be a little difficult,' said the Doctor.

'How come? They said they'd help.'

'And I'm sure they'd want to.' The Doctor thrust his hands in his pockets. 'But technically speaking, a foreign embassy, even a temporary one, is foreign soil. Sending troops into 17 Carlton House Terrace would be tantamount to invading Germany!'

'So maybe we better handle it ourselves. You, me and the Op.'

'Who?'

'My operative. Name's Jimmy, but everyone calls him the Op.'

The Doctor looked round. 'Where is he?'

Dekker turned his coat collar down and then up again and scratched his chin.

The tubby little man reappeared.

'How does he *do* that?' asked the Doctor, feeling the situation spiralling ever further out of his control.

'Damned if I know. You only see the Op when he wants you to see him. Where's the heap, Jimmy?'

The Op jerked his head towards the nearest corner.

'Maybe we better go in the Op's jalopy,' said Dekker. 'The Rolls is kinda conspicuous for this operation.'

They followed the Op around the corner and squeezed into an ancient Morris saloon. The Op got behind the wheel. 'Where to?'

'17 Carlton House Terrace,' said Dekker. 'We're going to invade Germany!'

Peri's interrogation was taking place in the back sitting-room, a high-ceilinged room with files piled high on wooden trestle tables. Presumably, thought Peri, they hadn't got the dungeon fitted out yet.

Von Ribbentrop himself was handling the proceedings. He had changed into his black SS uniform specially for the occasion, a design intended to strike terror into the heart of any victim. In Nazi Germany perhaps it would have worked. Peri, however, wasn't impressed. He looked like a reject from some cheap war movie. She'd had enough. The folding wooden chair she'd been pushed into was hard and uncomfortable.

A thuggish-looking SS man, the one who'd slugged her, stood on guard at the door, just as when she'd been bundled out of the car into this crummy room.

Von Ribbentrop had then vanished. Nobody had spoken to her.

Peri had waited and waited. No doubt all this was supposed to break down her morale.

Peri had just got bored, and mad.

Eventually, von Ribbentrop had reappeared, this time dressed up in all his military glory. Now, Peri looked up at him and yawned.

'Why the fancy dress?'

Von Ribbentrop was scandalised. 'This is the uniform of a *Gruppenfuehrer*, a general in the SS. The rank was awarded to me by the Fuehrer in person!'

'Well, enjoy it while you can,' said Peri. 'When he finds out what you've been up to he'll probably bust you down to corporal.

What do you mean by kidnapping an innocent American citizen?' She remembered the Doctor's story at the bank. 'A very wealthy and important American citizen, too.'

'Nonsense. You are an American agent. It is useless to repeat your cover story. We have checked and it is full of holes. There is no American millionaire by the name of Capability Brown. The only person of that name our researchers uncovered was an English landscape gardener of the eighteenth century.'

Mentally cursing the Doctor's weird sense of humour, Peri said, 'We wealthy heiresses never travel under our real names. We always use an alias, it keeps off the fortune hunters.'

Von Ribbentrop eyed her narrowly. 'What, then, is your real name?'

'Never you mind,' said Peri airily. 'It might be Rockefeller, or it might be Rothschild. You'll find out. And when you do, you'll be in trouble. Daddy will probably buy Berlin and pave it over for a parking lot.'

'Nonsense,' said von Ribbentrop, a little uneasily.

Feeling on shaky ground, Peri hurried on. 'What's more, my guardian, Doctor Smith, is an important diplomat.'

'That too is a lie,' stated von Ribbentrop, with pleasure. 'Our geographers can find no such country as the Republic of Santa Esmerelda.'

'It's a very small country,' said Peri helpfully. 'About twice the size of Hyde Park. North-north-west of Paraguay, I believe. You could easily miss it.'

'More nonsense!' shouted von Ribbentrop. 'You are foreign agents, spies and saboteurs, enemies of the Reich! Now, for the last time, I want the truth. Who are you, and who is the Doctor? What is your real mission here?'

Peri didn't reply.

'You will do well to answer my question,' said von Ribbentrop. 'Remember –'

Peri said, 'You're not actually going to say it, are you?'

The interruption made von Ribbentrop stumble in his tirade. 'Say what?'

'"We have ways of making you talk!" And anyway, you haven't used, "We will ask the questions!" yet. Isn't that supposed to come first?'

Von Ribbentrop looked so baffled, so helplessly angry, that Peri almost felt sorry for him. She burst out laughing. 'It's no good. You'd better stick to the garden fêtes and lunch parties. You're not cut out for this sort of thing. You're just not scary enough.'

'Am I not?' snarled von Ribbentrop. He calmed himself. 'Well, perhaps not. I am, after all, a gentleman. But I have those on my staff who are – what was your word – scary...' He nodded towards the thug on the door. 'Take Sergeant Schultz, here.'

'Your expert on socking people with truncheons? *You* take him.'

'Precisely. You have already sampled his ministrations. A caress behind the ear, a few minutes' dizziness. A firmer tap, half an hour to an hour's sleep. But Sergeant Schultz has other talents.' A note of gloating cruelty came into von Ribbentrop's voice. 'A sharp tap on the knee, the elbow, the shins, the bridge of the nose – such blows as these produce intolerable pain. I have seen men – and women too – screaming with agony under Sergeant Schultz's – caresses.'

He turned and beckoned and the squat figure of Sergeant Schultz came forward. He slapped a rubber truncheon into his palm, and Peri jumped.

Von Ribbentrop leaned forward. 'You see, Miss Brown,' he whispered. 'We really do have ways of making you talk.'

Peri didn't answer. Suddenly nothing was funny any more.

'Will you answer my questions? Or shall I leave you to the good Sergeant?'

Ribbentrop leaned forward, his face close to hers. Peri flinched. She could smell his too-powerful cologne, he must have slapped more on specially for the interrogation. Nice.

Again the rubber truncheon slapped into Schultz's palm.

'Well?'

There came a sudden tremendous hammering at the front door.

Chapter Twenty-Six
Raid

Carlton House Terrace at dusk looked as aristocratic as it sounded. It was a street of impressive mansions, most of them detached and standing in their own grounds.

Jimmy's shabby little car definitely lowered the tone as it crawled past the opulent houses. Apparently quite untroubled by this, the Op parked the car and pointed across the street.

'Seventeen!'

Dekker was in the front seat beside him, the Doctor in the back. The car was so small that both had their knees under their chins.

Number Seventeen was just as impressive a building as its neighbours, but it had a shabby and deserted air. There were shutters up at the windows and the heavy wooden front door was scratched and faded. The Doctor guessed it was a disused Foreign Office house, on loan to the German government until their own embassy was redecorated. Redecorated, presumably, in a style sufficiently grandiose to satisfy von Ribbentrop's vanity.

It had been cunning of Peri's captors to put her in von Ribbentrop's charge. As long as this house was technically an embassy, it was covered by diplomatic status. Even with evidence that Peri was being held there – and the Op's testimony was all they had – it would be impossible for the lawful authorities to demand entrance.

'Jimmy watched the place for a while after they took Miss Brown inside,' said Dekker. 'Says it seemed pretty deserted, not much coming and going.'

'Von Ribbentrop won't have his full staff over here yet,' said the Doctor, thoughtfully. 'Maybe we won't have too many to deal with.'

He wondered if the half-dozen failed SS assassins had made it back to London yet. They weren't the sort of people one could easily reason with, and he doubted they'd respect a pacifist stance. In any case, a full-scale battle with machine-guns in Carlton House Terrace... it simply wouldn't do.

Dekker's voice interrupted the Doctor's musings. 'What do you say, Doctor? Are we going in?'

'Oh, I think so,' said the Doctor. 'I don't like to think of Peri in Nazi hands. And a quick commando-style raid stands a better chance than an attack in force.' He looked at Dekker and the Op. 'You two don't have to come, you know. This is highly illegal!'

'Try and keep me away,' said Dekker. 'How about you, Jimmy? You in?'

The Op nodded, 'Yep.'

'OK,' said Dekker. 'How about we use the old speakeasy routine?'

'Right,' said the Op.

'Speakeasy?' repeated the Doctor.

'Jimmy and me hadda crash our way into quite a few illegal booze joints in Chicago. We developed a kinda routine. Got the bag, Jimmy?'

'Sure.'

The Op fished a carpetbag from under the front seat and put it in Dekker's lap. Dekker opened it to reveal an assortment of gleaming tools. He fished out a large crowbar and a small sledge-hammer and passed them over to the Doctor.

'That oughta do it. Got a bottle?'

Jimmy produced a bottle of bourbon.

'Nearly full too,' said Dekker. 'Pity to waste it.' He opened the bottle and took a swig, offered it to the Doctor who shook his head, then handed it back to the Op, who took a swig himself and then tipped a little down his own shirtfront.

'OK, Jimmy, drive over and park right outside the door - we may need the motor for a quick getaway.'

As the car pulled away, Dekker briefed the puzzled-looking Doctor on the speakeasy technique.

'Remember,' he concluded, 'it all depends on speed. You gotta get them confused, hit them quick and hard, be in and out before they know what's happening. Got it?'

'Yep!' said the Doctor.

The car drew up outside Number Seventeen and they all got out.

At the same moment as the banging on the door started, a telephone on a table in the corner started to ring. The sound echoed clamorously through the big empty room.

There was still more hammering on the front door, and a voice raised in a raucous shout.

Doubly distracted, von Ribbentrop dithered for a moment. He stopped threatening Peri, straightened up, and crossed over to the telephone.

'Go and see who it is, Schultz,' he yelled. 'Tell them we will call the police if they don't go away!'

Pretty cool for a kidnapper, thought Peri, left alone on her chair. She listened as von Ribbentrop lifted the receiver and started speaking.

'Yes, I understand. The list? Yes, of course I have the list. I shall hand it personally to the Fuehrer on my next trip to Berlin... Of course I am aware of its importance, it never leaves my person.'

He tapped the top pocket of his tunic, and Peri heard the crackle of folded papers.

Moving as quietly as she could, Peri got to her feet...

Sergeant Schultz opened the front door to find himself facing a small, drunken man, reeking of bourbon whisky and brandishing a bottle.

'Hey, buddy!' yelled the little man. 'Where's the party? Look, I gotta bottle! Where's the party?'

Typically decadent American, thought Schultz scornfully. In his slow, careful English he said, 'This is the German Embassy. There is no party here. You will please go away, or the police I will immediately summon.'

The little man gave him a wounded look. 'Hey, don't be that way! Here, have a drink!'

He staggered forward, reeling past Schultz and right into the Embassy hallway. Schultz grabbed him by the lapels to throw him out, but the little man was surprisingly hard to shift.

Letting him go, Schultz reached for his rubber truncheon, but stopped, suddenly, as a gun was violently pressed against his ear. The holder of the gun had slipped, unnoticed, through the open doorway as Schultz had been concentrating on the drunken party-goer.

'OK, where's the girl? The American girl. Talk, or I'll blow your head off!'

'Yes, yes,' said von Ribbentrop. 'Tomorrow night. Everyone will act at the signal from the Fort. Very well, Count. Yes, I have the girl safe. Goodbye.'

He put down the phone, turned and saw that the American girl was no longer in her chair. She was standing up, quite close to him, holding the wooden kitchen chair high above her head.

Von Ribbentrop had just about time to register this before the chair came crashing down...

Peri stepped back as von Ribbentrop staggered and fell, wondering if the history books ever mentioned the fact that he was seen in high society for a while with a big red bump on the top of his head. She hesitated, wondering which way to go, looking at the open door. She didn't want to run into Schultz and his 'vays of making her talk'.

She became aware that the hammering and shouting at the front door had stopped, succeeded by a sinister silence.

Turning, she looked at the other end of the long room. There was a door there too. Maybe she could find a back way out.

She ran across and tried it. It was locked.

Peri ran back to the centre of the room, biting her lip as she looked for something to break down the door. There was nothing. Footsteps were fast approaching. She felt a surge of panic and glanced at von Ribbentrop's fallen body. She was really going to be for it, now.

Suddenly the locked door burst open with a splintering crash, revealing a somewhat dishevelled Doctor. He was clutching a sledgehammer and a crowbar.

'No wonder they call it housebreaking!' he said.

Peri rushed over and hugged the Doctor as he looked round the room, taking in the splintered chair and the unconscious von Ribbentrop.

'In the good old days, the heroine screamed and waited to be rescued,' he said reproachfully. 'Are you all right, Peri?'

'More or less!' She looked down at von Ribbentrop. 'Is *he* all right?'

The Doctor put down his housebreaking tools on a table, went over to the body, knelt beside it and felt for the pulse in the neck.

'He'll survive. Well, come along, Peri. Let's not hang about here chatting!' He picked up his tools and moved towards the door that led to the hall.

'There's a nasty type with a rubber truncheon that way,' warned Peri.

'I rather imagine Dekker's taken care of him. We make quite a cavalry all told! Come on.'

'Wait,' said Peri. She knelt beside von Ribbentrop and unbuttoned the top button of his tunic, taking out several sheets of folded flimsy paper.

'What's that?' asked the Doctor.

'I think it's some kind of list. He was talking about it to the Count on the phone. It seemed to be pretty important.'

'The Count, eh?' The Doctor nodded. 'And the Countess with him?'

'And they haven't aged a day.'

The Doctor sighed, his face grave. 'Is the list *for* the Count?'

'No,' said Peri. 'Ribbentrop was going to deliver it to Hitler himself.'

'Good girl,' said the Doctor. 'Hang on!'

Putting down his tools again he snatched some sheets of flimsy paper from the table and studied them.

'Yes, this should do the trick. A list for a list!'

He folded the flimsy sheets to the exact size of the papers Peri had taken, put them in Ribbentrop's tunic pocket and buttoned it neatly.

'When one comes across some top-secret information,' he hissed in a pantomime whisper, 'it's always better if they don't immediately know you know!'

Straightening up, he grabbed his crowbar and sledgehammer, and he and Peri ran though the door.

'This is your last chance,' snarled Dekker. 'Tell me where the girl is or I'll blow your brains all over the ceiling!'

Sergeant Schultz was, no doubt, cruel and stupid, but he was evidently no coward. He clamped his jaw shut and prepared to die a glorious death for Fuehrer and Fatherland.

Since he wasn't actually prepared to shoot Schultz in cold blood, Dekker was stumped.

'Let me smack him around a little,' said the Op.

Dekker shook his head. 'No time.'

'So shoot him!'

'No need to go to extremes, Mr Dekker,' said the Doctor. Dekker turned and saw Peri and the Doctor crossing the hall towards them.

Instantly, Dekker slammed the point-45 against the side of Schultz's head and the SS man dropped to the ground. 'Let's get outta here!'

As Dekker put the automatic back into his shoulder holster, a voice from above called, 'Halt! Nobody move!'

They looked up and saw von Ribbentrop's burly SS driver, standing at the top of the stairs. He was covering them with a Luger.

Dekker moved for his gun, but the Op was quicker and fired first.

The SS man staggered back, but didn't fall. Changing the Luger to his left hand, he fired. The bullet went over their heads. He was about to fire again when a bullet from Dekker's point-45 blasted him off his feet.

Dropping the Luger, he rolled down the stairs and lay still.

'Guess it just wasn't his day,' said Dekker, looking down at his diminutive colleague. 'You only just beat me!'

'Shaded you by a clear quarter second.'

Dekker looked down at the revolver in the Op's hand. 'Still using that point-38 peashooter, I see. Why don't you get a decent-size gun?'

'Don't need a cannon when I can shoot straight!'

'Gentlemen, please,' said the Doctor. 'Perhaps we could save the technical discussions till later?'

They hurried out of the Embassy, slamming the door behind them.

As the Op got into the car and started the engine, the Doctor said, 'Thank you, Mr Dekker. Your friend saved our lives.'

'The Op's the best,' said Dekker, opening the front passenger door. 'He could have put a slug between the guy's eyes, or clean through either one.'

'Charming,' shuddered Peri. 'So why didn't he?'

'My fault,' said Dekker. 'I told him the client didn't like killing!' He turned to the Doctor. 'I aimed for his right shoulder, but I can't promise you he's still alive. Sometimes you don't get much choice.'

'I know,' said the Doctor, sadly. 'Believe me, I know. Let's get away from this place.'

Dekker got in the front beside the Op, the Doctor and Peri got in the back, and the little car drove away.

Von Ribbentrop struggled painfully to his feet.

He touched the swelling bruise on top of his head and winced. Dazed and semi-conscious, he staggered into the Embassy hallway. He looked round, taking in the full extent of the disaster.

Sergeant Schultz lay bleeding and unconscious close to the front door.

Heinz Muller, his driver and bodyguard, lay in a spreading pool of blood at the bottom of the stairs.

The girl, of course, had gone.

Von Ribbentrop felt a sudden stab of panic.

The list!

He patted his tunic pocket and the wad of folded flimsy paper crackled reassuringly.

At least he still had the list…

'It's called the Chicago speakeasy technique,' explained the Doctor, proud of his new expertise. 'It's what you might call simple but effective!'

'How does it work exactly?' asked Peri.

'Somebody makes all the fuss he can to distract people at the front of the house, while somebody else smashes their way in at the back!'

'Well, it seemed to work, anyway,' said Peri. 'Thank you all very much! And thank your little friend for me too, Dekker.'

They were in the sitting-room at Hill Street, enjoying pre-dinner drinks. The Op had simply faded away.

'Why wouldn't he come in even for a drink?' asked Peri.

'Jimmy's not all that social,' said Dekker. 'I think this place is a little too high-toned for him.'

'Where did he go?'

Dekker smiled, 'He's around.'

The Doctor began studying the list that Peri had taken from von Ribbentrop.

'Is that thing important?' asked Dekker.

'Important is hardly the word,' said the Doctor.

Peri looked disappointed. 'Sorry. Old von Ribbentrop seemed so worked up about it I –'

'You misunderstand me, Peri. I meant that "important" just isn't an adequate description.' He raised his voice for effect. 'Vital, crucial and earth-shattering would be far more appropriate.'

'What is it exactly?' asked Dekker.

'It's a list of names, some of which I know and some of which I don't. Names and certain specific instructions,' said the Doctor. 'Peri, tell me again what von Ribbentrop said on the phone.'

Peri thought for a moment.

'He said, yes, yes, Count, he understood. He said he had the list, it was for the Fuehrer. And he said something about a signal from the fort, tomorrow night.'

The Doctor looked at Peri and Dekker. 'This may be the key to the entire conspiracy!'

He fished in his pocket, took out two visiting cards and went over to the telephone.

'Operator, I want to make two urgent calls. One to a Colonel Carstairs and the other to Mr Winston Churchill…'

Chapter Twenty-Seven
Trap

'I already know many of these names, Doctor,' said Carstairs.

The Doctor nodded. 'I rather thought you would. They're all Nazi sympathisers, I take it?'

'That's right,' said Carstairs grimly, 'Either open or hidden. People we suspect might operate as spies in the event of war, or be collaborators if, heaven forbid, we were ever occupied. Quite a few of them are already under surveillance.'

'Indeed,' mused the Doctor.

Carstairs looked up from the list, his face grave. 'But there are other names here… Names I would never have suspected.' He stood up and began pacing about the room. 'If all these people are Nazi sympathisers – and to be on von Ribbentrop's list they have to be – well, things are far worse than I thought. There are names here from Parliament, the Police, the Army, the Civil Service… An appalling number of members of the aristocracy… And not just here in London either, but all over the country. It seems the country's riddled with potential traitors!'

It was the following morning, and the Doctor and Peri were in the sitting-room of Carstairs' little house in Chelsea, waiting for Winston Churchill. The Doctor had been unable to reach him the previous evening, and had simply left a message that Peri was safe and that he had important news.

This morning Churchill had been tied up in a meeting in Downing Street. He had promised to join them for an urgent conference as soon as he was free.

Dekker and the Op were off on business of their own.

An attractive woman in her forties came into the room

carrying a laden tray. 'I thought you might like some coffee and biscuits,' she said in a high, clear upper-class voice.

The Doctor jumped to his feet. 'Lady Jennifer, how splendid to see you – ' He managed to bite off the word 'again' just in time.

Carstairs gave him a puzzled look and said, 'Doctor, Miss Brown, this is my wife Jennifer. Darling, this is the Doctor Smith I was telling you about.' He gave the Doctor a thoughtful look and added, 'Not our Doctor, of course, though the name's the same.'

'I can see that for myself, dear. How do you do, Doctor Smith, Miss Brown. And it's just plain Jennifer, please. I stopped using the title when Jeremy and I got married.' She smiled. 'I'm waiting till Jeremy gets his knighthood!'

'That'll be the day,' said Carstairs, smiling.

Lady Jennifer – the Doctor found it impossible to think of her as anything else – served them all with refreshments and then tactfully disappeared.

The Doctor picked up Ribbentrop's list. 'As you say, Colonel Carstairs, we have to assume that everyone on this list is a traitor-in-waiting. Now, the accompanying notes make it clear that all those named are to take certain unspecified actions "when they get the signal".'

'Von Ribbentrop said something about waiting for the signal from the fort', said Peri. She looked at Carstairs. 'Sounds like some kind of military set-up. Maybe the Army's going to try to carry out a *coup d'état*?'

'Nonsense!' said Carstairs indignantly. 'Oh, there are high-ranking military officers on this list, I admit, but the army as a whole is perfectly sound, believe me, and so are all the rest of the armed services. Anyway, these days, most forts are historical sites for tourists, not active military bases.'

'These people are spread out all over the country,' said the Doctor. 'How are they going to get a signal to all of them at one and the same time?'

'Radio sets,' suggested Peri. 'If they all had receivers that could pick up some central transmission from this fort...'

'Not very likely,' said Carstairs. 'The Broadcasting Corporation has more than enough trouble trying to cover the entire country. It's hard to see how some amateur set-up could do it.'

'Maybe they're *using* the BBC!'

'The British Broadcasting Corporation transmitting treasonous messages?' said Carstairs, shocked. 'Please, Miss Brown, some things are sacred!'

Peri, who was sitting by the window, saw a black limousine draw up outside. Before the chauffeur could open the passenger door, a rotund figure in a black overcoat and Homburg hat clambered out of the back and climbed swiftly up the steps.

'Mr Churchill's arrived,' said Peri.

They heard the ring of the doorbell, and a moment later Winston Churchill bounded into the room, followed by Lady Jennifer. It was obvious that he was in a state of great excitement. Waving away the offer of coffee he said, 'I bear grave news.'

They all looked expectantly at him.

'I was summoned this morning,' said Churchill, 'to attend an urgent meeting in Downing Street. The meeting was to discuss the momentous events of the weekend, and, in particular, to make various arrangements resulting from another meeting last night.'

He paused impressively, as if making a speech in Parliament. His mystified audience stared back at him expectantly.

The words 'Get on with it, Winnie!' came almost irresistibly to the Doctor's mind. Instead he said, gravely, 'Please continue.'

'In recent weeks, Mr Baldwin, the Prime Minister, has been conducting a series of negotiations and discussions with the King. Matters finally reached an impasse over the weekend.

Late last night, I was summoned to attend. I may be out of office, but my counsel is still sought in times of crisis. That is why you were unable to communicate with me, Doctor.'

'What happened, sir?' asked Carstairs.

'The King declared it his firm and unshakeable intention to marry Wallis Simpson and make her his Queen. Mr Baldwin informed His Majesty that this was unacceptable to the Government, the Church of England, and, indeed, to the British nation as a whole.'

'I'm not sure about that last bit,' said Peri. 'From what I hear, quite a lot of ordinary people are on his side.'

Churchill scowled at the interruption. 'Ordinary people perhaps, Miss Brown. The more responsible elements, however, are solidly opposed to it.'

In other words, the middle and upper classes, thought Peri mutinously. Some democracy!

'What happened next?' asked Lady Jennifer, who was always eager for royal news.

Churchill made another impressive pause. 'The King announced that if this was the case, he would surely abdicate!'

There were satisfyingly astonished gasps from most of his audience.

The Doctor seemed unruffled. 'Weren't you and Mr Baldwin surprised?' he asked.

'I cannot speak for the Prime Minister, but I myself was astonished,' said Churchill. 'Up to now His Majesty has shown every sign of a most distressing obduracy. Indeed, he seemed fully prepared to defy both Government and Church.'

'Suppose he'd persisted in that attitude?' asked the Doctor. 'What would have happened?'

'It is hard to say, Doctor. National upheaval, perhaps, of the most appalling kind.'

'It would certainly have been pretty sticky,' said Carstairs. 'But isn't this good news, in a way, sir? I mean, it's a pity things have come to this, but what with the King's fondness for Germany, and Mrs Simpson's links with von Ribbentrop – well, if he'd dug in his heels…'

'Thank heavens he's seen sense,' said Lady Jennifer. 'When he abdicates I suppose Bertie will have to take over.'

'Bertie?' queried Peri.

'The Duke of York,' said the Doctor, with an amused look at Lady Jennifer. To her, the royals were just a bunch of often troublesome relatives. 'The King's younger brother.'

'Bertie's terribly sweet,' said Lady Jennifer. 'But so shy, poor man. Of course, it's understandable – he's been overshadowed by his brother all his life. And that stammer! How he'll ever manage public speeches…'

'Perhaps he'll rise to the occasion,' said the Doctor solemnly. 'People often do, you know.'

'So they do,' agreed Lady Jennifer. 'And Elizabeth's very practical and sensible, I'm sure she'll be able to build up his confidence…'

Cutting off the flow of royal family gossip with another scowl, Churchill said, 'Something troubles you, Doctor?'

'Yes, it does,' said the Doctor. 'The expression "Too good to be true" comes to mind.'

'How so?'

'Well, Peri's right, you know. The vast majority of ordinary English people are behind the King. He was the People's Prince for years, and now he's the People's King. *They're* as besotted with *him* as *he* is with Wallis Simpson, so blinded by his charm they fail to see his faults. If he were to go over Baldwin's head and appeal directly to the country…'

'But he hasn't!' said Carstairs.

'Exactly!' said the Doctor. 'Why hasn't he? And don't tell me it's his sense of duty – by your own admission, that hasn't bothered him much until now! *So why throw in your hand when you appear to hold most of the cards?*'

There was a moment of silence.

Churchill broke it. 'You have some theory to propose, Doctor? Connected, I take it, with the reason for this conference?'

The Doctor gave him an account of Peri's rescue, and of the information they'd gained, and Carstairs showed him von Ribbentrop's list.

Churchill listened with concentrated attention, studying the list, scowling and shaking his head. Then he turned to the Doctor.

'A sinister discovery indeed, Doctor. And if the King still maintained his posture of defiance, it would be more troubling still. Perhaps some rash action *was* planned. Perhaps the unhappy King was foolish enough to lend some dastardly scheme his support. But surely he has now repented of it? As Colonel Carstairs implies, his coming abdication defuses the situation.'

'If his repentance is genuine, yes. But suppose it isn't? You yourself spoke of the obstinacy of the weak.'

'But all is arranged, Doctor,' said Churchill. 'Arranged largely in my presence, last night and this morning. Arranged, in my view, with precipitate speed. I begged all parties to take more time, to consider matters more fully but, alas, my advice was ignored. The King gave his full consent to all Mr Baldwin's proposals. The Instrument of Abdication has been drawn up and will be signed tonight. The King has asked to make a farewell broadcast to the nation and Mr Baldwin has agreed. Arrangements are in hand with the British Broadcasting Corporation even as we speak.'

'Really?' said Lady Jennifer. 'The first royal broadcast! How exciting! We must be sure to listen.

Is the King going to that funny-looking building in Portland Place?'

'Apparently not,' said Churchill. 'It appears that the mountain now has the technical ability to come to Mahomet. A temporary broadcasting studio is even now being assembled.'

'At the Palace?'

Churchill shook his head. 'No, no,' he said, rather impatiently. 'The King has asked to make the broadcast from Fort Belvedere. He felt he would be more relaxed there. Apparently it is technically quite feasible and the Corporation has agreed...'

'The fort?' interrupted the Doctor. 'What fort?'

'Fort Belvedere, the King's private hideaway,' explained Lady Jennifer. 'Down at Sunningdale, in Berkshire. He's had it for years. A big house on the edge of Windsor Great Park – sort of a mock-castle. It was somewhere to get away from the Palace – and a place to take his girl friends. They say Wallis has pretty well taken it over these days...'

She broke off, realising that the Doctor and Peri weren't listening. Instead they were staring at each other in mutual excitement.

'I'm sorry, Carstairs,' said the Doctor. 'It seems nothing is sacred after all.'

'What do you mean?' asked Lady Jennifer in mild surprise.

The Doctor turned to Churchill. 'The signal,' he said. 'It'll be transmitted to the nation from the Fort!'

Chapter Twenty-Eight
Preparations

Not many people can arrive unexpectedly at 10 Downing Street, demand an immediate meeting with the Prime Minister, and be shown inside – but Winston Churchill was one of them. Within ten minutes of his arrival he was facing Stanley Baldwin in his private office.

Baldwin was a dull, cautious man, who looked and sounded like John Bull. He had always disliked and distrusted the excitable and volatile Churchill.

'Well, what is it now, Winston?' he asked peevishly. 'You above all people should know how busy I am today. This morning's meeting…'

'It is with regard to this morning's meeting that I have come to see you, Prime Minister,' said Churchill. 'You may regard our present encounter as a continuation of it.'

'But everything has now been settled.'

'Possibly,' said Churchill, adding with sinister emphasis, 'but there have been certain developments.'

In a brief and eloquent speech, without mentioning the Doctor by name, he told Baldwin of von Ribbentrop's list, and the Doctor's theory. By the time he had finished, Baldwin was gazing at him in utter horror.

'This is a lunatic idea, Winston, even for you!'

'Perhaps so,' said Churchill. 'But I urge you to consider, Stanley – possibly, just possibly, it is the truth.' Wagging his finger at the horrified Baldwin, Churchill went on: 'Consider the consequences for the country, if a sequence of events such as those I have postulated should indeed occur. And consider also, Stanley, the consequences for you yourself.'

'What consequences?' asked Baldwin warily.

'His Majesty still has some fondness for me,' said Churchill. 'However, you he has never really liked. And since you are currently engaged in an attempt to thwart his desires and frustrate the dearest wish of his heart… Well, like many weak men, he has a vindictive streak. In your case, Stanley, I should hazard that a firing squad would be a distinct possibility…'

Baldwin looked appalled. For some time his mouth moved in silence as he attempted to find words to protest. Eventually, he sighed and looked the other man in the eyes.

'What can I do, Winston?'

'Nothing.'

'But if there is anything, anything at all in what you suggest…' Baldwin shook his head, worriedly. 'Either action or inaction could have the most terrible consequences!'

'I did not say that nothing should be done, Stanley,' said Churchill. 'I said that *you* should do nothing.'

'But I don't understand…'

'Leave everything to me,' said Churchill calmly. 'I suggest that you develop a diplomatic cold, which will render you unable to attend tonight's ceremony. Since I was a participant at last night's meeting, it is natural that you should delegate me to attend in your place.'

Baldwin looked at him with an expression of dawning hope. 'Go on, Winston.'

'If I am wrong, and nothing untoward occurs, then no harm has been done.'

'And if you are right?'

'Before I leave, you must give me full written authority to act as I see fit to preserve the security of the state. I shall need a similar document for Colonel Carstairs.'

Baldwin hesitated. 'But suppose things go wrong? Suppose whatever measures you take become public? There could still be the most appalling scandal…'

Churchill played his master stroke. 'If things go wrong, if there is any kind of scandal, you may simply disown me, and report that I exceeded my authority. I give you my word, I shall bear all the blame.'

Baldwin clearly found the offer irresistible. 'Very well, Winston,' he said. 'It shall be as you wish.'

Pulling a sheet of official notepaper towards him, he selected a pen, dipped it in a silver ink-well, and began to write…

'And so you lost her,' said the Count.

'Really, Joachim,' said the Countess. She shook her head sadly, though there was a gleam of amusement deep in her sapphire-blue eyes. 'We deliver a dangerous American agent into your hands, and you let her go!'

They were in the sitting-room of the temporary German Embassy. It was a large and draughty room with much of the furniture still covered in drapes.

'I did not let her go,' said von Ribbentrop, petulantly. 'She was taken from me by her friends – with considerable brutality, I might add.'

The Countess shrugged. 'No matter. The girl is not really so very important.'

'Then why did you tell me she was an American agent, and place her in my custody? One of my staff was gravely wounded and another was brutally assaulted. Both have had to be flown back to Germany. Even I myself suffered injury…' He touched the bruise under his thinning hair and winced.

The Countess looked shocked. 'You don't mean to tell me the Doctor actually struck you? Or was it his hireling, Dekker?'

Von Ribbentrop did not reply.

'Not the girl?' said the Countess. She laughed outright. 'Oh, my poor Joachim…'

'You have not answered my question,' said von Ribbentrop

angrily. 'Why did you urge me to kidnap the girl?'

'It seemed at least a possibility that she was an American agent,' said the Count. 'We placed her in your custody because you have diplomatic immunity – and because we have no facilities for guarding prisoners.'

'We wanted to use her as a way of putting pressure on the Doctor,' said the Countess. 'Unfortunately you didn't hold her long enough for us to achieve any results. It is not important. After tonight we shall deal with the Doctor and the girl – and the Doctor's hired killer – at our leisure.'

Von Ribbentrop rose and paced nervously about the room.

'You realise that I can have nothing to do with tonight's... event until it is successfully concluded? The Fuehrer was most insistent upon this point. I cannot send SS men to assist you. Indeed, at the moment I have none to send.'

'From what we have seen of your men we are better off without them,' said the Countess. 'What happened to your incompetent assassins, by the way? The ones who failed so miserably to ambush the Doctor?'

'They did not succeed in reaching the Embassy until some time after the raid,' said von Ribbentrop stiffly. 'Far too late to be of any help. I do not tolerate failure, my Countess. I sent them straight back to Berlin with the wounded. Replacements are on their way, they will arrive tomorrow.'

'Tonight, Sir Oswald's Blackshirts will serve our purpose,' said the Count. 'It is important that, initially at least, this is a purely British occasion.'

'Once you have succeeded it will be a different matter,' said von Ribbentrop, eagerly. 'The Fuehrer has authorised me to sign an immediate treaty of alliance. And then, if you need a few battalions of SS to assist in keeping order... Once things are settled we can discuss your business concessions.'

'Business concessions?' said the Count.

Von Ribbentrop, a keen moneymaker all his life, gave him a

baffled look. 'The business concessions in England and Germany for your Consortium. You will not find the Fuehrer ungrateful, and you truly deserve your reward.' He attempted a lighter note. 'After all, I assume you are not doing all this purely to amuse yourselves?'

The Count and Countess exchanged smiles.

'No indeed,' said the Countess. ' That would be absurd, would it not?'

A few minutes later, von Ribbentrop found himself alone. An odd pair, those two, he thought. Here one minute, and gone the next. And their lack of interest in the business concessions he had promised… As if money meant nothing to them.

Von Ribbentrop resumed his pacing up and down the room. He looked at the big radio set. It was going to be a long day, and a momentous one.

He wondered when he would be able to see Wallis again. Her time would be taken up for a while, but eventually they would meet. He smiled at the thought.

How many men could say they had a queen for their mistress?

Carstairs gazed approvingly around the comfortably furnished officers' mess. He downed his whisky, his host raised a finger, and a mess waiter appeared with two more drinks.

'I must say, Roddy, you chaps do yourselves very well,' said Carstairs.

'We're the Guards,' said Roddy simply. 'We deserve the best.'

Carstairs grinned affectionately at his old friend. Tall and thin, wearing an immaculately-cut uniform and a totally unnecessary monocle, Colonel Rodney Fitzsimmons was almost a parody of the languidly elegant Guards officer. Carstairs had fought beside him in the trenches, and knew that beneath all the stock aristocratic affectations was a tough and shrewd professional soldier.

He took a sip of his whisky.

'Well, I think that concludes the briefing, Roddy,' he said. 'Quite clear on what you have to do?'

'Oh yes, I think so,' said Roddy. 'Training manoeuvres, just outside London.'

'That's right.'

'With live ammunition…'

'Right again.'

'I'm pretty clear on the what, old boy. Bit shaky on the why.'

'Not your concern,' said Carstairs. 'You've seen my authority. Yours not to reason why, and all that…'

'Oh, quite,' said Roddy. 'I'm just a simple soldier, all I do is obey orders. Must be a fearful strain on you chaps in Intelligence, having to think all the time.'

'Ghastly,' said Carstairs, smiling. He finished his whisky and stood up. 'Well, better be off, got a lot to do.'

Roddy rose as well.

As they walked towards the door he said, 'I say, everything's – everything's all right, isn't it, Jeremy?'

'It will be,' said Carstairs. 'So long as you follow your instructions. See you this evening – in the park.'

Having dealt with the Prime Minister, Winston Churchill was now tackling a much tougher proposition – Sir John Reith, Director of the British Broadcasting Corporation.

Unusually tall, with a balding head, a beaky nose and an intimidating stare, Reith listened silently to Churchill's series of requests.

'This is an extraordinary business.' Reith said dubiously, when Churchill had finished. 'I cannot pretend that I am happy about it. To act in this way behind His Majesty's back…'

'You have seen my authority –' began Churchill.

Reith held up his hand to silence him.

'This is the British Broadcasting Corporation, Mr Churchill.

We are not subject to the commands of politicians – however eminent.'

Churchill realised that it would be fatal to try to bully Reith, or even to give him direct orders. He summoned up all his powers of persuasion.

'Upon this day, Sir John, the Corporation – *your* Corporation – can do England a great service. Or, through no fault of its own, it can be tainted by association with traitorous infamy.'

Still unconvinced, Reith sat silent, brooding.

Suddenly, Churchill remembered that Reith, like himself, had served in the War, and was fiercely proud of the fact.

'Sir John,' he said, 'I speak to you not as a politician, but as a fellow soldier. I appeal to you to play your part, to do what is best for the defence of England. I can do no more. The matter is now in your hands.'

Still Reith stared into space, palms lay flat on his desk. Then, at last, he picked up the phone, dialled and waited for a moment.

'Engineering Officer? How are the arrangements for the royal broadcast proceeding? Good, good...' He looked at Churchill and sighed. 'Now, I have a rather extraordinary task for you...'

In the drawing room at Fort Belvedere, British Broadcasting Corporation engineers were setting up the equipment for His Majesty's speech to the nation.

It was insufferably hot in the big room. The central heating was on full blast, and a fire blazed in the grate.

The perspiring engineers worked on...

In his study nearby, the King strode nervously up and down, rehearsing his speech.

Curled up like a cat in an armchair by the fire, Wallis Simpson watched him. 'You don't have to learn it, you know,

David,' she said, impatiently. 'It's a radio broadcast, not a public meeting. Nobody can see you, you can read the thing. I was talking to one of the engineers. All you have to do is to remember not to rustle the paper too much.'

The King stopped his pacing and gazed adoringly at her. 'If I just read it, it will sound stilted. Darling, our whole future together depends on the public's response to this speech. I've simply *got* to get it right…'

He resumed his pacing and muttering.

Wallis sighed.

Outside Fort Belvedere, lorries drew up in the gathering dusk and black-shirted figures jumped down. The rank and file carried staves and truncheons, while officers and sergeants had guns.

Their leader, a tall, beaky-nosed man with a moustache, immediately took charge. 'Take up positions inside and outside the house. Let anyone in who wants to go in, but let nobody out without authorisation from me.'

'What, not even the King, sir?' joked somebody.

'No,' said Sir Oswald Mosley. 'Not even the King!'

In the Doctor and Peri's sitting-room in Hill Street, Winston Churchill drained his glass of champagne and immediately held it out for Rye to refill. He looked anxiously at Carstairs.

'Have we done all we should? All we possibly can?'

'I think so, sir,' said Carstairs. 'I've checked with Roddy and everything's in place.'

'And Sir John?'

'The engineers are still working, but he's confident they'll be finished in time.'

'And all the necessary surveillance has been undertaken?'

'Yes, sir. Everyone's covered.'

'What about von Ribbentrop?' asked Peri.

'Von Ribbentrop is lying low in his temporary embassy. The only ones we've lost track of are the Count and Countess.'

'Don't worry,' said the Doctor, grimly. 'They'll turn up when it's time. Something tells me they wouldn't miss this for worlds.'

'I hear much of this pair of mysterious foreign aristocrats, Doctor,' rumbled Churchill, 'but I have yet to meet them. I am somewhat at a loss to understand their part in all this.'

'To be honest, so am I,' said the Doctor.

He wondered if Churchill would connect the current Count and Countess with the pair in the chateau when they met. Perhaps they were deliberately keeping out of his way.

'Are they in alliance with von Ribbentrop and his Nazi crew?' Churchill went on.

'I'm sure of it,' said Peri. 'They were definitely involved in my kidnapping. I got the feeling they were using von Ribbentrop. You know, as their pawn.'

'That's a very good way of putting it, Peri,' said the Doctor. 'Ever since we first met, I've had the feeling they were playing some kind of game…'

'No doubt their roles will emerge in time,' said Churchill, dismissing the subject.

There was a knock on the door, and Rye showed in Dekker and the Op. Like Churchill and the Doctor, both were in evening dress. Carstairs was in full uniform, and Peri herself wore a simple black dress.

'Our party is complete,' said Churchill, who was clearly enjoying himself. The prospect of action always invigorated him. 'May I suggest a final toast, Doctor?'

The Doctor nodded to Rye who opened more champagne and saw that everyone had a full glass.

'Gentlemen, Miss Brown,' said Churchill. 'It is possible that nothing more will occur tonight than the signing of the Act of Abdication and His Majesty's farewell speech. If that proves to be so, we shall all have been present on a sad but indubitably historic occasion. If, however, as the Doctor suspects, some more dastardly scheme is in progress – well, our foes will find we are ready for them.' He raised his glass. 'To victory!'

The Doctor, Peri, Carstairs, Dekker and the Op all raised their glasses.

'To victory!'

Peri glanced at the Doctor and muttered under her breath: 'We hope!'

Chapter Twenty-Nine
Execution

Three cars were lined up outside the house in Hill Street: Churchill's limousine, the Doctor's Rolls Royce, and a green Bentley Continental sports car. This last, it transpired, belonged to Carstairs.

'I'd better leave first,' he said, 'I need to go on ahead and liaise with Roddy.'

He jumped behind the wheel and the big car roared off down Hill Street.

'Will you accompany me, Doctor?' asked Churchill. 'We can confer on the way.'

The Doctor looked inquiringly at Peri.

'You go ahead, Doctor,' she said. 'I'll ride with the US contingent!'

The Doctor and Churchill got in the back of the big limousine, and the car drew away.

The Op was already behind the wheel of the Doctor's Rolls. He nodded to Peri and said, 'Always wanted to drive one of these!'

Dekker held the rear passenger door open for Peri, then got in the front beside the Op. The car moved smoothly off after the others.

As the Doctor had half-expected, little actual conferring was done on the way down to Fort Belvedere. They had discussed their plan extensively during the day, considering and covering every possibility.

Churchill said as much himself.

'It is a good plan we follow, Doctor, carefully thought out.

'Either it will work or it will not.' He frowned. 'However, I cannot but remember the famous axiom of von Clausewitz. "No plan of battle long survives contact with the enemy!"'

'This one will,' said the Doctor. 'I hope!'

Churchill looked thoughtfully at him. 'You know, Doctor, since we met, I have been casting my mind back over the past. When I look at you I see my companion of Boer War days, untouched by the passage of thirty-seven years. Miss Brown too bears an uncanny resemblance to my companion's ward.'

The Doctor made no reply.

'I will tell you another strange circumstance,' Churchill went on. 'You will remember that Colonel Carstairs spoke of a Doctor Smith whom we encountered during the War? There is no physical resemblance of any kind between you and that man. And yet, somehow, when I think of that Doctor Smith, the two of you seem to merge in my mind. Colonel Carstairs feels the same. Curious, is it not?'

Winston Churchill, thought the Doctor once again, was a hard man to fool. 'It is, as you say, curious,' he said. 'But the world is full of curious things.'

'Then let me tell you of another. The body of the assassin that your friend Dekker shot from the tree at the royal garden party has vanished from the morgue. Vanished from a locked and guarded room.'

'Baffling,' said the Doctor.

Churchill laughed. 'Never fear, Doctor, I shall not press you to explain the inexplicable – especially not tonight. Perhaps we can discuss these matters at some other time.'

The Doctor smiled agreeably, and the car sped on. Soon they had left London behind, and were driving through darkened countryside. Eventually the road narrowed, cutting through dense forests. The headlights of the Doctor's Rolls chased them through the rear window.

'Not far now, Doctor,' said Churchill.

The road abruptly opened out on to a broad gravel drive. At the end of the drive was a brightly-lit building, its battlements and turrets standing out against the night sky.

The two cars drew up before the building.

'Well, we are here,' grunted Churchill. 'Fort Belvedere. I have occasionally visited His Majesty here in happier times.'

They got out of the car, while behind them, Peri, Dekker and the Op did the same. Dark shapes appeared from the shadows, and suddenly they were surrounded by black-shirted figures.

'Who are you?' barked one of them. 'State your business.'

'I am Winston Churchill, and my business is with the King. This lady and these gentlemen are my guests. Stand aside!'

Churchill barged his way through the encircling figures, the Doctor close behind him. Dekker and the Op did the same, shielding Peri between them.

Suddenly Peri realised that Dekker was carrying a bulky musical instrument case.

'Brought your harp to the party, Dekker?' she whispered.

'Sure, why not. Maybe somebody will ask me to play!'

As the little group marched up to the door, it was opened by a liveried footman.

They passed through into an octagonal ante-room with a black and white floor. More black-shirted figures stood on guard. Beyond was a huge, elaborately furnished drawing room. Classical paintings hung on the walls, and there were yellow satin curtains at the long windows. Chintz-covered armchairs, Chippendale tables and even a grand piano all clamoured for the eye's attention. A cheerful fire blazed in the big grate.

Still more blackshirted figures stood at intervals around the walls.

In one corner of the room, the Broadcasting Corporation technicians had set up their temporary studio. It consisted of a chair, and a table with a microphone. The set-up was surrounded, Peri saw, with a tangle of large and clumsy equipment.

The King came forward to greet them, Wallis Simpson by his side. He was in evening dress. Wallis wore a magnificent cloth-of-gold gown and a diamond tiara in her hair. It looked very like a crown. The King's eyes were glittering with excitement, but Wallis looked strained and tense.

'Winston!' said the King exuberantly. 'I didn't expect to see you tonight. Where's Baldwin?'

'The Prime Minister presents his apologies, Your Majesty. A sudden cold…'

'A sudden attack of cold feet, more likely!' said the King.

'Mr Baldwin has asked me to take his place,' Churchill went on. 'May I present my guests, Your Majesty? Doctor Smith, and his ward Miss Brown, who you have already met, and two American friends of Miss Brown's. I trust Your Majesty has no objection?'

'No, no, the more the merrier,' said the King carelessly.

Churchill looked round at the Blackshirts lining the walls. 'Your Majesty chooses strange escorts for this solemn occasion,' he said, reprovingly.

'I know you don't care for Mosley, Winston, but he and his Blackshirts have always been loyal to me. I need loyal friends at a time like this.'

'I have some guests of my own,' said Wallis Simpson. 'Mr Churchill, may I introduce Countess Andrea Razetki and Count Ludwig Praetorius.'

The Count was in full evening dress, with stars and orders and medals blazing on his breast. The Countess wore a magnificent scarlet evening gown, with diamonds shining in her hair.

Churchill studied them both with keen interest. 'We have met before, I think. In France, some twenty years ago. You bear the ravages of time remarkably well, Countess.'

The Countess smiled. 'Thank you, sir,' she said.

'You, Mr Churchill, on the other hand, look considerably older,' said the Count. 'It is to be hoped that you are now wiser.'

Churchill merely gazed impassively at the elegant figure.

'I'm glad you're here, Winston,' said the King, hurriedly. 'You've always been my friend, a real tonic to me. You're just in time to hear my broadcast.' He looked across at the technicians and called, 'Are you chaps ready? Mustn't keep the nation waiting.'

'Ready, Your Majesty.'

The King gave a boyish grin. 'Pay attention, now, Winston. You're in for a surprise!'

'Your Majesty forgets that I have already seen the text of your speech. I assisted Mr Baldwin with the final draft.'

'Oh, that's all over and done with,' said the King dismissively. 'Just you listen to *this*!'

He strode over to the improvised studio and sat down, taking a sheet of paper from his inside pocket.

Peri saw Dekker and the Op drift after him, as if fascinated by the proceedings. Dekker was still carrying his violin case.

The King looked at the technician, who was pale and tense, and asked, 'What about the introduction?'

'All handled from the other end, Your Majesty. Just start talking when that green light goes on.'

There was a moment of tense silence. Then the cue light came on and the King began to speak, in slow, measured tones.

'People of Britain! This is the voice of your King. You know of the personal turmoil in which I have been involved. You know that there has been a plot by those in high places to prevent me from marrying the woman I love. I have decided that I cannot face the heavy burden of my duties without Wallis by my side.'

Churchill and the Doctor exchanged glances. This was the crucial point of the speech.

'I have also decided that I will no longer tolerate this interference with my wishes,' the King went on. 'I shall marry Wallis Simpson, and she will be my queen – and yours! I have therefore decided to dismiss the Government!'

Churchill closed his eyes and clenched his fists. The Doctor said nothing, and raised a finger to his lips to stop Peri speaking.

The King continued. 'For a time I shall rule directly as your monarch. In due time, a new and more loyal form of government will be established. Even now, those loyal to me are engaged in seizing the reins of power. I have the help of Sir Oswald Mosley and his loyal organisation of Blackshirts, and of my friend and ally Chancellor Adolf Hitler of Germany. Stay in your homes, remain calm and await further instructions. Goodnight.'

The Doctor looked at Churchill. 'Well, he did it!'

'Indeed he did,' said Churchill, sadly.

Jumping up, the King embraced Wallis and came hurrying over to the Doctor and Churchill. He turned to Churchill.

'Isn't it splendid? We'll get rid of that old fool Baldwin and you can be my Prime Minister. Better still, you can be my Chancellor.' He looked at Churchill's solemn face and said, 'Well, what do you think?'

'I am appalled, Your Majesty. Shocked and horrified by this act of monstrous folly.'

The King scowled. 'Be careful, Winston, this is close to treason.'

'It *is* treason,' thundered Churchill. 'But the treason, Your Majesty, is not mine, but yours!'

The King's face twisted with anger. 'Arrest him!'

Blackshirts moved forward, but Churchill held up his hand.

'Wait!' he boomed. The King was so taken with the authority in his voice that he nodded, holding up a hand.

Churchill turned to the King and said quietly, 'I have to

inform Your Majesty that the speech you have just made has not been broadcast. It has however been recorded – and can, if necessary, be used in evidence at your trial for high treason. Everyone on the list of your treacherous associates is under observation. When the signal fails to materialise, it is likely that most will do nothing. However, anyone who *does* take any treasonous action will be instantly arrested.'

Suddenly the Count raised his voice. 'Seize that recording!'

Blackshirts surged towards the terrified technicians – and stopped, this time at the sound of a shot.

The Op, standing in front of the improvised studio, had just fired his gun in the air.

'It is only one man!' shouted the Count. 'Shoot him, someone. Trample him down!'

The Blackshirts surged forward again.

Standing beside the Op, his open music case at his feet, Dekker stooped down and came up with his tommy-gun in his hands. He fired a single burst high above the heads of the advancing Blackshirts.

The noise was terrifying. The intimidated Blackshirts froze.

From outside, as if in response to the shots, there came the boom of a field gun.

Beckoning to Peri, the Doctor ran across to the windows.

They pulled back the yellow satin curtains to reveal rank upon rank of soldiers lined up outside.

The light from the windows glinted upon fixed bayonets.

The Doctor raised his voice. 'This building is now totally surrounded. Remain where you are and wait for instructions. If you have weapons, lay them down and step away from them.'

The Doctor moved over to the King and spoke in a low voice. 'Your Majesty, a studio has been set up in the Augusta Tower at Windsor Castle. Sir John Reith, Director of the British Broadcasting Corporation, is waiting there, with members of your family. You will go there now and sign the Instrument of

Abdication. At ten o'clock this evening you will deliver the speech announcing that abdication to the nation. The speech you originally agreed with Mr Churchill and Prime Minister Baldwin.'

The King was white-faced and trembling.

'And if I refuse?'

'You will be arrested and put on trial for high treason, Your Majesty' said the Doctor sombrely.

'But you can't do that! I'm the King! Winston, tell him.'

'The matter is deadly serious, Your Majesty' said Churchill.

'The English love their monarchs,' said the Doctor. 'But they still chop off their heads if they get above themselves.'

The brutal words had their effect. Wallis Simpson grasped the King's arm.

'Do as they say, darling. We're beaten.' She looked at Churchill. 'Believe me, I never wanted this. That damned Count and Countess gave him the idea.'

The King said, 'If I do as you say – what happens afterwards?'

'The original agreement stands,' said Churchill. 'You will be given the title of Duke of Windsor and a generous income. As soon as all the necessary arrangements are completed, you will leave the country and live abroad.'

'And Wallis?'

Churchill turned to Wallis Simpson.

'I advise you to change and pack. You, madam, will be leaving the country tonight.' He turned back to the King. 'Once you are both established in residence abroad, you may marry whenever you please.'

Wallis kissed the King briefly, gave them all a comprehensive look of hatred and ran from the room.

'Wait for me in France, darling,' called the King. 'I'll come to you, I'll never give you up!'

Colonels Carstairs and Fitzsimmons came into the room at the head of a squad of soldiers.

Under Colonel Fitzsimmons's supervision, the guardsmen began rounding up the subdued Blackshirts and leading them away.

Carstairs came over to the King and saluted. 'If you will come with me, Your Majesty? My orders are to escort you to Windsor Castle.'

They watched as the King followed Carstairs from the room.

The Doctor looked at Churchill and saw tears in his eyes. He beckoned to Dekker and the Op and touched Peri's arm.

'Everything seems to be well in hand, I think we might slip away.'

Peri looked round the crowded room. 'Doctor, what about the Count and Countess?'

'What about them?'

'Well, shouldn't we do something about them?'

'I don't think we can, just at the moment,' said the Doctor, looking round. 'They appear to have vanished!'

Chapter Thirty
Departures

Next day, Carstairs and Winston Churchill came round for morning coffee – or rather, at Churchill's suggestion, for morning champagne.

'How did things go at Windsor Castle?' asked the Doctor.

'Very well,' said Carstairs. 'He signed the Instrument of Abdication and read the speech as good as gold.'

'I know, we caught the end of it,' said Peri. 'Quite touching, really. What was that last bit about the new King…'

'"And now we have a new King,"' quoted Churchill. '"I wish him and you, his people, happiness with all my heart. God bless you all. God save the King." One of my better efforts, I think!'

'Saying that last bit must have cost him something,' said Peri. 'After all his efforts last night…'

'I don't know,' mused Churchill. 'One would almost think that he had forgotten it already. This morning he is wrangling about the financial settlement and planning the wedding of the century! He has a curiously childlike temperament.' He raised his glass. 'My thanks for all your help, Doctor. We must arrange a suitable celebration.'

'I'm afraid this will have to be it,' said the Doctor. 'Miss Brown and I are leaving almost immediately. We have business elsewhere.'

Churchill looked disappointed. 'I was hoping to have a long talk with you, Doctor. I wished to ask your advice about the future.'

'I'm sorry. We really must go, mustn't we, Peri?'

'Afraid so.'

Churchill shook them both warmly by the hand.

'I wish you well, Doctor.'

'And I you, sir,' said the Doctor. 'And I will give you one piece of advice about the future, if I may. There are hard times ahead, for you and for England. But don't despair and don't give up. You'll reach the broad sunlit uplands of prosperity, right enough.'

'A fine phrase, Doctor,' said Churchill. 'I may use it in my next speech.' As he left the room they heard him rolling the phrase over his tongue. 'The broad sunlit uplands of prosperity...'

'I'd better go too,' said Carstairs. 'Nice to meet you –' he paused. 'I almost said, "Nice to meet you again"... Goodbye, Doctor, Miss Brown... Oh, by the way, there's no trace of the mysterious Count and Countess anywhere. I hear von Ribbentrop's gone scuttling back to Berlin. Perhaps they went with him...'

When the signal failed to materialise, and the abdication speech followed soon afterwards, von Ribbentrop ordered up his big private *Junkers* aeroplane and fled to Berlin.

He didn't *think* he was implicated in the failed coup, but all the same... A diplomatic absence seemed indicated.

Next morning he was summoned to see the Fuehrer, who had already heard the news and was far from pleased.

'Abdicated! An English king who was our friend and he has abdicated!'

'I am sorry, my Fuehrer. All arrangements were in place – but something went wrong.'

'What about these Consortium people who were behind it all,' demanded Hitler. 'Can't they tell you anything?'

'I'm afraid not, my Fuehrer. They have disappeared.'

Something crackled in von Ribbentrop's tunic pocket and he said hurriedly, 'All is not completely lost, my Fuehrer. I have a list, a surprisingly long list, of those in England sympathetic to our cause. Some of them in very high places.'

He took the list from his tunic pocket and handed it to the Fuehrer.

Hitler studied it for a moment and then looked up and frowned. 'The list is in code?'

'No, my Fuehrer, in clear. A list of important names –'

'Three pairs of socks, five pairs of underpants, six vests… This is a laundry list, you imbecile!' Hitler sprang to his feet. 'Fool! Idiot! Incompetent swine!'

Terrified, von Ribbentrop turned and fled. An inkwell crashed against the wall by his head as he ran from the room.

In the outer office, Martin Bormann looked up in surprise as von Ribbentrop hurried past.

'The Fuehrer is – distressed,' gasped von Ribbentrop. 'I must return immediately to England!'

He disappeared down the Chancellery stairs.

Bormann listened for a moment to the shouts and screams, the sounds of splintering furniture coming from Hitler's office. The Fuehrer was becoming distressingly prone to these attacks of uncontrollable rage. What was the name of that latest psychic consultant, the one who seemed to have such a calming effect…

He picked up the telephone.

'I wish to place a call to Doctor Kriegsleiter…'

The Doctor finished writing and handed the completed papers to Dekker.

'There you are, Mr Dekker, a complete power of attorney. With that, you can pay off the house rent, house bills and car hire, pay off any other outstanding debts, and, most importantly, pay for the invaluable services of yourself and the Op, plus a handsome bonus.'

Dekker studied the papers and gave the Doctor a worried look. 'With this I could also rob you of your last cent, Doctor.'

241

'Yes, I know,' said the Doctor. 'But you won't, will you?'

Dekker sighed. 'No, I guess I won't.'

'Spend whatever you need to spend and leave the rest on deposit at Cholmondeley's, for myself or for my descendants.'

'OK,' said Dekker. He stood up. 'Well… If you're ever in the area…'

'I'll look you up,' said the Doctor. 'I promise.'

Dekker shook hands with the Doctor and then with Peri. 'If you ever run into a girl called Ace…'

'I'll give her your love, shall I?' said Peri.

'That's right,' said Dekker. 'Give her my love.'

He went out of the room just as Rye was coming in.

'Will there be anything further, sir?'

'No thank you, Rye,' said the Doctor. 'Mr Dekker will settle up and make all the final arrangements. Many thanks for all you've done.'

'My pleasure, sir.' He permitted himself the faintest of smiles. 'It's been much more exciting than working for the Duke.'

Rye slipped out of the room and the Doctor turned to Peri. 'That takes care of everything, I think.'

'With two rather large exceptions.' She stared up at him and tugged on his sleeve. 'What about the Count and Countess?' she implored.

'What about them? We put paid to their little scheme.'

'They may have others.'

'I'm sure they have.'

'Don't you want to stop them?'

'I don't want to make chasing them a full time job.'

'Who were they, Doctor?' said Peri. She shivered. '*What* were they?'

'Put them from your mind, Peri,' said the Doctor. 'Come on. Let's go and take a last look at the garden, shall we?'

They went out into the high-walled area, and Peri jumped back with a gasp of horror.

There was a dead body lying on the lawn. It was the would-be assassin from the veldt and from the garden party, just as he'd been when he fell from the tree, face down with a gaping wound between his shoulder blades.

Suddenly the Count and Countess appeared. They might have been lurking in the bushes for ages, but somehow Peri didn't think so. They just… were there. The Count wore a long overcoat, and the Countess wore a travelling cloak. She was holding an automatic in her hand.

The Count had a long cane. He stripped off the wooden sheath to reveal the sword inside.

'I hear you are leaving, Doctor,' he said. 'We too must depart – but we have one or two things to attend to first.'

'We thought you might like another look at your handiwork,' said the Countess.

'The Doctor didn't kill him,' said Peri, even as she said the words feeling guilty for endangering Dekker.

'He paid the man who did,' said the Count. 'We shall destroy Mr Dekker at our leisure – but first we shall deal with the true cause of our friend's death.'

The Doctor looked at the Countess's automatic. 'You gave that to a friend of mine once. I don't suppose…'

She smiled. 'I'm afraid not, Doctor.'

The Doctor looked at them, thoughtfully. 'The relationship between you two seems… How can I put it – variable?'

'You could say so, Doctor. In South Africa we were opponents. In France we were allies – until I changed sides on a whim. Here we were allies too – in a wonderful, poetic scheme which you have entirely wrecked, Doctor, costing us a life. You must pay for that, with your own and that of your friend.'

'First satisfy my curiosity,' said the Doctor. 'Allies and opponents in what?'

'In the Game,' said the Count. 'The Game that never ends.'

'All the wealth, all the pleasures of this world are within our grasp,' said the Countess. 'We are rich, we do not age – and we are bored, Doctor, so bored...'

'You don't age? Where are you from?' Peri challenged.

'We have moved through time so often and lived so long... We have changed so much, seen past and future alter around us time and time again...' The Countess threw her head back and laughed. 'Do you know, I'm not sure we any of us remember.'

'So you tinker with history – to amuse yourselves?'

'But it is such a fascinating game, Doctor,' said the Count. 'A kaleidoscope. Touch one piece and the whole picture changes.'

'Think of the new scenario you spoiled, Doctor,' said the Countess. 'Winston Churchill dead before World War Two. England under a Nazi king allied to Hitler. How fascinating to discover how the future would alter. Now we shall never know.'

'And you do all this just for fun?' said Peri, horrified. 'You can't do that!'

'How do you know how much of your own time was shaped by us, child?' the Countess asked, still clearly amused. 'We may have brought you into being!'

'We are Players,' said the Count arrogantly. 'Masters of Time. We can do as we will.'

'Now, satisfy *our* curiosity,' said the Countess. 'Like us you travel through time, you even change your appearance. Tell us what *you* are, Doctor, before you die.'

'First I will tell you what *you* are,' said the Doctor sternly. 'You call yourselves Players, Masters of Time? I call you vandals. Evil children who throw a slab of concrete on the track, derailing the train of history for the pleasure of hearing the smash and the screams of the dying. Moronic hooligans who throw grit in the machinery of history for the fun of hearing it grind screaming to a halt.' The Doctor's voice was filled with withering scorn. 'Don't humans cause each other agony enough, without you adding to it for your amusement?'

Peri had never heard him sound so stern – or so angry.

The Count and Countess stood white and shaken under the lash of his scorn.

Recovering, the Count said, 'And what kind of superior being are you, Doctor?'

'I am a Time Lord. My race is far from perfect but we respect time, we understand it, and we have powers that are beyond your petty comprehension.'

'Time Lord or not, you have no more concern with time, Doctor,' snarled the Count, raising the blade of his swordstick. 'It is time for you to die.'

The Countess trained her automatic on Peri's heart.

The Doctor took a step forwards, placing himself between the Countess and Peri.

'You'll achieve nothing by killing us,' he said. He looked down at the assassin's body. 'I'm sorry your friend here had to die – but, after all, he who lives by the sword...'

'We are not concerned with justice, Doctor,' hissed the Count. 'Only with revenge!' He drew back the swordstick, preparing to lunge for the Doctor's heart.

The Doctor didn't flinch. Instead his eyes widened in pleased surprise as he gazed past the Count as if at someone behind him.

'Mr Dekker! In the proverbial nick of time,' he cried.

Both the Count and the Countess turned – to find nothing but the garden wall.

'Now, Peri!' thundered the Doctor. He grabbed the Count's sword arm.

Peri lunged for the Countess's gun. The Countess drew back, but not fast enough. Peri felt the cold metal of the automatic under her hands and the strength in the Countess's wrists.

For all her elegance the woman's grip was like steel. If only Dekker really had come back...

The Doctor grappled with the Count for possession of the swordstick. Like Peri, he found his opponent unexpectedly strong.

'A fine Player you turned out to be,' said the Doctor mockingly. 'Falling for the oldest trick in the book!'

The Count didn't bother finding a witty riposte. Instead he kicked the Doctor in the stomach with brutal force, propelling him back against the far wall. His head slammed against the brick and he slid to the ground.

The Countess tightened her grip on Peri's wrists, holding her locked, immobile.

'Give up my dear,' she said lightly, as if this were some after-dinner amusement. 'It's all over. There's nothing you can do to save your friend now.'

Peri watched in horror as the Count strolled almost idly across to the fallen Doctor. The blade of the swordstick glinted in the dappled sunlight.

'Look out, Doctor!' Peri shouted.

The Doctor didn't seem to hear her. He was shaking his head dazedly as if to clear it. The Count prepared to deliver the killing thrust.

'No!' screamed Peri.

Abruptly she twisted round, trying to throw the Countess off balance and reach the Count before he could act.

Instead she tumbled over the corpse of the would-be assassin and almost fell.

Abandoning the struggle for the gun, she grabbed at the Countess's dress to save herself.

Turning the gun on Peri, the Countess fired – at the very moment that Peri's weight spun her round.

The gunshot echoed round the high walls. Birds clattered out from the trees, leaving a silence hanging over the garden.

Peri kept her eyes tight shut for a moment, convinced she'd been shot. Then she heard the Countess gasp.

She opened her eyes. The Count was staring straight at her, his face twisted in an expression between a mocking smile and the dawning of absolute outrage. There was a red spot on his forehead. As Peri watched, blood welled from it. Then the Count toppled forwards to land at the Countess's feet.

Carefully, the Doctor rose, his expression grave. He beckoned to Peri and she moved warily round to stand beside him.

The Countess stood staring down at the body of the Count. She let the gun slip from her hand as her body began to convulse and tears streaked down her face.

Peri darted swiftly forward and snatched up the gun, but the Countess ignored her. She threw back her head and actually clutched her sides.

Suddenly Peri realised – the woman was laughing.

The Doctor stepped forward and knelt by the Count, feeling for a pulse. He nodded, gravely. 'He's dead.'

'I imagine I'll be in trouble for this,' said the Countess, dabbing daintily at her eyes with a lace handkerchief. 'I don't think the rules make provision for such an unusual event!'

The Doctor jumped up angrily. 'Your game never ends, does it? You've killed one of your own kind and all you can think of is how it affects some stupid rule.'

The Countess smiled. 'Surely you understand by now, Doctor? All that matters is the Game.'

'Even coming here to avenge that unfortunate young man was just a diversion for you, wasn't it?' accused the Doctor. 'You couldn't care less about the fate of a living soul!'

Peri looked down at the Count's body and shuddered.

'Don't you dare judge me,' warned the Countess, her eyes flashing. Then, her anger disappearing, she smiled, slightly. 'However...' She took a step towards the Doctor.

Peri raised the automatic warningly, ready for another attack.

But the Countess was charm itself as she approached the Doctor.

'We have so much in common, Doctor,' she purred.

'We most certainly do not!' said the Doctor, appalled.

'You walk through time as we do,' she said. 'You meddle, you manipulate humans as we do.'

'No,' said the Doctor, looking sternly down at her. 'I do no such thing. My motives for any... interference are very different from your own.'

The Countess looked up at him. 'How could I have been so foolish as to wish to do you harm?' She smiled, completely composed, as if nothing untoward had occurred. 'You're too powerful, too important, to be allowed to escape our Game just yet. And now you've caused the death of two of us. They must be replaced...' She reached up and adjusted the Doctor's tie. 'I think you must join us in our entertainments, Doctor. You will make a splendid Player!'

'Never!' said the Doctor. 'In any event, Peri and I are about to leave this parochial patch of Earth far behind us.'

'Oh, but you'll be back, Doctor. Your face may look different, your form may change, but...' She nodded. 'You'll be playing our Game again.'

'No,' said the Doctor, his voice rising a fraction. 'I want no part of it.'

'The choice is yours, Doctor,' said the Countess. 'You can become a Player, like us. Win again, perhaps, as you have done today. Or you can be a Piece, ours to control.' She turned and stepped demurely over the Count's fallen body. 'And then... The hand of the Player must never be seen. So how will you ever be able to tell whether the moves you make are your own – or ours?'

The Countess turned and walked towards the open French windows.

'No you don't!' yelled Peri, raising the automatic. 'You can try playing your stupid Game from a prison cell. We can get you locked up on Murder One – you just killed someone, unless it's slipped your…'

Peri's words trailed away. The Countess hadn't gone into the house. She'd just vanished. Peri turned away from the French windows to find the corpses had disappeared too.

There was only the Doctor standing there now, a troubled frown on his face.

'No,' Peri heard him mutter. 'Never!'

'Doctor…' she said tentatively.

The Doctor turned as if awakening from some nightmare.

'Time to go, Peri,' he said.

He took something that looked like a gold watch from his waistcoat pocket – the device he'd used to put the TARDIS in parking orbit when they'd arrived in Green Park.

He opened the back and touched a control – and suddenly the air was filled with a familiar sound.

All at once, there was the TARDIS, blue and square and oddly anachronistic, standing in the middle of the little lawn.

The Doctor produced his key, opened the door, and ushered Peri inside. He followed her in, closing the door behind them.

Moments later, with a defiant wheezing, groaning sound, the TARDIS dematerialised.

Envoi

The space was filled with voices, old and young, male and female, every timbre and every accent.

An angry voice cut through the tumult.

'Two Players killed? And one of them at your hands!'

The voice of the Countess was cool and amused.

'An unfortunate accident. We are all subject to hazard.'

'Yet you allowed this Doctor and his companion to live?'

Again the furious hubbub arose.

'Vengeance!' called a voice and other voices took up the cry.

'Vengeance! Vengeance! Vengeance!'

'No!'

The sheer authority of the arrogant old voice silenced them. 'The death of the Count was due to hazard – the Countess bears no blame. She has done well. By allowing the Doctor to live, she provides us with a worthy opponent in some future Game.'

'The Doctor refused to play,' objected the angry voice.

'He will play,' said the Countess confidently. 'His pride will allow him no choice.'

The old voice said, 'Remember, we are Players. Hazard adds to the spice of the Game. We mourn our brethren, accept our losses and move on. The Game is endless.'

The voices blended into a chorus, speaking as one.

> *'Winning is everything – and nothing*
> *Losing is nothing – and everything*
> *All that matters is the Game.'*

BBC DOCTOR WHO BOOKS

THE EIGHT DOCTORS *by Terrance Dicks* ISBN 0 563 40563 5
VAMPIRE SCIENCE *by Jonathan Blum and Kate Orman* ISBN 0 563 40566 X
THE BODYSNATCHERS *by Mark Morris* ISBN 0 563 40568 6
GENOCIDE *by Paul Leonard* ISBN 0 563 40572 4
WAR OF THE DALEKS *by John Peel* ISBN 0 563 40573 2
ALIEN BODIES *by Lawrence Miles* ISBN 0 563 40577 5
KURSAAL *by Peter Anghelides* ISBN 0 563 40578 3
OPTION LOCK *by Justin Richards* ISBN 0 563 40583 X
LONGEST DAY *by Michael Collier* ISBN 0 563 40581 3
LEGACY OF THE DALEKS *by John Peel* ISBN 0 563 40574 0
DREAMSTONE MOON *by Paul Leonard* ISBN 0 563 40585 6
SEEING I *by Jonathan Blum and Kate Orman* ISBN 0 563 40586 4
PLACEBO EFFECT *by Gary Russell* ISBN 0 563 40587 2
VANDERDEKEN'S CHILDREN *by Christopher Bulis* ISBN 0 563 40590 2
THE SCARLET EMPRESS *by Paul Magrs* ISBN 0 563 40595 3
THE JANUS CONJUNCTION *by Trevor Baxendale* ISBN 0 563 40599 6
BELTEMPEST *by Jim Mortimore* ISBN 0 563 40593 7
THE FACE EATER *by Simon Messingham* ISBN 0 563 55569 6
THE TAINT *by Michael Collier* ISBN 0 563 55568 8
DEMONTAGE *by Justin Richards* ISBN 0 563 55572 6
REVOLUTION MAN *by Paul Leonard* ISBN 0 563 55570 X

THE DEVIL GOBLINS FROM NEPTUNE *by Keith Topping and Martin Day*
ISBN 0 563 40564 3
THE MURDER GAME *by Steve Lyons* ISBN 0 563 40565 1
THE ULTIMATE TREASURE *by Christopher Bulis* ISBN 0 563 40571 6
BUSINESS UNUSUAL *by Gary Russell* ISBN 0 563 40575 9
ILLEGAL ALIEN *by Mike Tucker and Robert Perry* ISBN 0 563 40570 8
THE ROUNDHEADS *by Mark Gatiss* ISBN 0 563 40576 7
THE FACE OF THE ENEMY *by David A. McIntee* ISBN 0 563 40580 5
EYE OF HEAVEN *by Jim Mortimore* ISBN 0 563 40567 8
THE WITCH HUNTERS *by Steve Lyons* ISBN 0 563 40579 1
THE HOLLOW MEN *by Keith Topping and Martin Day* ISBN 0 563 40582 1
CATASTROPHEA *by Terrance Dicks* ISBN 0 563 40584 8
MISSION IMPRACTICAL *by David A. McIntee* ISBN 0 563 40592 9
ZETA MAJOR *by Simon Messingham* ISBN 0 563 40597 X
DREAMS OF EMPIRE *by Justin Richards* ISBN 0 563 40598 8
LAST MAN RUNNING *by Chris Boucher* ISBN 0 563 40594 5
MATRIX *by Robert Perry and Mike Tucker* ISBN 0 563 40596 1
THE INFINITY DOCTORS *by Lance Parkin* ISBN 0 563 40591 0
SALVATION *by Steve Lyons* ISBN 0 563 55566 1
THE WAGES OF SIN *by David A. McIntee* ISBN 0 563 55567 X
DEEP BLUE *by Mark Morris* ISBN 0 563 55571 8

SHORT TRIPS *ed. Stephen Cole* ISBN 0 563 40560 0
MORE SHORT TRIPS *ed. Stephen Cole* ISBN 0 563 55565 3

DOCTOR WHO: THE NOVEL OF THE FILM *by Gary Russell* ISBN 0 563 38000 4

THE BOOK OF LISTS *by Justin Richards and Andrew Martin* ISBN 0 563 40569 4
A BOOK OF MONSTERS *by David J. Howe* ISBN 0 563 40562 7
THE TELEVISION COMPANION *by David J. Howe and Stephen James Walker*
ISBN 0 563 40588 0
FROM A TO Z *by Gary Gillatt* ISBN 0 563 40589 9